BE WITH ME

AN ADAIR FAMILY NOVEL

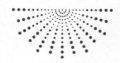

SAMANTHA YOUNG

Be With Me

An Adair Family Novel

By Samantha Young

Copyright © 2022 Samantha Young

ALSO BY SAMANTHA YOUNG

One King's Way (a novella)

On Hart's Boardwalk (a novella)

Hart's Boardwalk Series:

The One Real Thing

Every Little Thing

Things We Never Said

The Truest Thing

The Adair Family Series:

Here With Me

There With You

Always You

Young Adult contemporary titles by Samantha Young

The Impossible Vastness of Us

The Fragile Ordinary

Other Titles by Samantha Young

Warriors of Ankh Trilogy:

Blood Will Tell

Blood Past

Shades of Blood

Drip Drop Teardrop, a novella

Titles Co-written with Kristen Callihan

Outmatched

Titles Written Under S. Young

Fear of Fire and Shadow

War of the Covens Trilogy:

Hunted

Destined

Ascended

The Seven Kings of Jinn Series:

Seven Kings of Jinn

Of Wish and Fury

Queen of Shadow and Ash

The Law of Stars and Sultans

True Immortality Series:

War of Hearts

Kiss of Vengeance

Kiss of Eternity: A True Immortality Short Story

Bound by Forever

ABOUT THE AUTHOR

Samantha Young is a *New York Times*, *USA Today* and *Wall Street Journal* bestselling author from Stirlingshire, Scotland. She's been nominated for the Goodreads Choice Award for Best Author and Best Romance for her international bestseller *On Dublin Street*. *On Dublin Street* is Samantha's first adult contemporary romance series and has sold in 31 countries.

Visit Samantha Young online at http://authorsamanthayoung.com

Instagram @authorsamanthayoung

TikTok @authorsamanthayoung

Facebook http://www.facebook.com/authorsamanthayoung

Want book updates, exclusive excerpts, bonus content and a chance to enter newsletter only giveaways? Join Samantha's mailing list:

https://authorsamanthayoung.com/subscribe-to-sams-newsletter/

ACKNOWLEDGMENTS

For the most part, writing is a solitary endeavor, but publishing most certainly is not. I have to thank Stacie Ervin and Kalie Phillips for reading Eredine's story before everyone else and providing such amazing insight into her character. I appreciate you guys more than you know. Also, thank you to my lovely friend Catherine Cowles for also reading an early version of *Be With Me* and providing support throughout the whole writing process. Love you loads!

Of course I have to thank my amazing editor Jennifer Sommersby Young for always, *always* being there to help make me a better writer and storyteller. Thank you!

Thank you to Julie Deaton for proofreading *Be With Me* and catching all the things. You have an amazing eye for detail and I'm always reassured my stories are going out into the world in the best possible shape.

And thank you to my bestie and PA extraordinaire Ashleen Walker for handling all the little things and supporting me through everything. I appreciate you so much. And miss and love you loads.

The life of a writer doesn't stop with the book. Our job expands beyond the written word to marketing, advertising, graphic design, social media management, and more. Help from those in the know goes a long way. A huge thank-you to Nina Grinstead at Valentine PR for your encouragement, support, insight and advice. You're invaluable to me and I hope you know how much I cherish you.

Thank you to every single blogger, Instagrammer, and book lover who has helped spread the word about my books. You all are appreciated so much! On that note, a massive thank-you to the fantastic readers in my private Facebook group, Sam's Clan McBookish. You're truly special and the loveliest readers a girl could ask for. Your continued and ceaseless support is awe-inspiring and I'm so grateful for you all.

A massive thank-you to Hang Le for once again creating a stunning cover that establishes the perfect visual atmosphere for this story and this series. You amaze me! And thank you to Regina Wamba for the beautiful couple photography that brings Eredine and Arran to life.

As always, thank you to my agent Lauren Abramo for making it possible for readers all over the world to find my words. You're phenomenal, and I'm so lucky to have you.

A huge thank-you to my family and friends for always supporting and encouraging me, and for listening to me talk, sometimes in circles, about the worlds I live in.

Finally, to you, thank you for reading. It means the everything to me.

PROLOGUE

EREDINE

Eight years ago

L os Angeles, California
United States

STARING at the map of Scotland on the laptop screen, I tried to picture myself in the place labeled Ardnoch, right on the northeastern coastline of the mainland. Having never been there, it wasn't a simple task.

"Ardnoch," I murmured, trying out the sound of it in my mouth.

So foreign.

And yet, what Lachlan Adair offered was a life there, not

completely unlike the one I lived now. Just safer. Much, much safer.

You trust him? the voice, a memory, asked in my head.

Yes. Despite everything I'd been through, I trusted Lachlan Adair. I trusted my gut. If there was something I'd always been able to trust, it was my gut instinct. Granny called it my sixth sense, said I inherited her gift of perceiving a person's goodness or wickedness. My friends used to say I caught a person's "vibe" because, eventually, my instincts about someone usually turned out to be true. I'd only been wrong once or twice in my entire life.

Those people I'd been wrong about had a gift too—they could make you believe in their goodness, so you never saw their wickedness coming.

It unnerved me to know that my sixth sense didn't always get it right, but I knew deep in my soul I was right about Lachlan Adair.

Life was so surreal. One minute, I was hopeless, feeling angry and powerless, and the next, a Hollywood actor, of all people, offered me a chance to start over. It wasn't like he and the bodyguard who went everywhere with him were my saviors. Nah, screw that. They were just presenting an opportunity. I'd pay them back.

I'd work my ass off to live life on my own terms again.

Granny always said there was no shame in taking help when you needed it, as long as you had exhausted all other avenues. Well, I'd exhausted them all.

This was what I had left. And I hated it. I hated I had to rely on a wealthy man to get me the hell out of Dodge, especially when it was a rich male (he wasn't a *man*) who had—

Furious tears thickened my throat, and I threw the thought of *him* out of my mind.

He'd taken too much already.

I wouldn't let him turn me into an angry, bitter woman.

Concentrating on the map, I scrolled over Scotland, taking in the place-names I'd never heard of, some beautiful, some unpronounceable … all thousands of miles away.

A knock sounded on the door. "It's Lachlan," he called out in his lilting brogue.

"Come in."

My pulse picked up as the hotel room door beeped and Lachlan entered with Mac, his bodyguard, at his back. Well, not his bodyguard anymore. Mackennon Galbraith was now the head of security at Ardnoch Estate.

Lachlan had explained that he'd renovated his family's castle and estate in the Highlands and turned it into a members-only club for TV and film professionals. It only opened a few weeks ago, and Lachlan was in LA to spread the word among his peers. Our meeting had been by chance, and thank the Lord, because I didn't know what might have happened if he and Mac hadn't appeared in my life when they did.

I didn't know why Lachlan was so determined to help me, but he offered me a position at his estate. He needed a yoga/Pilates instructor, and I *was* one.

Both men wore small smiles as they sat across from me in the hotel suite's living room. Lachlan hid me here after I'd uncharacteristically blurted my entire story to him. With everything I'd been through, I wanted to fight against my instinct and remind myself that no one was this kind. Yet, that wasn't true. Granny was. She'd have helped a stranger on the street.

What other choice did I have? So many had been taken from me.

Lachlan sighed and leaned forward. "How are you feeling?"

A little tired of that question. "Okay. What now?"

"We're ready to get moving."

3

"Just one last thing," Mac said, searching my face with a concerned frown. "Name change. You need to do that before we can get you out of here."

"Do you have a new name in mind?" Lachlan asked. "Something far removed from your real name or any family member's name. Something he can't figure out."

Name change.

My stomach flipped unpleasantly as I stared down at the laptop screen. This was it. I really was rewriting my life. Leaving everything behind. So much pain and grief ... but it also meant leaving behind who I'd been before the horror overtook everything. And I'd liked that girl. She had a good life.

Tears stung my eyes and nose as a pretty-looking place-name caught my attention on the map. I turned the laptop and pointed to it. "How do you pronounce this?"

Lachlan leaned forward to peer at it. "Eredine? It's pronounced Ery-Deen."

My lips twitched. He pronounced it differently from how it looked, but I liked it. Weirdly, somehow, it fit. "That'll do."

"It's bonny." Mac gave me a sympathetic smile.

"Surname?"

"Willows," I said without thinking. *The Wind in the Willows* had been one of Granny's favorite children's books. "Eredine Willows."

"It's perfect." Lachlan stood up. "We'll get you out of here ... Eredine."

Eredine.

So strange.

So foreign.

I tried to pull the name on like a sweater. Make it fit. Sighing past the tightness in my chest, I stood too. "I'm going to pay you back."

"I don't want that."

4

"I do." I lifted my chin stubbornly. "I have my granny's house I can sell. If you help me sell it, I can use the money from that to pay you back for this. I need to. And I'm not asking."

Everyone thought because I was soft spoken and reserved that I was a pushover. They soon found out they were wrong.

Lachlan's eyes sparked with understanding. "Okay."

"Okay, then." My hands shook as I reached to close the laptop. "When do we leave?"

1

EREDINE

Present day

S utherland
  Scottish Highlands

I MOVED to close the bedroom door when Lewis called out sleepily, "Light!"

"I got you, buddy," I answered softly, pulling the door almost shut. A crack of light from the hallway filtered into Lewis's bedroom. Having already put a sleeping Eilidh to bed, I made my way quietly downstairs to Thane's open-plan living room and kitchen.

It had been a good night with the kids. Since it was New Year's Eve, I let them stay up a little later, but I could tell by ten they were fighting sleep. We were watching our second Disney movie of the night when Eilidh fell asleep on the couch and Lewis drowsily agreed that it was time for bed.

The wall clock above the dining table said it was just past eleven. I grabbed a drink from the fridge and settled into Thane's massive sectional to watch the New Year's Eve shows broadcasting from Edinburgh and Glasgow.

Memories of New Year's parties in LA prodded at me, but I shook them off, and the accompanying dread, and tried to concentrate on what the Scots called "Hogmanay" celebrations. The TV flickered in the room's dim light, the images flashing in a blur. The volume was low so as not to wake the kids, and my ears pricked up at a noise from the laundry room.

It sounded as if the laundry outer door had just opened and closed.

Pulse pounding in my ears, I swiped the heavy paperweight from the coffee table and crept toward the laundry room. I couldn't hear anything but the blood rushing in my ears.

Maybe it was Regan?

But why would it be? She'd left now that she and Thane were no longer seeing each other.

I wanted to speak, call out hello, but fear closed my throat.

Determined, I stepped into the doorway of the laundry and slammed my hand down over the light switch.

The long, narrow room illuminated, but there was no one, nothing. The outer door sat closed, untouched.

My pulse slowed.

So I was jumpy these days. What was new?

Shaking my head at myself, I placed the paperweight back on the coffee table and retrieved another drink from the kitchen.

I heard it too late.

As I was crossing to the couch, the floorboards creaked at my back. My heart leapt into my throat as I spun around.

This was when everything should go dark.

That was how it happened.

Instead, I faced him.

Terror froze me to the spot.

I couldn't scream. Couldn't run.

"I finally found you," he said lovingly. "All these years, and I finally found you."

No.

No!

Then he grinned, and my mouth opened on a silent scream at the sight of his teeth, all sharpened into vicious points. My pulse raced so hard, I was sure I would die.

No.

Please.

He lunged, teeth to my throat, sinking in—

Jaymes Young's song about loving someone until infinity blared in my ears, and my eyes flew open as I let out a strangled cry.

Daylight streamed into my bedroom, and the rushing in my ears slowed as I came out of the nightmare.

Just a nightmare.

My limp hand fell to my forehead. I was clammy with sweat.

"Shit," I whispered.

At the continued sound of one of my favorite songs ringing through the room, I realized it was my ringtone—someone was calling me. I scrambled for my phone on my bedside table and saw it was my friend Arran. "Hey," I answered quickly.

"Thank bloody goodness," Arran grumbled in his Scottish accent. "I was about to break down the door."

"What?" I sat up. "Where are you?"

"Where I am most days at six o'clock in the morning. On your stoop, waiting for you."

"What?" On my porch? "What time is it?"

"You slept in," he answered, amused.

"Oh, Lord." I launched out of bed, hurrying out of my

9

small bedroom, down my tiny hallway, and out into the main living space of my lodge.

Sure enough, Arran Adair stood outside my big front window, waving comically.

I hit the code on the alarm panel by the door to disarm night mode and let Arran in.

He grinned down at me and lowered the phone from his ear. I did the same, hanging up as I stepped back to allow him entrance. "Sorry. My alarm didn't go off." I hated sleeping in.

"No problem. I'll make a protein shake while you ..." He trailed off as his eyes moved up my body and locked onto my head.

"What?" I patted it frantically, finding only the silk wrap that protected my curls during sleep.

"So this is what you look like in the morning. It's awesome." The bastard's grin couldn't be any bigger.

I flushed, but not at his teasing. Unfortunately, as much as I wanted to ignore it, Arran's smile gave me butterflies. Like a kaleidoscopic monsoon of butterflies. A best friend should not give a girl butterflies. And he definitely should not make me tingle in my yoga pants, if you know what I mean.

I ignored his comment. "You make the shakes. I'll hurry to get ready." Every weekday, we ran along Ardnoch Beach for a workout. I'd been doing it alone for years. Arran ran early in the morning, like me, and when we bumped into each other that first time, he'd given me no choice but to become his running partner.

"Nice jammies."

My step faltered as I became acutely aware of my tiny sleep shorts, tank top, and lack of bra. Almost feeling his eyes burning into my ass cheeks, I experienced a flare of arousal mixed with annoyance, a familiar feeling around Arran. Without looking at him, I flipped him the bird and disappeared down the hall to the sound of his rich laughter.

Even though I'd only have to shower again after our run, I rinsed off because I was sweaty from my nightmare. Not wanting to think about the bad dream where the past and my fear had merged, I dried and changed into running clothes—sports tank and yoga pants. It was pretty much my everyday uniform because of my work at Ardnoch Estate, a massive private property that belonged to Lachlan and Arran (and the three other Adair siblings). Lachlan, an ex-Hollywood action star, had turned it into an extremely lucrative members-only club for TV and film industry professionals. The level of privacy and security at Ardnoch made it the perfect place for me to work.

I'd just sat down at my vanity to fix my hair when there was a knock. "You decent?"

"Depends who you ask," I quipped.

Arran laughed. "Was that a yes?"

I glanced around my room a little nervously. "Yes."

The door opened, and he strode in with tall glasses filled with green juice, a barely palatable protein powder mixed with water. His eyes found me, and he placed mine on the vanity.

"Thank you. I'm sorry I'm making us late."

"Don't be." Arran wandered around my room, and I tried not to tense up as he ran his fingers over my jewelry box and peeked into my wardrobe. No one had been in this space except me. I didn't want to be uptight about him nosing around, but I fought the urge to spring to my feet as he reached for the handle on the built-in closet.

"Hey, nosy, there's nothing in there for you." I tried to keep my tone light, but I could tell by the way Arran's lips pinched he heard the slight panic in my voice.

Whatever he saw in my face softened his expression. "Sorry. I am a nosy bastard. Just never been back here before." He shrugged and sat on the end of my bed, gulping his drink and making a face.

I relaxed a little as his gaze darted around the room again. Though I was born in Chicago, I lived most of my life in California, so I'd brought a little California contemporary to my beachy bedroom. All whites, soft blues, and wood tones.

Our eyes met as he looked back at me.

He stared in that intense way of his.

Arran Adair looked a lot like his brothers. He was the youngest among the men, but Arrochar, their only sister, was the youngest of the Adair brood. Arran probably looked most like Lachlan, strange considering I'd never felt any attraction toward Lachlan. He was like a big brother to me. With somewhat slightly smoother features, Arran wasn't as rugged as his eldest brother. But they shared the same striking azure eyes and dark blond hair. While Lachlan sported a short beard these days, Arran fluctuated between the smooth look and unshaven scruff. He was tall at six feet two, broad shouldered, slim hipped, a rangy, athletic physique that caused all those aforementioned tingles. I liked that he was taller than my five ten.

Not that he needed to be taller than me for any reason.

Especially not romantic ones.

I had no intention of becoming romantically involved with anyone.

Arran's eyes narrowed slightly as he stared at me. "What are you thinking?"

Flushing, I turned away and quickly applied moisturizer. "Just wondering if you mean to stay and watch me like a creeper."

"Aye, I was planning to," he deadpanned.

My lips quirked as I reached to unwrap my hair from the microfiber towels I used to protect my curls from frizz.

A heavy tumble of twisted strands spilled down my back,

and I caught Arran's eyes in the mirror. "Seriously, you sure you don't want to run without me?"

"Nope." He took another sip of his shake. "I'm fascinated by your morning routine."

"That's because you're weird," I teased. Since we were going on a run, I decided not to waste time untwisting my hair and twisted it up into a ponytail.

I then applied a little makeup, nothing too heavy since sweat would melt it off. Just enough where I didn't look like Arran had woken me from a nightmare. Arran watched the process of me fixing my hair and makeup as if it truly captivated him.

"I'm done," I announced and took a long drink of my shake, only to get caught in Arran's striking eyes again.

Sometimes he stared at me like he was visualizing me naked. If any other guy gave me those vibes, I'd feel violated. The thought of Arran being attracted to me, however, made me feel too hot, my skin too tight.

I raised an eyebrow at him as he continued to stare.

His lips quirked, but the intensity in his expression didn't dissolve. "I think I enjoyed this behind-the-scenes peek into your routine a little too much. I'm a wee bit hot and bothered."

Watching me do my hair and makeup?

Rolling my eyes, I stood and strode past him. "Stop flirting."

This was our routine. Arran Adair was an even bigger flirt than his slightly older brother Brodan. I threw out the thought of Brodan because it made me feel guilty—being attracted to brothers—and hurried into the kitchen to collect my purse and keys.

Anyway, Arran was just like his brother. They both flirted with women all the time. Arran's flirting with me meant nothing, just as Brodan's flirting with me had meant nothing.

We were all friends.

Brodan and I were just friends.

Arran and I were just friends.

Arran. And. I. Were. Just. Friends.

We were.

Truly.

I hadn't really wanted to be friends with him considering my attraction, but Arran Adair was the human equivalent of a boundary bulldozer. Unlike every other member of the Adair family who didn't want to push or intrude on my personal space, Arran was all about that.

And weirdly, it didn't bother me.

I'd grown to trust him these last six months.

Which was a big deal.

Believe me. Once upon a time, I'd relied on that sixth sense, the one Granny said I could trust until my last breath. But then Lucy Wainwright happened. No one had ever fooled me like Lucy had. It was beyond unnerving. And suddenly, even the people who I knew cared about me seemed like a threat.

Until Arran.

Arran ... I had to believe my instincts about Arran were right.

"I can't stop flirting with you." Arran wandered into the living room, placing both our glasses in the sink. "You're stunning, and sometimes it dazzles me." He approached with a wicked grin. "Looking at you is like looking at the sun."

Ignoring the warm feeling he evoked and the racing of my pulse, I grimaced. "Stop wasting such excellent material on me, Arran. We're just *friends*."

He gasped in dramatic outrage, hand to his chest. "*Best* friends."

I fought a laugh and lost. "Are we in kindergarten now?"

"It's called nursery school," he corrected and then kissed

me quickly on the tip of my nose, the scent of his cologne surrounding me for a brief second. "And friends can flirt."

"I suppose it's good practice," I said to his back as I locked up.

"Sure." He shrugged, throwing his keys up and catching them as he bounded down my steps with the energy of a teenager. More times than I'd care to admit, I'd wondered what all that energy in bed would be like.

I missed sex.

So. Much.

Groaning under my breath, I hurried to my car and was glad for the fifteen-minute drive to Ardnoch Beach that counted as a reprieve from Arran and his sexiness.

My phone connected to my car, and I hit my favorite playlist. But as I followed Arran out of my driveway and through the woodlands surrounding my place, my phone rang, cutting off the music. The car screen announced the caller.

"Yes?" I drawled.

"I'm calling because I missed you," Arran teased.

I laughed at his nonsense. "You missed me in the ten seconds we've been apart?"

"Aye. Also, I had the sudden urge to once again ask, why the hell are you driving that thing?"

I shook my head as we turned onto the main road. "Hey, this car is environmentally friendly and gets me from A to B." After my old Defender broke down beyond the point of repair, I'd done the sensible thing and bought a Smart car. But I've been longing for something bigger.

Arran did not fail to make fun of my car at every opportunity.

I mock glared at his fancy Range Rover. All the Adairs drove Range Rovers because of the deal Lachlan got for using the cars as the estate's official fleet. Lachlan had offered to provide one for me, but he'd done enough as it was.

"How do you even fit? Your gorgeous legs are longer than the entire car."

Not true. But okay, it wasn't the best car for a tall person. And Arran was even more flirtatious this morning than usual —it was discombobulating.

"I'm hanging up now." I reached for the End Call button on my steering wheel.

"No, I'll stop, I'll stop."

"Arran, I'll see you in ten minutes."

"But I like your voice."

He said it with such seriousness that for a second, I wondered if he was being genuine or if it was just his usual flirting.

Nah.

Arran couldn't help himself.

"See you soon." I hung up, my music filling the car once more.

I didn't know how I allowed this friendship to develop into something I'd come to rely on, but I did know that believing Arran's flirtations to be real was a surefire way to hurt us both.

2

ARRAN

Months of waiting and waiting for planning permission to come through, and finally, we had holes in walls and an addition going up in the back of the Gloaming.

I strode through the construction site that was the old restaurant, bar, and hotel, my hard hat in place, my hands itching to do some demo. However, I'd promised Lachlan I'd leave it to the professionals. As such, I served as the project manager to liaise with our contractor instead.

My phone rang, and speak of the devil. I grinned as I answered. "Checking up on me?"

Lachlan chuckled. "Just wanted to see how things are going."

"So, checking up on me. It's looking good. I'm sure we'll run into a problem at some point today, but we're making nice progress."

"And the windows?"

We had to special order windows to replace the old ones. In Scotland, you could only replace sash-and-case windows in historical buildings like the Gloaming if they were beyond repair. Unfortunately, all of them were, which meant replacing every single window with as close a match to the originals as possible. That was expensive business. We also had to match the new windows in the rear addition. I wanted to make sure we found the right people to do it. "I've narrowed it down to two companies."

"We need to order them pronto, so try not to take too long deciding."

"You said you trusted me to do this," I reminded him, my tone teasing, but truthfully, I needed to know my big brother had faith I could manage this renovation.

It had shocked me when Lachlan proposed buying the Gloaming together. Gordon Wallace owned it for years, his father before that, so it had become a staple of Ardnoch, a much beloved local haunt. I knew a few people in the village were uncertain about my family taking it over and renovating, but I was determined to prove we were honoring the old girl. That Lachlan even considered me for a joint business venture, too, was humbling.

He was finally treating me as the man I'd become versus the reckless wee shit I'd once been.

I wanted to prove that his faith in me was not misplaced.

But I also needed him to prove he trusted me.

"I do, I do." He sighed. "I just know what renovations are like after doing it with the castle. Time pulls away from you. Coordinating a renovation on a historical building is a juggling act."

"I know. But I've got this."

"Good. Well, call me if you need anything. You coming to dinner Sunday?"

Lachlan and Thane took turns hosting weekend dinners every other week. "I wouldn't miss it."

It was true.

18

I couldn't believe it was true, but coming home had turned out to be exactly what I'd needed all along.

We hung up and I pulled out my tablet to mull over the window companies before my contractor, Bill, found me to ask about the plumbing in the addition.

EREDINE LEANED against the side of that ridiculous car, staring up at the Gloaming as if lost in thought. I hadn't been joking this morning when I told her that sometimes the very sight of her dazzled me. She was the most stunning person I'd ever met, inside and out. There were many things I didn't know about Eredine, things my curiosity itched to discover. She discomfited me a wee bit.

Yet, having met so many people on my travels, I could say with certainty that despite her many secrets and mysteries, Eredine Willows oozed a goodness, a kindness, a gentleness that renewed my faith in humanity. She reminded me of the softness and light in this world. Even if she hadn't been stunning to look at (which she was), Ery would still be the most beautiful woman I'd ever met because of that light inside her, a glow never diminished by the haunted look in her eyes.

I knew something had existed between her and my brother Brodan. I didn't know if anything physical happened or if feelings had been exchanged, but I'd witnessed a spark between them at Lachlan's wedding. For months, I'd been trying to build the trust between me and Ery so I could ask her.

Yet, as much as I loved and owed Brodan, if they had a past together, it wouldn't stop me. Whatever was between them, he was foolish enough to leave her behind. As far as I was concerned, that told me everything I needed to know. I knew my brother, sometimes even better than he knew himself. And if Brodan truly wanted her, he'd be here.

But he wasn't.

I was.

And if it took me another six months to make my way past Ery's defenses, enough for her to let me in, to tell me what she was running from, to convince her to go on a date with me, then I was here for it.

Because I'd never felt this drawn to a woman before.

Eredine was worth whatever tension might arise between me and Brodan when I made my move … but we'd get through it. My brother and I had survived worse.

Something in me settled as I approached Ery. Those gorgeous hazel-green eyes dropped to meet my gaze. She gave me a small smile, and a wee swoop of nerves buzzed in my gut. Not that I'd ever admit that to anyone, especially not my siblings. I'd never hear the end of it.

This morning I'd been a bit too nosy, wandering into her bedroom under the guise of bringing her a protein shake, but I wanted to know everything about her. And watching her get ready for the day had been extremely satisfying in an unnerving, possessive way. Very few people, and not any in the last few years, as far as I was aware, had the privilege of seeing Eredine in her bedroom doing her hair and makeup. Now I had. And as I'd sat and watched her, I couldn't help but imagine having that pleasure in the mornings after making her come.

"That is quite an intense look on your face," Ery teased as she pushed off her car and sauntered toward me. The feminine sway in her hips killed me more each day. "What were you thinking about?"

"You don't want to know." I winked at her, and she rolled her eyes, already turning to walk down Castle Street.

Falling in beside her, we'd stepped away from the car

park outside the Gloaming, which served as the main car park for the village, when a Range Rover slowed beside us. I curled a hand around Eredine's elbow, drawing her to a stop as I was unsure where the vehicle intended to go. It halted beside us, and the passenger window rolled down to reveal a vaguely familiar youthful face. I guessed she was one of Lachlan's club members. Peering past her at the driver, I didn't recognize her.

The passenger flicked a look at Eredine before turning her attention to me, smiling flirtatiously. "You're an Adair, right?" she asked in an American accent. "I'm sure I saw you at Lachlan's summer party thing last year."

Something about her tone bothered me, but she was a guest, so I gave her a respectful nod. "Yes, I'm Arran. Can I help you with anything?"

Her gaze moved past me to the Gloaming. "We heard this place did good food, but it looks closed."

"It's under renovation at the moment."

"Right." She glanced at her companion. "Inverness?"

"There's An Sealladh, Ms. Benning," Eredine offered. "A restaurant about fifteen minutes outside the village, right on the water."

Ms. Benning?

I knew that name, and I knew the young woman's face, but I couldn't quite recall her first name. What I did know was I didn't like the way she zeroed in on Ery, tone haughty. "Aren't you the little Pilates instructor?"

What the fuck? Her condescending tone when she said *little* made me grind my teeth.

Eredine's expression never wavered as she politely answered, "I'm the Pilates instructor for the estate, yes."

Benning's eyes flicked to me and then back to Eredine. "Huh." She sighed heavily, her nose wrinkling like she was annoyed. "Un Shalag, did you say?"

21

"No." I shook my head at her butchering the Gaelic. "An Sealladh." I spelled it. "You'll find it on your sat nav. Your GPS."

She beamed at me. "Thanks. There must be something in the water here because all of you Adair boys are spectacular. And of course, there's Mac. What I wouldn't give for an Adair/Mac sandwich." She laughed flirtatiously while I tried not to shudder at the thought.

"Right. Well ..." I placed a hand on Ery's back to lead her away. "Enjoy your day, Ms. Benning."

"Hey, if you see Mac, will you tell him I was asking for him?" she called out as the Range Rover moved slowly past us.

"Only if you want Arro to eviscerate you," Ery muttered under her breath.

Mackennon Galbraith, the head of security at Ardnoch Estate, was my sister Arro's fiancé. It hadn't surprised me, after observing the two of them upon my return to Scotland, that they'd ended up together. Mac was thirteen years older than Arro, which had proven a sticking point for a while, but they were perfect for each other. The age difference didn't matter.

I laughed at Ery's response because it was true, and gave the woman a nod out of respect for Lachlan before the SUV drove down Castle Street well over the twenty-mile-per-hour speed limit.

"I rarely say this, but I really dislike that woman," Eredine confessed as we continued to Flora's Café for lunch.

"Who is she?"

She quirked an eyebrow in surprise. "You don't know? I thought you knew."

"She's familiar, but I can't place her."

"Iris Benning. Hollywood's latest darling. She's been nominated for two Oscars, and this is her third visit to the

22

club in the past year. She was in my class just this morning, and I overheard her talking about Mac like he was a piece of meat." Ery scowled. "One of the other guests told her that Mac was engaged, and she said she didn't care."

"Mac can take care of himself," I assured Ery.

"It's not the point. Mac has told her himself that he's not interested, and she's still going for it like she's entitled to him just because she wants him. That's harassment."

Suspicion prickled the back of my neck at Eredine's passionate response to Iris Benning. "You're right," I agreed. "But like I said, Mac won't put up with it, and Lachlan won't either." One thing I admired most about Lachlan was that he didn't give a shit who someone was or how much money they had—if they crossed the line with someone he cared about, he wouldn't put up with it. His wife, Robyn, told me he'd thrown the actor Sebastian Stone out of Ardnoch, ending his membership, for accosting Robyn on the estate. Then about eight months ago, Stone hit the global headlines when several women came forward to accuse him of sexual assault. The Oscar winner had been canceled, losing the part of a title character in an upcoming TV show as he awaited trial.

I'd wondered if Lachlan had a hand in unearthing those women, but he wouldn't admit to anything. After finding out he'd cut Arro's ex-boyfriend off from the culinary industry for assaulting her, however, I wouldn't put anything past Lachlan when it came to avenging his family.

"I know." Ery brought me out of my musings. "Mac won't stand for it. He's so in love with your sister, he wouldn't allow anyone to jeopardize that."

Hearing something akin to longing in her tone, I studied her profile as we walked. "Do you want that?"

She looked at me in confusion as we stopped outside Flora's. "Want what?"

"What Mac and Arro have?"

Eredine smiled, that sweet, perfect fucking smile. "No one will ever have what they have. It's something truly special."

I furrowed my brow. "Don't you think my brothers have that with Robyn and Regan?"

"What they have is special, too, of course ... but Arro and Mac ..." She tilted her head in thought. "It's literally like they're two halves of a whole. When she moves, he moves and vice versa. It's always been that way. I was so afraid they'd never find a path to each other because I knew they'd never be complete until that moment."

Something a little like shame filled me because I'd seen it, too, on the rare occasions I'd come home. Deep down, I knew Arro was miserable without Mac. But I'd stayed away. I hadn't talked to her about it. I'd left her.

Thank Christ it had all worked out for her in my absence.

"Hey, you okay?" Ery asked.

"Fine," I lied. "Let's eat before our lunch break is over."

Holding the door for Ery, I waited for her to enter the café first, and she thanked me with a small, secretive smile I wanted to kiss right off her lips. She smelled of the same perfume she wore every day—light and floral, not overpowering. I'd fantasized about waking up to that perfume on my bedsheets too many times to count.

Letting go of the door, I moved to her side and drew to an abrupt halt at the redhead walking toward the exit we blocked.

She faltered, too, her big eyes round with surprise. "Arran?"

I shook my head, sure I was seeing things.

But nope.

There she was.

Monroe Sinclair.

"Roe?" I gaped at her.

Monroe swallowed nervously, staring up at me. She was still short, curvy, and bloody adorable. In fact, she barely looked older than the last time I saw her, which was … shit … eighteen years ago. "How … how are you?" she asked.

Letting out a surprised chuckle, I moved toward her and lifted her into a hug. Monroe let out a shocked gasp, but thankfully, it petered into a giggle as she hugged me back. Placing her on her feet, I turned to find Ery watching us with a frown. "Ery, this is Monroe. She was Brodan's best friend growing up, and I haven't seen her"—I turned back to Roe—"in eighteen years."

Roe frowned, stepping out of my embrace. "It has been a long time, hasn't it?" Her focus moved to Eredine. "So nice to meet you."

"Eredine." She nodded at Roe, her bland smile uncharacteristically unfriendly.

Confused by Eredine's cool greeting, I looked back at my old friend. A quick glance at her left ring finger told me she wasn't married—surprising—considering that was all Monroe had wanted when we were kids. To be a teacher, a mum, and a wife. She'd called them simple desires. Yet, as I knew well, nothing in this life was simple. "What brings you back?"

She tucked a lock of her gorgeous red hair behind her ear. "I … I got a job at the primary school. Mrs. Welsh retired, so a position opened up."

"They finally got rid of that old boot?" I hooted, not caring if anyone heard me. Mrs. Welsh had been a teacher at Ardnoch Primary when I was a child, and she was an auld witch. Apparently, my nephew Lewis hadn't enjoyed having her as a teacher either.

"Arran," Monroe admonished as if we were kids again, like those eighteen years hadn't passed.

"I only speak the truth."

Her lips twitched. "Well, she's gone, and I'm here. My mum hasn't been keeping well, so the timing was right."

"Sorry about your mum. But I'm glad you're home." I wondered if anyone else knew Roe was back. If anyone had told Brodan. Guilt filled me, and I unconsciously took a step away. Her gaze flickered to my feet and then to my face. Her smile grew strained.

"Okay, well, I need to get going. It was nice to run into you. And nice to meet you, Eredine." Monroe walked around us.

But I couldn't just let her walk out like that. "Does Arro know you're back?"

She glanced over her shoulder. "You're the first Adair I've bumped into."

"Arro would love to see you, Roe."

"I'm not so sure about that." Her smile fell before she briskly turned and marched out of the café.

"Can I get you a table?" Flora's voice drew my head around.

Shrugging off the unexpected trip down memory lane, I gave Flora a big smile. "Bonny Flora. We'd like the best seat in the house."

She tittered, cheeks flushing. "Och, you. This way."

I pulled Ery's chair out at the small table near the window and then took the seat opposite. Our feet touched beneath it as her eyes narrowed. "There's definitely a story there."

"Where?" I pretended to peruse the menu.

"With the beautiful redhead who just ran away from you like the hounds of hell were nipping at her heels."

I glanced around the café, finding more tourists than locals, but still. Looking back at Ery, I answered quietly, "Not here."

She nodded in understanding and looked down at the small menu. I wanted to breach the distance between us and smooth away the frown between her brows. Who did she think Monroe was to me? Did Roe make her jealous? I didn't want Ery to be jealous. There was no reason. But I felt an annoying tug of satisfaction at the thought of her being possessive over me.

Because I sure as hell wouldn't have liked it, I realized, if she'd hugged a man the way I'd hugged Roe.

Fuck.

If it wasn't bad enough that something might exist between Brodan and Ery, Monroe Sinclair, the girl I was pretty sure Brodan had once loved, was back in Ardnoch. A girl I'd slept with because I was a selfish kid who hadn't realized just what she'd meant to Bro.

What a clusterfuck.

3

EREDINE

It bothered me how much it bothered me that Arran still hadn't told me about Monroe, the stunning redhead he'd treated with such warmth in Flora's two days ago. We'd jogged together yesterday morning before work, and still, nada, even though he'd promised me "later."

It shouldn't irritate me this much. However, I'd realized in that moment that while Arran was a giant flirt, I could tell the difference between sincerity and just him being charming. And he'd been genuinely happy to see Monroe. Of course, he would be happy—she was gorgeous. But *who* was she to Arran? He'd said she was Brodan's best friend, but it seemed like there was something more between her and Arran.

Something more than friendship, maybe.

I hated it bothered me, that Monroe's arrival made me a little panicky. I didn't understand it, and truthfully, I didn't want to.

Yet I still was desperate to know who she was. I needed to know.

I just couldn't face why.

Arran never raced ahead of me, even though his legs were longer and stronger. He kept pace, our breathing almost in sync as the sand offered resistance during our run along Ardnoch Beach. Gulls cried overhead and the early morning sun broke through the hazy mist, the rays of pale gold light shimmering above the North Sea. A cool breeze rushed pleasantly across my hot skin.

I glanced at Arran. Concentration furrowed his brow as he ran, and I felt a little swoop in my belly as I studied his handsome, familiar profile.

Screw this.

I slowed to a stop, my hands resting on my hips as I drew in a breath.

Arran glanced over his shoulder and halted. He walked back toward me, breathing a little faster, heavier. He had this way of searching my face, and I couldn't tell if he was memorizing me or looking for something hidden. "What's up?"

Looking out toward the water, I shook my head. "Can we just walk for a bit?"

"Of course."

Meeting his eyes again, I saw the questions within—he knew something was bugging me. Shit.

I walked with my eyes directed down to my feet, and Arran fell into step beside me, so close his arm brushed mine. Goose bumps rose on my skin in the wake of his touch. Surreptitiously, I tried to widen the gap between us.

"So ..." I attempted to sound as casual as possible. "You never told me about Monroe."

Feeling his stare, I forced myself to look at him. He appeared... uncertain.

"What is it?"

Arran sighed, running a hand over his hair, his biceps flexing with the movement and causing a rush of inconvenient tingles between my thighs.

I wrenched my gaze away.

"I, uh …" Arran's eyes burned into my cheek. "I don't know what I can tell you because I don't know what happened between you and Brodan. If anything."

Shocked, I stumbled to a stop and gaped at him. While I was pretty certain every member of the Adair family had noticed an attraction between Brodan and me, no one had mentioned it. Least of all Brodan.

Arran raised an eyebrow, but he had a hard glint in his eyes that I didn't like. "Well?"

"Nothing happened between me and Brodan," I answered honestly, surprised that I no longer felt bitter about that. A year ago, I would have felt a complicated mix of relief that Brodan hadn't pushed for more than quiet flirtation, and bitterness that he didn't feel I was worth working a little harder for. It wasn't fair to Brodan that I resented him for it, especially when I had no intention of getting romantically involved with him. "We've flirted in the past, but that's it."

"You don't have feelings for him?" Arran sounded gruff.

Something about that, and the way he looked at me, made my breath catch. My chest felt tight and my hands itched to touch him, and I didn't understand myself or this attraction at all.

How could I have been attracted to Brodan for so many years and now find myself drawn even more powerfully to his brother? I felt guilty about it, like I'd led Brodan on, even though nothing happened between us—and even though nothing would ever happen between Arran and me either.

"Ery?" Arran persisted.

I didn't want to lie.

Not to Arran.

"I was attracted to him."

Arran frowned. "Was?"

I shrugged. "Was. And nothing happened."

He seemed to let this sink in, and I wasn't imagining when his shoulders dropped with relief. My stomach flipped at the thought of what that meant, and I wanted to be alone, so I didn't have to deal with this complicated situation.

"So, if I tell you details about his romantic history, it won't bother you?" Arran asked.

I'd seen Brodan pictured online with different women over the years, celebrity dates on his arm for glamorous events, so I knew he wasn't a monk by any stretch. Once upon a time, it stung a little.

Now … worryingly … I didn't feel jealous. Or possessive. Not like I'd felt when Arran picked up Monroe and hugged her like she was the best thing he'd seen in years.

That stung more than I wanted to acknowledge.

"Nope," I answered sincerely.

He didn't bother to hide the relief in his expression as he cracked that boyish smile that unleashed my butterflies. He resumed strolling, and we fell into step as he flicked me another assessing look. "Monroe is Brodan's age. But since there's only a year between me and Bro, as you know, he and I were close. So close, in fact, that … um …" He rubbed the back of his neck, looking a little sheepish. "The two of us were girl mad when we were kids. Started fucking around with the lassies really young because we looked older, so we could get older girls."

I smirked, not at all surprised to hear those two were little Lotharios running around Ardnoch, breaking hearts.

"We even …" Arran sighed heavily. "We were selfish wee pricks and more than hedonistic. Ery, we shared girls."

I raised an eyebrow. "What do you mean?"

"If I'd enjoyed a girl and she was up for it, I sent her Brodan's way, and vice versa."

Not liking that at all, I stayed silent.

"Arro tried to warn us that one day we'd hurt someone

without meaning to, but we were so bloody sure of ourselves."

Realization dawned, and I drew to a stop. "Monroe?"

Arran winced and stared out at the sea, a muscle ticking in his jaw. "She was one of Brodan's best friends since primary school. He was her protector. Reading between the lines, she didn't have the best family life, and Brodan wanted to make her feel like she had a family with us. She was good friends with Arro, too, as they got older, even though there were a few years between them." He looked at me now. "Bro never made a move on her. He was always fucking around with other girls, so I never imagined there was anything more between them."

Oh, Lordy. I knew what was coming.

"Brodan left for uni, but Monroe couldn't afford to live at school, so she got into Inverness and commuted. They still saw each other, we all did, but Bro was gone, and I was pissing Lachlan off by not going to college, kicking around Ardnoch, getting into trouble ..." Regret flashed in his eyes. "Bro was twenty, and, um, he started dating this one girl at uni, so I didn't know ..." He bowed his head and sighed. "I should have known."

"You slept with Monroe," I guessed.

Arran lifted his head and nodded. "We were seeing more of each other because we were both in Ardnoch. She became one of my closest friends. Then one night we had a bit too much to drink, and we had sex."

Jealousy bloomed hot and fierce and horrible inside me.

Damn.

Why him?

He was complicating everything.

"Brodan found out?" I asked quietly, forcing the words past my stifling possessiveness.

"Aye." Arran nodded, his remorse evident in his bright

eyes. "Timing couldn't have been worse. He surprised us with a trip home, and we were in my room at the castle. He caught us mid act."

"Oh, hell." That couldn't have been comfortable.

"And I honestly thought he was going to kill me." Arran's countenance shuttered, and I could tell he was back in the memory. "I've never seen Brodan lose it like that. Thane was always the hot-tempered one. Brodan, contrary to all the wild stories about him in the papers a few years back, was always the calm kid. Aye, he was a Jack the lad, sleeping around, but he was never unpredictable or wild. But when he saw me with Roe, he lost his fucking mind. To this day"— Arran looked at me, his expression considering, searching almost—"he has never admitted that he was in love with her. But I think back and I see things I was too self-involved to notice then."

The thought of Brodan loving someone else might have hurt months ago, but now I felt nothing but sadness for him. I realized whatever feeling I'd had for Brodan, it was only a crush, an infatuation. I hadn't ever truly known the man. Not like I know Arran. "If he loved her, why wouldn't he have done something about it?"

"Christ knows. But my brother had never lifted his hand to me, and he beat the utter crap out of me that night."

"Whoa." I couldn't imagine Brodan doing that, but to be fair, a few years back, around about the same time Robyn came into our lives, we'd all been worried about him. Brodan had been photographed in the tabloids hitting a bouncer outside a club, behavior so unlike him.

"It devastated Roe. She felt guilty," Arran continued. "She left a few weeks later, and I never saw her again, until this week."

I nodded, but my curiosity got the better of me. "Did you love her?"

Shame flushed high on his cheeks. "No. I think it might have been forgivable if I had. But I was just an eighteen-year-old arsehole who could only think with his dick, and she was beautiful."

Relief filled me. "Oh."

"Do you think I should tell Brodan she's back?"

"Yes," I answered immediately. "If he comes to visit and bumps into her without a warning ... don't let that happen to him." Something occurred to me. "Maybe he'll come home if he knows she's here."

His eyes lit with amusement. "That wouldn't bother you?"

No, it really wouldn't. "I don't know if you've noticed this about me, Arran, but I'm a secret romantic. How amazing would it be if your brother found happiness with his childhood best friend?"

Chuckling, Arran slid his arm around my shoulders and drew me into his side for an affectionate hug. It felt beyond nice to be tucked into his body. I wanted to nuzzle my face against his neck, but refrained. "I love your heart, Ery, but I don't think that's how things would pan out. It's been eighteen years since they saw each other. Whatever love Brodan had for Roe is probably long gone now."

I thought of Monroe and the panicked look on her face when she first saw Arran.

I suspected that for her, the past was still very much a part of her present.

4

EREDINE

While I led the small class of celebrities through the cool-down exercises, I could feel Iris Benning eyeballing me. She'd been doing it throughout this afternoon's session.

I hadn't seen the actor since the beginning of the week when she'd encountered Arran and me outside the Gloaming, but when she'd turned up to a Pilates class this afternoon, I got the distinct feeling she was itching to ask me something.

"Push into your heel, stretch your right calf muscle. That's it," I encouraged, looking around the studio to make certain everyone was following carefully. "Okay." I stood out of pose and then lowered myself to my mat. "Last one, and then you're free."

The class tittered as they mimicked my position.

"It's your favorite stretch," I teased. Even though it was mine, I knew not everyone loved it. "Knees bent, place your right foot over your left knee and gently draw your knee to your chest." Turning my head on the mat, I searched everyone, saw they were good, and said, "Now the other knee."

A few minutes later, the class was on their feet, rolling up their mats. When I first moved to Ardnoch to run one of Lachlan's fitness studios on the small loch on his estate, I'd been a little starstruck at first. Yes, I'd lived in LA most of my life and seen more than my fair share of famous people, but I'd never instructed them in an intimate studio. Funny how quickly I got used to it, how easy it was to remind myself they were just people, good, not so good, funny, complicated people.

One of them had even become a close friend.

But she'd been one of those rare folks with a special gift. She was wicked, so very wicked, but, Lord, did she have a gift for making people believe she was good. Lucy Wainwright was a high-caliber actor who'd befriended me, gained my trust, gained all our trust, and then she'd terrorized Ardnoch, including me, all because she was obsessed with Lachlan. No, she was obsessed with herself, and she'd decided that Lachlan was the only man worthy of her.

She did just about every diabolical thing a person could do to have him. She almost killed Robyn and Lachlan. She wrecked my studio, which emotionally took me back to a traumatizing place. And she hadn't operated alone. Her accomplice, Fergus, worked as a mechanic on the estate and had been a longtime family friend of the Adairs, another of Brodan's close childhood friends. He was working on an old car for me before Lucy shot him.

Truth be told, Lucy had shaken my faith in my gut instinct.

But not today, as Iris Benning waited until every other person left my studio before she approached. I felt it in my gut that Iris Benning was not a nice person and that I needed to be careful around her.

"Eredine, right?" She smiled falsely.

I didn't bother replying because she'd just spent an entire hour in my class while people said my name.

Her smile wavered, annoyance flashing in her eyes. "Right. Well, I've noticed that you're kind of chummy with the Adairs. I've seen you with Lachlan on the estate and then you were cozy with the younger one who looks like him in town the other day."

I waited, wondering where this was going, sensing I would not like it.

At my continued silence, her smile dropped entirely. "I've also seen you with Galbraith."

Oh, here it was.

"Do you speak?" she spat.

Patiently, I replied, "I'm waiting for the question."

Her jaw clenched. "I want Mac's number and thought you might have it."

I did. "If you have a security issue and would like to talk with Mr. Galbraith, you only have to ask Wakefield or Stephen"—Ardnoch's butler and underbutler—"and they will arrange a time for you to speak with Mr. Galbraith."

Iris sneered, and it amazed me how lovely she'd seemed before I met her compared to how plain and mean she appeared now. "I need to talk to him, and I'm pretty certain he'll want to talk to me too, if you catch my meaning. Which is why I'm asking if you have his cell number."

Lord, she was delusional. "I can't give out staff members' private contact details to you."

"So, you have his number?"

"Ms. Benning, Mr. Galbraith is engaged to my friend."

She smirked. "Men are not monogamous creatures, and I've seen the way he looks at me. Now give me what I asked for."

Was she wackadoodle? True uneasiness filled me. What

was it about this place that attracted the crazies? "Ms. Benning—"

"Let's cut the crap." Iris stepped toward me. She was tall, so we were face-to-face. "I want Mac's number, and unless you want me to get you fired, you're going to give it to me."

Though rage burned through my blood at her threat, I stayed outwardly calm. "Fired?"

Her lips twisted cruelly. "I'm an excellent actor, Pilates Girl, and I'm pretty sure everyone will believe me when I say that you hit me in a fit of rage for no good reason."

What?

Was she insane?

Struggling to control my breathing, I clenched my fists, hating the satisfaction I saw in her face as she took in my reaction.

"Well? Mac's number?"

Feeling sick to my stomach, but refusing to be cowed by this awful woman, I replied, "You've made a huge mistake, Ms. Benning."

"Don't you threaten me," she snapped, getting in my face, and I feared this was about to escalate.

"Step back," I replied quietly. "Step back now. There are cameras in this studio," I warned her.

Her eyes widened as she retreated, glancing up toward the corner of the room. She spotted the CCTV Lachlan installed after Lucy and Fergus trashed my studio. Iris blanched. Her gaze flicked to me. "I'll just say you threatened me. Which is true." Then she stormed out of the studio.

"Damn it," I muttered, running a shaky hand down my face.

LACHLAN'S EXPRESSION HAD DARKENED, a human representation of a thundercloud.

"She said what?"

Still sick to my stomach, I repeated word for word what Iris Benning said to me.

My boss and friend pushed away from the desk in what we called his stage office. It was a fancy reception room just off the great hall used to talk with club members. His actual office was a small, practical room in the staff quarters. "That nasty, dangerous wee ..." He petered off in a growl of anger.

He then lifted the phone off his desk and hit a button. "Mac," he barked, "I need you in my stage office now." He hung up, his attention returning to me.. "Are you all right?"

"I'm fine," I promised him, even though I was still shaken.

Lachlan rounded the desk and leaned against it. "I'm sorry I put you in this position."

"You didn't. You weren't to know what she was like."

"But I knew she was bothering Mac. I just didn't realize it was this bad. And to threaten you ... did she honestly think she'd get away with that? That I'd believe her over you?"

Yes. But I had to wonder if deep down, Iris thought no one would believe a Black member of staff over a White club member. She was a fool, if so. She didn't know Lachlan at all. It also made me wonder if she'd done this before. How many people she thought below her had she hurt to get what she wanted?

It made me seethe, though no one would ever know.

I was a swan, floating calmly across the water, but no one could see my feet kicking like hell beneath.

"Thank you for trusting me," Lachlan said.

I gave him a small smile. "Of course. You're a good boss, Lachlan, and an even better friend."

His lips quirked, but his eyes were still filled with anger and concern. A knock at his door brought our heads around as Mac Galbraith entered. He took in the sight of us and closed the door. Sensing the obvious tension, he scowled. "What happened?"

ARRAN

It was a good thing the kids were around to hog my attention because every second they weren't asking me a question or demanding a story, my attention was drawn to Eredine.

She'd seemed fine after our conversation on the beach a few days ago. I'd been assured from her demeanor that whatever feelings she'd had for Brodan had been shallow and fleeting.

But for days now, Eredine had been quiet and introspective, and when I tried to ask her if anything was the matter, she blew me off.

It was fucking irritating.

I wanted her to tell me when she was having a shit day. I wanted to be that person she could vent to.

Something was up. I could feel it.

As I took a bite of the fajitas Lachlan and Robyn had cooked for our weekend family get-together, I watched Eredine smile at something Arro said at the other end of the table. What was with that? Ery usually sat with me.

Had I pushed her away by being honest about Monroe, about how I used to treat women? Surely, she knew from the fact that I had a permanent case of blue balls, I hadn't touched another woman in eight months.

It was the longest I'd ever gone without sex.

And it was bloody unpleasant.

Sensing my stare, Eredine looked over and frowned. "What's wrong?" she mouthed.

Aye, wasn't that the question of the hour?

Before I could respond, my niece, Eilidh, who just turned seven but acted like a deranged forty-year-old half the time, announced loudly, "I'm done! Uncle Arran, will you come watch a movie with me now?"

"I'm done too." Lewis, my nine-year-old nephew, pushed his plate away.

Thane, my second-eldest brother and their father, said from beside me, "Then you both may be excused from the table, but Uncle Arran is still eating."

Eilidh frowned at me, and I tried not to laugh as she said with extreme disappointment, "You're so slow, Uncle Arran."

"Apologies, my lady." I bowed my head.

She giggled and slipped from the table. "You can make up for it later."

Snorting, I nodded, but found my gaze drawn back to Eredine. Her eyes were lit with affection as she grinned at me.

My heart lurched in my chest.

Thane nudged me, and I reluctantly pulled my focus from her.

My brother gave me a searching look. "I hope you know what you're doing there."

Indignation filled me. "What does that mean?"

His expression softened. "I'm not worried about her, wee brother. I just don't want *you* to get hurt."

"Excuse me!" We heard a gasp, and I looked around just in time to watch Arro jolt back from the table and bolt out of the room.

"Is she all right?" Thane asked over my head to Mac.

41

Mac, concern etched in his brow, left the table with a mute nod to march after her.

"Everything's cooked properly, right?" Lachlan glanced frantically from plate to plate. "Usually Robyn cooks the chicken," he said, inspecting his half-eaten tortilla, "but the smell was giving her the boak."

"The what?" Regan asked.

"Making me feel sick," Robyn translated.

"Ooh, that's a new one." Regan looked at her fiancé, Thane. "You've never used that phrase before."

"It's not exactly a sexy word," he muttered dryly, eyeing Robyn with suspicion.

"What is it?" I asked, looking at my sister-in-law.

"Nothing," he murmured before taking a drink.

It took less than five seconds for my attention to be drawn back to Eredine. Even as Eilidh and Lewis started fighting over the TV remote in the living room and Thane yelled in my ear for them to quit, I didn't tear my gaze from her. She was watching the hallway where Arro and Mac had disappeared, a pinch of worry between her brows.

I could still hear Lachlan clucking over Robyn to make sure her food tasted all right, that he'd cooked everything okay, like he was a fucking mother hen. And I wondered if I really wanted to do that to myself. Give myself to another person so completely—it would change me. Thane, Lachlan, and Mac had changed. Not dramatically, but in small ways. Well, maybe Mac's transformation was a wee bit more dramatic than that of my brothers.

But as Eredine turned those gorgeous hazel-green eyes on me, I realized I had no choice.

I wanted to see what could be between us more than I could remember wanting anything.

Eredine's gaze flew over my head and widened with concern. "Arro, are you okay?" she asked.

Everyone turned to watch my sister walk back into Lachlan's large, open-plan living area with Mac's arm around her shoulders. Her cheeks were pale. They halted before the table, sharing a look with one another before Arro heaved a sigh. "I guess there's no better time to tell you since we're all here together ... We're having a baby."

"Oh, bloody hell." Lachlan shocked us all by slumping back in his chair.

Arro scowled. "Not really the response I was hoping for, big brother."

He blanched. "No, it's not that." He looked to Robyn, but her back was to me, so I couldn't make out her expression. But then she turned to Arro and Mac, and she seemed ready to burst into laughter.

"Um ... You will not believe this." Her eyes flicked to Mac, her *father*. "But I'm pregnant too."

The table exploded into a chatter of surprise as we all flew from our chairs to congratulate the couples. When the hugging and exclamations died down, Robyn asked Arro, "How many weeks are you?"

"Fourteen."

"Holy shit," Robyn huffed. "I'm fourteen weeks too."

"Could this family get any weirder?" I asked. Because Robyn had married Lachlan, and Mac (Robyn's dad) was engaged to Arro, Lachlan's sister, that meant that any kids each couple had would not only be cousins, but Arro and Mac's child would be half uncle or half aunt to Lachlan and Robyn's child because Robyn would be Mac's child's half sister. It was weird before, when Arro was technically Robyn's new soon-to-be stepmother via Mac and sister-in-law via Lachlan, but now she'd be auntie to Lachlan and Robyn's baby. And the final cherry on top of the weirdness... Mac would be grandfather to Robyn and Lachlan's baby.

Fuck, that hurt my brain just trying to work it out.

And now the kids will be the same age.

Robyn snorted. "So we conceived—"

"Don't," Mac cut her off belligerently, and Arro pinched her lips tight to keep from laughing. "No. Nope. Fucking no."

"Mac, there are children present," Regan admonished primly.

"Sorry. But no. We are not discussing the details of this strange, bloody situation." Mac glared at Lachlan. "This is all your fault."

Lachlan's indignant expression did it for me.

I laughed, and hearing Thane's laughter join mine just made me laugh harder.

"I AM STUFFED."

I turned from my seat on the steps of Lachlan's back deck to see Eredine slipping through the bifold doors before closing them behind her. She smiled, illuminated by Lachlan's deck lighting, before sitting beside me.

"I think Lachlan and Robyn made all that dessert to distract us."

My lips twitched. "There is no distracting anyone from the fact that they most likely conceived a child in the same week. It's fucking hilarious."

"Not for Mac." Ery nudged me. "Give the guy a break."

"You laughed."

Eredine snorted. "Who wouldn't, to be fair?" She glanced at me. "Hey, you're going to be an uncle again."

I grinned at the thought. I loved Eilidh and Lewis. In fact, I felt sad when I thought about all the years I'd missed with them. But I was trying my damnedest to make up for it. "I'm looking forward to more miniature Adairs running around.

If they are as funny as the current minis we've got, it'll be grand."

"I don't think there will ever be another Eilidh and Lewis Adair."

"Truth." I thought about the hardship those two wee ones had been through. Not only had they lost their mother to a brain aneurysm months after Eilidh was born, a man who was stalking Regan had traumatized them. He'd taken the kids and tied them up in the guest house where I was currently staying. Just the thought of anyone touching those precious kids filled me with rage. "They amaze me, you know. So resilient."

"They are."

The night it happened, Eredine was babysitting. The intruder, Austin, hit Ery over the head, twice, with a baseball bat. She was so damn lucky there was no permanent damage. A miracle, in fact. If that bastard hadn't toppled over the edge of a cliff while fighting with Regan, I'd hunt him down and kill him myself.

"So are you." I pressed my leg against hers. "You amaze me too."

Eredine looked down at where our legs touched.

"Ery."

"Mmm?" Her gaze moved toward the sea. The moon rippled over the water, and we could hear the waves hitting the cliff bottom.

Lachlan and Thane had built mirror-image houses on the land here in Caelmore, a tiny plot not far outside Ardnoch. Land stretching along this part of the coastline belonged to the Adairs, and Thane, an architect, had designed two more houses a little farther down the coast. One for Mac and Arro, and one for me. Planning permission had been slow, just as it had been for the Gloaming, but we broke ground on the houses a few weeks ago.

Thane had a contractor project-managing the whole thing, and I was trusting my brother to get the house done so I didn't have to think about it on top of the Gloaming renovations.

I was looking forward to no longer living in Thane's guest annex.

Studying Eredine's profile, I thought of how I'd asked for her input with the house design and how she'd shyly but slowly offered her opinion. I'd thought I'd made serious progress with her, that I was the one person she could truly trust.

But something happened, and she hadn't told me about it, and it was pissing me off beyond reason.

For so long, I was not the guy people trusted.

I needed to be that guy for her.

But I didn't want to force it.

"Nothing," I murmured, staring out at the water.

Silence fell between us as I stewed and tried not to grow visibly frustrated, thinking that maybe I'd never get past Ery's walls. That nothing would ever happen between us.

Then I felt the press of her knee against my thigh, and I turned to look at her.

She looked unbearably sad.

I hated seeing her like that. "Ery?"

"You can't tell anyone because it's club business," she said, "but I had an altercation with a member this week."

Anger, instant and blazing, lashed through me. "Altercation?" I gritted out.

Eredine squeezed my arm. "Nothing physical," she assured me. "It was with Iris Benning."

I frowned. "The actor who stopped us outside the Gloaming?"

"Yeah." Eredine proceeded to tell me what happened between them.

46

"That scummy wee cow." I glowered in outrage. How fucking dare she! "What happened? And if you say Lachlan didn't boot her off the estate, then I'm afraid I'll have to rip my brother a new one."

She leaned into me. "You know Lachlan better than that."

I relaxed infinitesimally.

"But he couldn't just throw her out like he did with Sebastian Stone. Mac had to stop him from doing just that and reminded him he had a board to consult. Thankfully, between Mac's accusations of harassment and what occurred between me and her, they didn't take long to come back with their unanimous decision to cancel her membership and have security escort her out of Ardnoch."

"I can't imagine she took that well."

"Probably not."

Sliding my arm around her shoulders, I hugged her to my side. Eredine tensed for a second before she relaxed into me. "Is this why you've been quiet all week?"

"Aren't I always quiet?" she teased.

I chuckled. "More so than usual."

Ery nodded. "I just ... I know there are more good people than bad, and most of our guests are really nice and respectful. But knowing there are people like Iris Benning out there in the world makes me sad. I don't understand them. I don't understand that need to cause others pain. To be so focused on obtaining what you want, you don't care who you hurt or destroy to get it."

"Hey." I gently grasped her by the chin to turn her face to look at me. Staring into those haunted eyes, I wished like fuck I could take away every bad thing that had happened to this woman. But first I needed to know what those things were. "I'm sorry if you've met more than your fair share of shitty people ... but do you know how much more of a miracle it is, then, that you are who you are, Ery?"

"And who do you think I am?" she whispered.

My chest suddenly felt too tight and my words came out hoarse. "You are good. From the tips of your toes to the ends of your curls ... you're nothing but good, through and through."

Her eyes widened as the air charged and crackled between us. "Arran ..."

Rational thought left me as my eyes dropped to her perfect mouth, and my head descended—

"There you are, Uncle Arran!" Eilidh's voice was like a lasso, jolting me from Eredine.

She stared up at me wide-eyed before Eilidh's arms came around Ery's neck. Eilidh pressed her cheek to Ery's, and her entire expression melted into warmth and affection.

"Hey, sweetie." She rubbed Eilidh's arm. "All okay?"

"Yup." Eilidh pressed a quick kiss to Ery's cheek. "Mum told me to come get you because her and Aunt Arro are talking about the weddings." Arro and Thane would be sharing a wedding day this summer. Eilidh's dark blue gaze cut to me. "Uncle Arran, will you come help me win against Lewis on the Nintendo? He's being really annoying and smug."

My lips twitched at her use of the word *smug*, and I nodded. "Come on, then."

We stood, and I tried to catch Eredine's eyes to see how she was feeling about our near kiss, but she wouldn't look at me.

And I was worried that pretty much said it all.

5

EREDINE

While I usually had time between my morning and afternoon classes to leave the estate for lunch with either Arran or one of the girls, Monday was not that day. Perhaps to counteract a weekend of eating and drinking, Mondays were always my busiest.

For almost two years, I'd eaten lunch in the studio on the first day of the week, until Lachlan had enough of me being antisocial and maneuvered me into the staff lunchroom at the castle. To my surprise, the men and women who worked at the spa—a separate building a short drive from the castle —ate their lunch here, too, since the estate chef served the staff lunch. The food was fantastic, making it worth the trek over.

I began a friendly acquaintance with a couple of the spa ladies and ate with them every Monday.

Call it my Spidey senses or whatever, but I knew as soon as I walked into the lunchroom today that something was up. I felt eyes on me from all over, and as I approached the pass-through where we place our order, I glanced over my

SAMANTHA YOUNG

shoulder at the spa girls and noted they were watching me too.

Unease shifted through me, but I chose an option off today's small menu. The kitchen staff member in charge today, Ali, said he'd give me a shout when it was ready.

Sucking in a breath, I walked toward the table, eyeballing the girls.

"Hey," I said quietly as I took the empty chair they'd left for me.

They exchanged a look, and then Michelle, a masseuse from Inverness, said, "Notice anything strange in your classes this morning?"

I couldn't say that I had. I frowned. "Not really."

She raised an eyebrow. "Considering the gossip, I thought you would have noticed."

I tensed. "What gossip?"

Natalia, a young woman originally from Glasgow, had escaped her massive Scottish-Italian family there for a little privacy up here. She shared a lodge on the estate with a few of the other young staffers. She leaned toward me. "Iris Benning told anyone she could that you're a snake who lied and got her thrown out. A few of the members were gossiping about it at the spa this morning."

"Saying what?" I gritted out, anger filling my belly.

"Iris told them not to trust you. They were ..." Natalia shot a look at Michelle, who scowled. "They were talking about whether they'd come back to your class."

Pulse racing at the thought of my classes becoming obsolete, I forced myself to remain calm as I rewound through my memories of this morning's sessions. None seemed any smaller, and I'd felt no weirdness from the members. We'd had a very good turnout for my yoga/mindfulness class in particular. It was those mindfulness techniques, in fact, that stopped me from overreacting to stressful situations such as this.

And thank goodness, because if what they were saying was true, then wouldn't my classes have been smaller? Someone would have said something, surely? Lachlan would have gotten complaints from members and said something, no?

"I didn't hear that," Michelle interjected. "I just heard that Iris Benning was shooting her mouth off about you."

"Me too," Anne-Marie, a nail technician who lived in Ardnoch, added, expression reassuring. "I didn't hear anything about boycotting your classes."

"I think most of them are probably well aware that Iris Benning is a rotten apple." Jacinda, the spa's oldest staff member, an experienced freelance physiotherapist who only works Mondays, shook her head. I could tell she was annoyed they'd even brought this to my attention. "Anyone who's crossed paths with that woman knows it. And this isn't the Golden Age of Hollywood. That kind of behavior doesn't stay buried anymore. Soon enough, the world will know who Iris Benning really is. So don't you let her worry you a bit, Eredine," she said kindly.

I gave her a small smile. "I won't."

"Good."

A call of my name drew me from the conversation. In the time it took me to collect my lunch and return to the table, I'd convinced myself to focus on Jacinda's advice. There was always gossip among the staff here because we'd all signed nondisclosure agreements that meant we couldn't discuss anything that happened inside the club with the outside world. So we only had each other to unload it on to. But the gossip always died down within a few days when they found something else to talk about.

"I honestly thought it was a myth." Anne-Marie giggled as I sat down.

Jacinda snorted while Michelle wore an envious expression.

Just before taking my first bite of grilled salmon and rice salad, I asked, "What's a myth?"

Anne-Marie beamed. "The G-spot."

I nearly choked on my mouthful, and the ladies laughed. "Sorry," I said once I'd swallowed, my cheeks flushed. "I wasn't expecting that."

"Neither was I." Anne-Marie cackled. "But my God, where has it been all my life?"

Now *I* felt envious.

"You've honestly never had a man hit your G-spot before?" Jacinda frowned.

"Hey, I'm not sure I have," Michelle answered, her lip curled in disappointment. "And I'm ten years older than she is."

Natalia shook her head. "You need to get that man of yours told."

"Aye, don't I know it."

"Do it doggy style," Anne-Marie instructed. "Seriously, I was totally against it because I always thought it would be impersonal, but oof ..." She waved a hand over her face like she was getting hot just thinking about it. "He hit me so deep, and at this angle—"

"We get it," Michelle cut her off. "You're embarrassing Eredine."

"No, you're not," I promised Anne-Marie while trying not to be annoyed at Michelle for using me as the excuse. "I'm thirty-two, not a shy virgin."

"You're thirty-two?" Natalia's eyes almost popped out of her head. "Give me your skin-care regimen. You look my age."

Granny had taught me to take care of my hair and skin from the age of twelve. "Thanks."

"Not a shy virgin?" Michelle pounced, eyeing me. "So, why do we never hear about your sexual exploits?"

Because I hadn't had sex in eight years.

Oh my Lord.

Eight years.

Maybe my hymen had regrown. Who knew?

I missed sex.

Not that I'd ever been a casual sex kind of girl. I'd always been in a relationship with the person I was intimate with, but I'd had this one boyfriend before everything fell apart, and he was the first guy I'd met who seemed to care if I had a good time. We'd had some pretty great sex together.

I *really* missed sex.

Squirming, I crossed my legs under the table and speared my fork through a piece of salmon, a little too aggressively. "I'm very private," I finally said.

"So, you're not banging the headboard with Arran Adair?" Anne-Marie teased.

Unamused, I shot her a look that made her smile fall. "More gossip?"

"Sorry. I didn't mean anything ..."

"It's fine." I shook my head. "Arran and I are just friends."

"How can you be just friends with him?" Natalia huffed. "He is gorgeous."

"Not as gorgeous as Brodan," Michelle said. "Did you see his last film? I kept rewinding the scene where he comes out of the bathroom naked, and though they didn't let you see his dick, they certainly let you see his arse. And what an arse it is." She closed her eyes as if replaying the scene in her head.

I squirmed uncomfortably again because not that long ago, I'd fantasized about Brodan Adair, and now I barely even thought of him. And while the mention of Arran bothered me, I only felt a flicker of annoyance on Brodan's behalf for being objectified. Not that he'd mind.

"I'd take Thane over the others any day." Jacinda pointed her fork at us. "Now that is a *man*."

Anne-Marie sighed dramatically. "Well, I'd actually take them all. Orgy style."

"You try one sexual position outside of missionary, and suddenly you're into orgies," Michelle teased.

Anne-Marie cackled, and we all laughed with her, but my smile covered the gloom that had fallen over me.

It was a gloom that came for me now and then, and more often lately. While I knew I wasn't capable of a relationship with someone anymore, I longed to be touched again. I missed kisses and caresses and the feel of a man moving inside me.

I'd never considered casual sex before because I needed to trust the person I was with, and it seemed impossible to find both.

Envy for these women who could reach for sex when they wanted it, could enjoy life to the fullest, scored through me. Arro, Regan, and Robyn might crack jokes about their sex lives, but they didn't go into detail because of the connections. Regan and Robyn, sisters, were with Arro's brothers, and Arro was with Robyn's father. It was too weird for them to chat about, saving me from those conversations.

But I envied them too. They'd all more than insinuated they were delighted with their sex lives.

The Adair men and Mac Galbraith apparently knew how to satisfy their women.

An image of a naked Arran braced over me, his hips thrusting against mine, flashed before my eyes, and heat blazed through me. My fork fell from my fingers, clattering against my plate, drawing the ladies' attention.

"Are you okay?" Michelle asked, concerned.

"Fine. Just done. Didn't mean to drop my fork like that." I laughed softly, trying not to look mortified. I wished them all a great afternoon and took my plate up to empty it before passing it through the kitchen's wash-up window.

Unfortunately, now that the image of Arran had entered my mind, I couldn't get it to stop replaying. Over and over and over ...

6

ARRAN

"**D**id you get my email?" My contractor, Bill, approached me as soon as I stepped into the Gloaming.

My mind, as per usual, was preoccupied with Eredine. This morning on our run, she'd been distracted again. She'd barely looked at me. I tried to recall if I'd said or done anything to upset her, but I'd been my usual self.

Frowning, I shook my head. "Problem?"

"Aye, you could say that. Follow me."

Bill led me past the bar and into the ground-floor great room used for events. This very room had hosted Ardnoch village's anniversary ceilidh every year for as long as I could remember. The village's anniversary of becoming a royal burgh was much celebrated, and this year was our 393rd. Scheduled for a few weeks' time from now, the ceilidh had been relocated to our town hall, just for this year. To say the locals weren't happy was an understatement. However, they'd show up, even if they whined about the venue change.

Stopping at the entrance to the event room, Bill pointed

upward where we'd exposed the building's structure. "Joints are rotten. It's a wonder this bloody thing hasn't collapsed."

My stomach twisted at the thought. "What does this mean?"

"I had the engineer come out early this morning, and he says it all needs replaced."

Looking at how spectacular the space looked with the ceiling removed, I frowned as I studied it. "If we're having to replace these, could we just vault the ceiling? Leave it open."

"Oh, aye, we could do that. That would look grand."

"Right. Well, if you can get me the added cost of replacing these, that'd be great. I'll talk with Lachlan, make sure he's on board with the vaulting, and then I'll let you know."

"Perfect."

I strode back out into the bar area, untouched for the moment with renovations focused elsewhere, and I pulled out my phone to call Lachlan. The email banner notifications on my screen alerted me to Bill's email but also to another that froze me on the spot.

Indignation churned in my gut as I tapped on the notification.

The email from blackwidow0101@gmail.com opened up to one line: **Don't think I've forgotten about you.**

Deleting the email, I ground my teeth and took a breath before hitting Lachlan's number. For a few years now, I'd received these ominous one-line emails that all said roughly the same thing, about not forgetting me or about watching me. Since nothing had come of them, I'd decided it was just some bored crazy on the internet sending random emails.

After everything that happened with my family, however, there was a moment when I paused to think about the emails. One came every few months. But if I mentioned it, my family would overreact, and, quite rightly, considering what they'd been through. I didn't want to worry them over something I was ninety-nine percent sure was a prank.

"Morning," Lachlan answered on the fifth ring.

"Do you want the good news or the bad news first?"

He sighed. "Please do not tell me people are picketing outside the Gloaming about the anniversary ceilidh?"

I snorted. "Please don't tell me that's been a threat."

"I wouldn't put it past them. You'd think they'd be happy. I offered to pay for the whole bloody thing this year as recompense for the change of venue. Do they care? No. We changed their precious routine, and I am fielding calls every fucking day asking me if this or that will still happen this year or how not to use the fucking caterer Gordon used every year because no one really liked the food. Fuck."

I covered another snort because I could hear how stressed he was, and it shouldn't be funny.

"I can hear you smiling," he snapped. "Aye, you wouldn't be smiling if you were the one dealing with this shite."

A chuckle escaped before I could stop it. "If it makes you feel any better, I can't walk through the village without someone stopping to lecture me about what we should and shouldn't be doing to the Gloaming."

"No one likes change, apparently." My big brother sighed, sounding exhausted.

At once feeling like a shit for making light of his stress, I asked, "Everything else okay?"

"Och, I'm just a bit knackered. I can't seem to sleep."

"Worrying about Robyn?" I guessed.

Lachlan hesitated, but then confessed, "Every minute of the day."

Our mother, Vivien, died when I was barely three years old, after giving birth to Arro. A blood clot killed her. I didn't remember her, but Lachlan and Thane, being the eldest, did. Even Brodan had memories of our mother. I remembered

58

our aunt Imogen more. She was our dad's sister, and I remember her stepping in to help because Dad checked out after Mum died. However, tragically, Aunt Imogen died in a hiking accident when I was seven.

The Adair men had an awful family history of losing the women they loved, and I knew from Thane the so-called curse had badly affected Lachlan in particular. He'd almost lost Robyn and pushed her away because of his fear of eventually losing her, anyway.

Maybe her pregnancy was bringing up some of that old trauma.

"She'll be fine, Lachlan. She's young and healthy."

"I know." His voice was hoarse. "Logically, I know that."

"You know I'm here, aye? If you ever need me or need to talk … I know I haven't been around in the past, but I'm here now."

"I know. I know that, Arran," he promised. "Thank you."

I didn't know what to say after that, emotion thickening my throat.

"So," Lachlan broke the moment of silence, "bad news first?"

"Ah, yes, that. About the great room ceiling …"

I SAUNTERED into Thane's laundry room, hearing the bustle of his family in the main living area beyond. Since I'd taken up residence in my brother's annex, Thane and Regan made it clear I always had an open invitation for dinner. So I followed my growling stomach into their place.

Unfortunately, when I stepped into the kitchen, it was to find Thane helping Regan into a jacket. They looked dressed up. Beyond them, Eredine played a board game with Eilidh and Lewis at the dining table.

Dirty dishes on the kitchen counter suggested they'd already eaten.

Thane frowned at me. "I thought you were out tonight." He glanced questioningly at Regan.

Regan shrugged, face a perfect mask of innocence. "I thought that's what he said." She looked at me, still guileless. "Didn't you say you were going out tonight?"

Confused, I shook my head. "Not that I recall."

"Oh, I must have gotten mixed up."

"But …" Thane sighed. "If I'd known Arran was here, we could have asked him to watch the kids instead of dragging Ery out."

"Watch the kids? Where are you going?"

"Date night." Thane slid an arm around Regan's waist. "We've got a table booked at North Star."

I raised an eyebrow. That was a pretty fancy restaurant and one of Arro's favorites. "Occasion?"

Regan shrugged. "We haven't had time alone in a while."

"Reason enough." I flicked another look at Eredine, anticipating an evening with her. "Well, I haven't eaten, so I'll just stick around if you don't mind. Any leftovers?"

Regan nodded to a tray covered in foil. "Left some behind just in case. Pop it in to reheat." She beamed. "Enjoy your night."

"Will do, thanks. Enjoy yours."

Thane eyed Regan with an expression that bordered on suspicious, but when she wrinkled her nose at him, he shook his head and turned to call out to the kids. "We're leaving."

"Bye!" They waved them away with barely a look, too engrossed in their game.

"Love you too," Thane said dryly before he led Regan toward the exit. "We'll be back by eleven."

"Have fun, kiddies," I said quietly. "No pulling over for car sex on the way home."

The immediate bloom of red on Regan's face revealed that was exactly what they were planning on doing. I howled with laughter.

Lucky buggers.

Thane cut me a mock glare over his shoulder before they walked out of sight. I heard the front door open and shut a few seconds later and turned to Ery and the kids.

Eredine gave me a small smile. "You staying? Regan said you were out for the night."

"Regan was mistaken," I answered, quite chuffed with how the evening was panning out, and even more so that Ery was making eye contact. After her bizarre behavior this morning, I'd worried all day that maybe I'd fucked up unknowingly. "Let me heat this up and then I'll come over to play."

"You'll be on my team, Uncle Arran," Eilidh decided.

"You got it, cutie."

My niece beamed, and fuck, my heart … Seriously, the kid could ask for the last penny in my bank account, and I'd hand it over with no qualms. She had me wrapped around her tiny pinkie finger.

Not long later, I approached the dining table, plate of reheated steak pie and mash in hand, and slid into the seat beside Ery. Her hair was loose tonight, tumbling in long, shining waves down her back. I'd never paid much attention to a woman's hair beyond if it was nice, but Ery's played a pivotal role in my fantasies about her. Mostly just seeing it sprawled across my bedsheets, but also wrapped around my fist as we fucked.

I shifted uncomfortably in my seat. "Changed your hair?"

Ery glanced at me in surprise. "Yeah."

"I like it!" Eilidh announced. "Why don't you wear it like that more?"

"One: because I feel lucky to have curls like mine and I

like my hair curly. Two: it takes forever," Ery replied with a wry twist to her lips. "First, I have to straighten my hair and then put this wave in it."

"That doesn't seem like much work." Eilidh frowned. "Maybe we could do that to my hair!"

My niece was also blessed with natural dark curls, but I had a feeling her father might not be amused by anyone taking a straightener to them.

Eredine agreed apparently. "Um, maybe when you're older."

"Can we get back to the game?" Lewis frowned at us, especially me, as if I'd somehow betrayed the brotherhood by mentioning hair in the first place. "Bloody Nora."

While I choked on a piece of steak pie, Eredine admonished gently, "Lewis Adair, we do not use that kind of language."

"Sorry," he murmured.

"Apology accepted. Now, back to the game."

It had been unseasonably hot all day, and the evening was no different. And while Thane had designed a home that stayed cooler than most in the summer, it was still muggy inside, and the kids were growing crabbit.

"Let's play a wee game of football," I suggested. "We'll probably get a breeze coming up off the water."

The kids jumped to it, scattering from the table to grab their trainers.

Ery slowly stood and pulled her thick hair into a ponytail. It was a wonder she had a hair tie that could hold it. "You're staring," she murmured.

"Am I?" I sounded hoarse even to my ears.

Her eyes widened a little, and then she pushed back from the table. "I'll get my sneakers."

I was not ashamed to admit that my eyes followed her perfect arse out of the room. Groaning, I scrubbed my hands down my face and tried to get it together. I was better than some horny wee teenager who couldn't control his attraction to a beautiful woman.

I hoped.

Getting up, I strode across the room and slid the already-open bifolds back against the wall. I was right. The sea's cool breeze felt bloody marvelous.

T-shirt sticking to me, I whipped it off and tucked it into the back of my jeans. Finding the football already outside, I created goals with the large rocks we kept in the back garden for such occasions. A fence wrapped around the yard to protect the kids from the cliff's edge.

The sea was calm beneath perfect skies, weather more suited to summer than spring, and I could hear soft waves lapping against the coast unimpeded.

"I'm taking my shirt off too!" Lewis yelled as he hurried down the deck toward me, already flying out of his T-shirt. "Feels good." He stood arms wide, letting the breeze flow over him. "Good plan, Uncle Arr."

I stifled a laugh and even more so when Eredine appeared with Eilidh, and then stuttered to a stop at the sight of me.

Her eyes dragged over my body, and I saw her hands clench at her sides. I also noted the way her breathing moved a little quicker than usual.

Fuck.

She was attracted to me too. No doubt about it.

For a second, I wished the kids weren't here so I could cross the distance between us and kiss the absolute hell out of her.

"Why do you have your shirts off?" Eilidh crossed her arms over her chest. "That's not fair."

"Do either of you have sun lotion on?" Ery yanked her attention from me to frown at Lewis as she walked down the deck steps. "You can't play like that without lotion on."

"The sun is low," I replied. "We've barely got an hour of it left. Can't do that much damage."

"Thane and Regan like the kids to have lotion on when it's sunny," she countered.

"Och, I'll put my shirt back on." Lewis sighed wearily, as if everyone was trying his patience this evening. He pulled his shirt over his head.

Ery glowered at me. "You too."

I smirked but nodded. Sauntering toward her, I pulled my shirt out of my jeans but stopped at her side to murmur in her ear, "Excuses, excuses."

"What?" She turned to glare harder, our noses almost touching.

My eyes dropped to her mouth, and I said, "All you had to say, gorgeous, was that my naked body is too much of a distraction. You didn't have to make up crap about lotion."

She huffed in a breath and pulled away from me. "Not an excuse. Skin cancer isn't a joke."

"True." I pulled on my shirt. "But don't think I'm buying it."

We stared each other down until Eilidh asked, "Why are you looking at each other like that?"

Ery broke our gazes first, turning to my niece with a bright smile. "We're sizing up the competition. Staring each other down. Because it's boys against girls, right?"

"Yes!" Lewis shot a fist into the air. "I'm so gonna win with Uncle Arr on my team."

I winked at him, but my amusement died when Eilidh yelled unhappily, "No! Uncle Arran is mine!"

I felt that tug in my chest again.

"That's not fair! You always want Uncle Arr on your team. You just had him on your team for the board game!" Lewis's wee face darkened with frustration.

"Hey, hey." Ery knelt beside Eilidh, who looked near tears. "Don't you want to be on my team, Eilidh-boo? I miss being on yours."

That seemed to surprise Eilidh, as if she hadn't considered it might upset Ery that I'd become her favorite since my arrival. "Really?" she asked quietly.

"Really." She tugged on one of Eilidh's curls. "You know what's so great about having lots of family and friends?"

"What?"

"There's always someone to be on your team. Just because Uncle Arran is on Lewis's team sometimes doesn't mean you don't have someone on yours. And the other great thing about family is that it teaches us to share our love. Sometimes Lewis will need Arran, and you have to be okay with that and vice versa, right?"

"Okay." Eilidh nodded like a little adult. "That makes sense. I'm happy to be on your team, Ery."

For that, Ery hugged my niece hard while I stood in awe that Ery could talk to the kids like that.

Eilidh's smile turned to a scowl as she pulled out of their embrace. "But we better win, Ery."

Ery's laughter made me grin as she promised to "whup our butts."

In the end, Lewis and I won, but while the boy crowed our victory on the short walk back inside, I did not feel triumphant. I felt impatient and possessive over Eredine Willows, and neither emotion was something I was proud of.

7
EREDINE

I loved my house.

My little lodge in the middle of the woods was my haven, surrounded by trees, with potted flowers scattered around the porch to add color in among all the heavenly shades of green. While I knew some of my girlfriends disliked the idea of me being out here alone (and so did Lachlan and the rest of the men in the family), I'd never felt afraid, until Lucy. After her arrest, Lachlan installed cameras and the alarm, so I was back to enjoying the house for the sanctuary it was. I wasn't a misanthrope who needed to be far away from people, but I'd always enjoyed silence and privacy. Now I wrapped both around me like a security blanket.

My days off were every other Saturday, alternating with Thursday, and every Sunday. On Sundays, I spent most of my time with the Adairs. I also babysat for Regan and Thane a couple times a month, which I loved, even if Arran had taken to hanging around. If I was being honest with myself, I didn't mind his presence at all.

This Saturday, however, my day off, I wanted nothing but

to curl up with a good book in my small lodge with no one but the chirping birds for company.

Alas, it wasn't to be. Morosely, and perhaps a little ungratefully, I gave my living room a sad face before I stepped outside and locked up. Regan had been working to start a book club for a long time now and had finally gotten us to agree to meet at Arro's for our inaugural meeting. Every member would take turns picking a book, and the first week had been Regan's choice as club founder. The thought made me smile as I got into my car. It all sounded so very middle school. However, Regan's pick had been as far from middle school as one could get.

As a voracious romance reader, she'd chosen a contemporary novel that was extremely emotional and spicier than anything I'd ever read. Enthralled upon finishing it, I proceeded to buy a bunch more titles for my e-reader. Regan would be so proud. I couldn't wait to tell her.

What I wouldn't be telling her, however, was that the romance novel had only made me miss sex more. It wasn't like I hadn't gone through periods of missing sex in the last eight years—of course, I had. But it had never been this insistent, and I was trying not to overanalyze the timing.

Sighing, I concentrated on driving. I was more than used to the crazy Scottish weather that could change from sunshine to snow in a second, so this weird week of summer temperatures in spring didn't surprise me. Today was another gloriously warm day. Last week I'd been wearing my winter jacket and boots, and now I wore a thin, long-sleeved T-shirt, shorts, and sneakers.

To be fair, we wouldn't consider this hot in California, but my blood had acclimated to the Scottish temps. And when the sun came out in Scotland, so did the skin. Had to grab our vitamin D while we had the chance.

Smiling at the fact that I now considered myself part

Scottish, I hummed along to the radio, enjoying the smell of sun lotion and the shade of my sunglasses.

Arro lived with Mac in a midcentury bungalow on the northern outskirts of Ardnoch village. Once their new house was built in Caelmore near Lachlan and Thane, she planned to rent the bungalow as a holiday let. Arran was building a house near Arro too. A big house. A family-sized house.

I ignored a panicky, fluttery feeling at the thought of my friend settling down with some faceless woman. It would be bye-bye friendship, then, wouldn't it? No wife would allow her husband such a close friendship with another woman.

Mood somewhat soured, I turned up the radio, blasting "Wrecked" by Imagine Dragons to drown out my feelings.

I lowered the volume when I slowed into Arro's residential area. As I pulled into her cul-de-sac, I noted Robyn's Range Rover and assumed she'd driven Regan here since they were neighbors.

Disconnecting my phone from my car after I parked, I noticed a text message from Arro.

Too nice to sit inside so we're in my back garden. See you soon!

Just like that, I didn't mind so much leaving behind my peaceful little lodge. I enjoyed Arro, Robyn, and Regan's company. They seemed to accept me for who I was and never pushed me to give any more than I could. My sixth sense told me from day one of meeting each of them they were good people, all unfailingly kind. Kindness was a big factor for me in choosing friends. Kind friends, plus a day outdoors, sounded good.

Walking quietly around the side of Arro's house, I heard the American-accented voices of Regan and Robyn. It was more than nice to have fellow Americans as friends in Scotland. It made me feel more at home.

But then I caught the sound of my name and stopped, staying hidden.

"We're all worried about Eredine," Arro said, her brogue carrying across the yard.

I frowned, leaning against the side of the house.

"I'm just saying maybe we shouldn't be sitting on that," Regan replied.

My heart rate picked up speed. *Sitting on what?*

"Or maybe we should," Robyn spoke, her tone stern. "Thane told Lachlan that you did something with Arran the other night. Set it up so he was there when Ery came over to babysit. What's with that?"

What? I gaped. I hadn't even asked why I was there if Arran was around to look after Eilidh and Lewis. I'd just been happy he was.

Argh. Regan!

"What?" Regan huffed. "They are good together."

"You know there's something there with Brodan," Robyn argued.

"I'm sorry, but Brodan would have already gone there with Eredine if he was serious about it, and Thane told me Brodan is extremely commitment phobic."

"That's true," Arro added.

A year ago, that might have hurt.

Now I saw it for the truth.

"Brodan or Arran or the man from Timbuktu, it doesn't matter. Eredine has shown no interest in a romantic relationship beyond an obvious crush on Brodan."

I flushed. *Obvious?*

"She's a grown woman, and if she wants a relationship, she'll go after one. You are not butting into her life that like."

Thank you, Robyn. Voice of reason!

"I have to agree, Regan," Arro said.

I heard a heavy sigh. "I wasn't trying to cause trouble. I

just … I was thinking about it, and Ery has been here, what, eight years? And in that time, have you ever seen her with anyone?" Regan asked.

Arro answered, "No. No one."

"That's eight years without sex. Eight looooong years. That is too long for a woman to go without."

Scowling in embarrassment, I considered getting back in my car. So, eight years *was* a long time. I knew that! I didn't need other people to remind me. Not that she knew she was reminding me, since they were talking behind my back.

Hurt pricked me.

So much for unfailingly kind.

"It's none of our business," Robyn reiterated. "Ery doesn't cross me as the type who does casual sex, so if your plan is to throw Arran at her to douse her dry spell, forget it. She'll never do that."

For some reason, that made me glower even harder.

"Aye, definitely not," Arro agreed. "I can't imagine Ery ever having a one-night stand with someone."

How did they know I hadn't? Hmm? I could have had casual sex!

I hadn't.

But they didn't know that for a fact.

They'd just pegged me as Miss Prude or something?

"You don't know that," Regan said, alleviating my annoyance. "None of us really know her."

And I was annoyed again.

Because that stung.

A lot.

Mostly because it was true, and I hated it was true, but I didn't know how to lower the walls that would make it not true.

Tears of frustration stung my eyes.

Sometimes I wished I were someone else. That I could

break free of the chokehold that kept me frozen in place, never moving while everyone else whirled around me, evolving, becoming more.

It might have been irrational, but it hurt that my friends saw me that way too.

"I know enough," Arro said, her tone firm. "She's kind and sweet and clearly loves this family. That's all I need to know."

Her words soothed the ache.

"Now, let's talk about something else because she'll be here soon, and I don't want her to overhear us talking about her like this. It's not nice."

"Guys, I only mentioned it out of love, I promise," Regan said, sounding remorseful. "I adore Ery."

"We know," Robyn assured her. "But let it go, sweetie."

I leaned against the side of the house, listening to them change the subject to Arro and Mac's new place and how it was coming along. Checking the time on my phone, I waited a couple minutes before stepping into the garden with a smile painted on.

The ladies looked happy to see me, and I tried to shrug off my annoyance with them for chatting about my love life and for assuming things about me. I couldn't really blame them for assumptions, since I never shared anything of personal substance. All they could do was guess.

Still, was I really some Mary Sue to them? A boring, sexless creature?

Ignoring that horrible thought, I asked, "How are you guys? Pregnancy treating you kindly?"

Arro and Robyn shared a look, and Robyn turned to me first. "We're opposites. I haven't had an ounce of morning sickness, but I can't sleep at night ..."

"While I'm sick every morning," Arro continued, "and sleepy all the time."

"Neither of you are showing yet."

"Oh, there's a little bump there." Robyn smoothed her T-shirt down, and I could see a slight swelling in her lower abdomen.

Arro stood and turned to the side to do the same with her shirt, and I could see her small swell. "Just a wee bit." She caressed her stomach protectively.

"And how are the menfolk?" Regan asked, eyes bright with amusement. "Thane told me he hovered constantly over Fran when she was pregnant with Lewis but was more laid-back with Eilidh."

Fran was Thane's deceased wife. I hadn't known her as well as I know Arro, but I'd liked Fran. She was warm and friendly and had a great sense of humor. She'd died from an aneurysm not long after Eilidh was born. Thane woke up and found her in bed beside him, just gone. Imagining how that must have been for him always brought tears to my eyes.

I'd assumed Thane would never settle down again, but to be honest, I never saw passion between him and Fran like what I'd witnessed between him and Regan. With Fran, it was their quiet, affectionate contentment I'd envied. With Regan ... his eyes barely left her if she was in the room. I'd caught them making out in his office one day, and the fire between them was something to behold.

In fact, although I'd told Arran there was something extra special about Arro and Mac's relationship, now that I really thought about it, the Adair siblings all loved their partners with an enviable fierceness. It was unreal how epic their love affairs had been, but I guessed the fates were making up for all the stalking, kidnapping, murder, and mayhem also thrown their way.

Robyn's expression abruptly changed. Her brow pinched tightly. "I'm worried about Lachlan. It feels a little more like hovering. He doesn't want me to go anywhere without him, but he's also really inside his head. I can barely get a conversation out of him."

"Why is he so worried?" Regan frowned. "You're young and healthy."

Robyn flicked Arro a look before shrugging.

Arro's expression shuttered a little. "It's because my mum died after giving birth to me, isn't it?"

A tense silence fell among us, and I wanted to reach a hand out to Robyn and Arro.

"I'm sorry. I didn't want to bring up something painful for you." Robyn gave Arro an apologetic look.

"It's all right. It affected us in different ways, but Lachlan was the oldest. He remembers her. Talk to him, Robbie. Don't let him spiral with this."

She nodded contemplatively but asked, "Dad isn't hovering over you and my soon-to-be little brother or sister?"

Arro grinned. "He's hovering a fair amount, but I think the normal amount."

"Good."

"Well, not to be completely rude, but no more pregnancy talk for the next hour," Regan interjected. "We can talk babies after we do book club. Books out, please."

As we did just that, I said, "I'm a new fan. Bought a bunch more romance novels after reading this one."

Regan's eyes lit up. "Really? I'll give you some recommendations."

"Great."

"I liked how it wasn't all just sex," Robyn offered. "The heroine went through this compelling journey, and although the hero was kinda bossy, like a certain man I know, she stood her ground with him."

"Like a certain woman we know," Regan teased.

"Can't let them steamroll you. Adair men are natural

leaders who think they know what's best for everyone. They need women who'll remind them to be team players." Robyn laughed.

I frowned because I wasn't sure Arran was like that at all. He was so easygoing. Though he had bulldozed his way into my life, so I guessed he had a bit of a bossy spirit.

"Those sex scenes were hot." Arro pretended to fan herself. "Seriously, Mac was especially pleased with my reaction to them."

"No." Robyn pointed a finger at Arro. "No, no, no, no, no."

Arro chuckled. "Sorry, I forget sometimes."

"You forgot when we just discussed it two seconds ago?"

Arro shot me a smirk, and I covered a snort by hiding behind my book.

Robyn grumbled under her breath while Regan smiled devilishly. "Oh, Thane loves my devotion to romance novels. This one time, he actually acted out this—"

"La, la, la, la, la, laaaa!" Arro stuck her fingers in her ears like a child, and I burst into laughter while Robyn high-fived Regan in thanks.

Dropping her hands to her lap, Arro scowled. "Okay, new rule for book club. We do not mention our sex lives."

Regan flicked a look at me, and I squirmed because now I knew what she was thinking.

I didn't have a sex life.

I dropped my gaze, feeling like an outsider.

That wasn't anything new, but for once, just once, I wished I felt normal. That I could join a conversation about sex with my friends and have it be based on current life, not on the relationships I had in my late teens and early twenties. Relationships that now felt part of someone else's life so long ago, they seemed so distant from who I'd become in Scotland.

ARRAN

THE FAMILIAR SIGHT of red hair stopped me in my tracks. Monroe Sinclair stepped out of Morag's, a grocery store and deli on Castle Street, with a bag in hand. She turned her head, saw me, startled, gave me a hesitant wave, and then hurried to the car park outside the Gloaming. I was too far away to catch up, so as I sauntered away from Flora's with a to-go coffee in hand, I didn't bother to hurry after her. She was in her car and driving in the opposite direction out of Ardnoch, presumably to her mum's on the eastern side of the village.

The reminder had me fumbling in my pocket for my phone as Zuzanna, the owner of an outdoor clothing store, walked toward me with her teenage daughter, Maja, at her side. I nodded hello to them and grinned as Maja beamed flirtatiously. "Hi, Arran!"

"Hello, lovely Maja." I winked at her, making her giggle, while her mother shook her head with a small smile. Hitting Brodan's number on my phone, the smile dropped from my face as it rang. When I'd first bumped into Monroe with Ery, I'd tried to reach Brodan, but I could only get him via voice mail and text. There was no way I was telling him about Monroe like that.

Since he still hadn't told us if he was coming home for the anniversary ceilidh, I had an excuse to keep calling until I got him.

To my shock, the line clicked on. "Do you know what fucking time it is here?" my brother grumbled.

I chuckled. "Sorry about that. I keep forgetting you're in Canada."

"Try not to." I heard him yawn loudly and felt a prickle of guilt.

"Shit, I am sorry for waking you."

"Don't be. I'm on set early every morning, so the alarm was just about to go off. Everything all right?"

Sighing, I took a sip of coffee before answering. "I was just calling to see if you're coming home for the ceilidh? It's been a while, Bro."

"I know, I know," he groaned wearily. "It's just been one project after another, and my manager says it's rare that it's like this, so I should enjoy it while I can."

"Aye, I get it." Disappointment filled me. "Is that a no, then?"

"I just … I'll see if I can squeeze in a quick trip, but I don't know."

My stomach churned as I prepared to mention Monroe.

"You still there?"

"Aye, I'm here."

"You okay?"

"Fine, fine. It's just, um … well, I thought you might want to know that Monroe is back in Ardnoch. Permanently."

A heavy silence fell between us.

"Monroe Sinclair," I stupidly added.

"I know who the fuck Monroe is, Arran," he snapped.

"Of course." An awkwardness I hadn't felt with my brother in a long time settled in. Jesus Christ, I'd give anything to take back that night.

"Family okay?" Brodan abruptly changed the subject.

"They're good."

"Arro and Robyn doing okay? Can't believe they're pregnant at the same time. More nieces or nephews or both, eh?"

"The more, the merrier," I offered, wincing at the small talk.

Brodan obviously couldn't take it. "I have to get up and get going. I won't be able to make it to the ceilidh, but give everyone my love. Bye, Arr." He hung up before I could say another word.

I scrubbed a hand over my face, wracked with guilt.

All these years, and Monroe was still a thorn between us.

Because of what Brodan considered my betrayal ... or because he'd never gotten over her?

As selfish as it was, I hoped like hell it was the latter, not just because I didn't want that kind of ugliness between me and my brother, but because of Ery.

One day soon, I hoped I'd have reason for another awkward fucking conversation with my brother, and it would really help things along if Monroe Sinclair, and not Eredine Willows, was the woman renting space in Brodan's head.

"Fuck," I muttered, very much not looking forward to that inevitable discussion.

Well, inevitable once I convinced Ery we'd be great together.

8

ARRAN

I t happened slowly. My personal dark cloud appeared above my head and stayed there over the subsequent days. At first I barely noticed it, but as the weeks passed, growing closer to the anniversary of a time I'd like to erase from my memory, it grew heavier and darker and harder to bear.

I could've become an actor like my brothers, for I shrugged on the part of carefree Arran and no one seemed to notice the grim clutch of the past dragging down my shoulders.

Except Eredine.

We'd switched roles. Gone was her distraction in place of mine. The last few days on our runs along Ardnoch Beach, she'd asked several times if I was okay. I'd flirted in return, evading her concern.

Part of me couldn't believe it had been four years since that tragic night in Thailand.

Horrible fucking coincidence it fell on the night of Ardnoch's anniversary ceilidh.

I stared at my reflection in the mirror, taking in the kilt

with the Sutherland tartan the Adairs wore. The dark green plaid with red, black, and white accents had been worn in this family for generations. While Clan Adair was actually from the Lowlands of Scotland, our particular offshoot of the Adairs had migrated north and broken away from the clan. We became more involved in the politics of Clan Sutherland, and our ancestors had opted to adopt the Sutherland tartan in lieu of the tartan worn by Clan Adair, which was actually Maxwell tartan.

I came from a long line of Scotsmen who left their home to start anew.

Only problem was, I'd eventually regretted my choice, missing my family. Missing Ardnoch. I wondered if any of my ancestors had missed their clan in the Lowlands.

The jacket I wore was dark gray to match my brothers' kilts. I looked the part.

But that cloud above my head felt almost unbearable tonight.

I grimaced at the mirror, trying to force a smile.

Fuck.

I barely drank these days, and tonight it seemed like a poor decision to do so, but maybe a glass or two of whisky would loosen me up. It would all be fine.

Thane and Regan were bringing the kids to the ceilidh, and my niece and nephew looked adorable. Lewis wore a wee kilt to match ours, and I managed a genuine smile when Regan took photos of us. Eilidh was on cloud nine wearing what she called a princess dress that matched the color of Regan's much sexier dark green gown.

"You look absolutely gorgeous," I told Regan truthfully.

"Stop flirting with my wife." Thane stepped between us to grab his car keys, giving me a warning look.

Affronted that he was genuinely annoyed, I scowled. "Not your wife yet, brother."

His eyes narrowed. "As good as."

"It was just a compliment, handsome." Regan patted her fiancé's arm while offering me an apologetic look.

Whatever Thane saw in my expression caused remorse to flicker across his. "Sorry. You and Brodan are just so similar that sometimes I forget you're also not."

"What does that mean?"

Instead of answering, Thane ushered the kids into the hall while Regan stayed behind to tell me quietly, "Brodan deliberately flirted with me to get a rise out of Thane when we first started dating."

That didn't sound like Brodan, but then again, he was all over the map these days. "What a prick."

Regan chuckled. "Yup."

Still, a wee dark part of me wondered if Thane's annoyance with me wasn't based on my own past mistakes. After all, I'd slept with Monroe, and even though she and Brodan weren't together when it happened, I often suspected my family saw it as a betrayal. Would they ever forgive me for it?

Deciding to curb my instinct to flirt, I got into the back of the SUV with the kids while Thane helped Regan into the passenger side.

"You do look beautiful, *Mo leannan*." I heard him murmur to her before they kissed softly.

"Yuck." Lewis wrinkled his nose, watching his parents.

Chuckling, I nudged him. "One day you'll want to kiss someone, and it won't be yucky to you then."

"I doubt it." He shot me a world-weary look. "And who would want to when I'm wearing a skirt?"

"Kilt," Thane and I said in unison, somewhat belligerently.

"As a Scotsman, you have to respect the kilt," I told my nephew with a grin. "And any non-Scot who calls it a skirt should fear for their life."

Regan groaned, "Arran, stop."

"It's true," Thane agreed. "No one calls a kilt a skirt in this family."

"Why can't I wear a kilt?" Eilidh asked, fluffing the layers of her dress's underskirt.

"No one is stopping you, sweetheart," Thane told her as we pulled away from the house. I noted Lachlan and Robyn's vehicle was already gone. "Next year, you can wear a kilt if you want."

I watched as Eilidh comically eyed mine and Arran's kilts and then her own dress. Her gaze shot back and forth in open contemplation. Then she abruptly decided, "Nah. You're fine."

Laughter shook my shoulders as my niece grinned, and I swear to God, for just a second, she blasted sunshine through that cloud over my head. It shamed me I hadn't been in their lives for as long as I should have.

THE TOWN HALL was on the street behind Main, a late-nineteenth-century building with a great room that catered to events like the ceilidh with its vaulted ceiling and big windows.

Lachlan's team had transformed the drab space into an explosion of Scottish tradition with tartan and heather and the scent of whisky heavy in the air. One room off the main hall served as the bar while a buffet-style spread was available in the other.

A ceilidh band owned the stage, and the main floor was perfect for dancing.

Laughter, conversation, and rhythmic clapping rose over the music as we entered the packed space. Suddenly, it felt very claustrophobic as people greeted us and I had to turn on the charm. The energy it took for what usually came so naturally was phenomenal.

A glass of whisky was definitely in order.

Lachlan approached with his arm around Robyn, and while she looked stunning, I stopped myself from saying so. My brothers and their fucking caveman possessiveness.

Mac and Arro found us seconds later, but instead of greeting them, I asked, peeved, "Where's Ery?"

"She just went to the restroo—"

"I'm here," Eredine's voice cut Arro off, and I whirled to face my friend.

Yet as I drank in the beauty before me, I felt anything but friendly toward her.

Ery's curls were smoothed into shiny, dark waves that tumbled down her shoulders. Instead of a dress, she wore a cropped, dark pink top and high-waisted, dark pink trousers that showed off a sliver of her toned stomach. In her high heels, she was maybe even a little taller than me.

She looked glamorous and heartbreakingly out of reach. Tonight, for many reasons, I was reminded that Eredine was too good for the likes of me.

That didn't stop me from wanting to touch every inch of her soft golden-brown skin. I wanted to daily, and I'd seen her bare stomach plenty of times in her yoga tops ... but in this situation, that flash of skin was more enticing than ever. I had to force my gaze to her eyes because I was immediately fantasizing about covering her stomach in kisses as I made her come with my fingers.

Fuck.

Swallowing past a lump in my throat, I said, "You're stunning."

Ery gave me a shy smile. "Thanks. You look handsome. *Everyone* looks great."

Reminded we were not alone, I turned as Ery joined our

circle and noted Lachlan, Thane, and Mac scowling at me like they were Eredine's overprotective fathers. Regan smirked knowingly, Robyn seemed contemplative, and Arro worried her bottom lip with her teeth.

"Why is everyone staring at Uncle Arran?" Eilidh piped up, and everyone dropped their gazes to where she held Thane's hand. Lewis stood at Regan's side. When I first moved back to Ardnoch, Lewis's utter dedication to his soon-to-be stepmum made me warm to Regan immediately.

"Aye, why is everyone staring at Uncle Arran?" I chirped, probably a little too enthusiastically to cover that I was dying inside. "Probably because he needs a drink. Anyone else?"

I took their orders, trying not to dwell on Eredine's beauty, and failing immensely.

A THIRD WHISKY was in my hand as I watched couples take to the dance floor. I'd danced the "Gay Gordons" with Eredine and "The Dashing White Sergeant" with Eilidh before hiding in the bar area for a while. The hooting and hilarity brought me back out, though, hoping against hope that the levity and joy of those around me might burst that damn cloud over my head.

Unfortunately, my mood only worsened as I watched a guy I didn't recognize ask Eredine to dance.

And she said yes.

I could tell by the look on Arro's face that she was surprised too.

The guy was good-looking. I could see that objectively.

Bloody hell.

Who was he?

My eyes narrowed as he smoothed his hand over Ery's

lower back, his fingertips almost touching her arse. That wee fucker ...

"Jared McCulloch."

I blinked, turning to look down at Regan, who'd appeared at my side. "What?"

"Eredine is dancing with Jared McCulloch. Collum's grandson."

Collum McCulloch was a local farmer, and he had a problem with the Adairs because he swore our ancestors had taken land from his family. I'd grown up avoiding the miserable auld bastard—he always had a harsh word for me.

I knew his granddaughter worked at Ardnoch Castle as a housekeeper, but I hadn't known there was a grandson.

"He moved here a few years ago to help Collum."

"Has anything ..." I took another sip of whisky. "Ery and him?"

Regan shook her head, expression much too knowing. "He actually asked *me* out last year."

I thought of Thane snapping my head off earlier. "Does my brother know?"

"Yeah. He wasn't too happy."

"Don't let him push you around by being a possessive arse," I muttered. I loved my brother, but he didn't own Regan.

"He's not like that, I promise. We both have gotten jealous in the past, but we feel secure with each other now."

"So, what was tonight? A special treat just for me? The untrustworthy black sheep of the family."

Regan frowned. "No, no, Arran. I think he just can't see when you're being charming and when you're being genuine."

"I don't know if that's an insult," I murmured with a smirk. Then my gaze hardened on Ery as she laughed at something Jared said. *He's too short for her*, I thought imma-turely. They didn't look right together at all.

"It's not an insult. An observation. See, to the casual observer, you are flirtatious and charming with all women. But if you look closely enough, it's obvious there's only one woman you're interested in."

Ery laughed again, and jealousy cut through me.

Was she interested in this guy? I'd only ever seen her laugh like that with Brodan.

My mind raced as the dark cloud began to drip, drip, drip on my head, every hit of its cold misery telling me I wasn't good enough for Eredine, anyway.

I threw back the rest of my whisky. "I'm getting another drink. You want one?"

"No, I'm—"

But I was already walking away before Regan had finished talking.

9
ARRAN

The whisky's numbing magic finally settled upon me, the pain of the past dulling as I wandered outside town hall for fresh air.

A cool spring breeze fluttered through my shirt as I weaved along the edge of the building, away from the smokers who'd come outside to light up. I'd abandoned my jacket inside, but fuck knows where.

Across the street on a bus stop bench sat a familiar kilted figure.

I squinted against the streetlamps.

Lachlan.

Concern filtered through my whisky fog, and I crossed the street to him.

He sat with a bottle of Clynelish in hand. A third of it was gone.

Without a word, I slid in beside my big brother, and he passed me the bottle.

I took a swig and passed it back, staring up at the sky full of a million stars but not a cloud to be found beyond the one over my head.

"Still worried about Robyn?" I asked Lachlan.

"I've been acting like an absolute prick," he spat in self-directed anger. "It's a wonder she hasn't left me."

I couldn't imagine Lachlan treating Robyn with anything but respect. "Somehow I doubt that."

"It takes a lot to make Robyn cry, and I made her cry last night. Because I'm a selfish arsehole."

"What happened?"

He shook his head. "She tried to talk to me about the baby, about my worries. She's been trying to talk to me for weeks, and I just ... I won't let her."

"Why?"

"Because I'm ashamed I'm not stronger," he answered immediately. "My wife is the strongest person I have ever met, and I am unraveling over her pregnancy because our mother died over thirty years ago. Pathetic, no?"

Compassion cut through my self-absorbed misery, and I patted my brother's knee. "You can't help your fears, big bro. They are what they are. They don't make you weak. Not facing them, not facing your wife, that's a different story."

He grunted. "Thanks."

"I'll always be honest with you." I shrugged. "Just fucking talk to her. I know Robyn's strong, but she's still human, Lachlan. She's not invincible. And she's pregnant for the first time. Do you not think she's scared of what's coming? Of being a mum? She needs you now more than ever, and you just need to fucking man up and communicate with her." I ripped the whisky out of his hand because I was equal parts sympathetic and annoyed.

After I'd taken a drink, he yanked the bottle back. "You know, you're bloody irritating when you're right."

"Aye." I sighed heavily. "Doesn't happen much, so I wouldn't worry yourself over it being a regular occurrence."

Silence fell between us as we passed the bottle back and forth, getting drunker by the second.

"Do you think because I'm a bag of shite right now that I haven't noticed your dark mood these past few weeks? And tonight"—he waved the bottle at me—"well, you didn't even get drunk at my wedding, and look at you now."

I grunted.

"What's wrong, Arran?"

Squeezing my eyes closed, memories assaulted me. Memories I wished were just a dream.

But they were real.

So damn real, it was a living nightmare.

Why was it so bad this year? Why was I so haunted?

KRABI PROVINCE, *Thailand*
  Three years ago

THERE WAS *nothing but midnight sky bleeding into black water, the moonlight rippling across its lazy waves. Ocean lapped at the shore in a rhythmic sound that lulled beachgoers to sleep on their loungers during the day.*

It was cooler at night this time of year, and I welcomed the whisper of a breeze on my skin as I took another swig of my beer and stared out at the water. Sometimes I wondered if I shouldn't just walk into it. Just walk in and let it take me.

Like it took him.

"So, this is what running a bar looks like?"

The familiar voice jolted me from my morbid thoughts. It was a voice I hadn't expected to hear.

Turning toward it, I saw my brother in the moon's glow, walking along the sand toward me. "Brodan?" I murmured, pushing to my feet, staggering as the world spun.

"Damn it." Brodan hurried to help me, but I pushed him off. His eyes dropped to my beer and then to the cooler at my feet filled with many more. "How many of those have you had?"

I curled my lip at the judgment in his tone. "Apparently, not enough." I'd been happy to hear my brother's voice only seconds ago. Now I wished he'd fuck off. "What are you doing here?"

"It's nice to see you too," he said, and I tried to focus on his face. Whatever he saw on mine made him curse under his breath. "Okay, I came because you've not been answering anyone's emails or texts, and I was worried. I paused a shoot to come find you."

"Sorry if I wasted your precious time." I stumbled back and fell onto my arse in the sand. But since it was where I wanted to be, I just shrugged and reached for another beer.

Brodan's hand curled around my wrist.

Anger boiled in my blood. "Let me go, Bro, or I will fuck you up."

"Considering you're half cut, I like my chances."

"You're a prick." I wrenched my hand away and tried to focus on the water.

I heard my brother sigh and then watched him out of my peripheral vision as he sat down beside me to stare out at the dark ocean. We hadn't seen each other in six months. I didn't suppose this was the welcome he'd expected.

"I always understood why you wanted to work at the bar here. The Highlands couldn't compete with paradise."

That felt like another dig, even though he probably didn't mean it as one. The truth was, I hadn't been running from the Highlands. I was running from who I'd been there. Overlooked by my father, not talented like Lachlan and Brodan or smart like Thane or passionate like Arro. I was the joke. In trouble constantly at school and even with the police. One day, I realized I didn't want to be that person. I didn't want that to be my label, and staying meant it always would be.

So I followed my wanderlust around the world, bartending

wherever I could to pay for the next flight or the next train to my next adventure. I'd stayed in Thailand the longest.

Bartending for my friend Kasem.

We ran his bar together and befriended people from all over the world as they came to the province for a piece of paradise.

We weren't alone, though. Colin had tended bar with us too. Until last summer.

And for the past year, paradise had become purgatory.

"You're miserable here," Brodan said, as if he could read my mind. "You're wasting away, Arran. You've lost weight. Come home."

I snorted. "Why should I listen to you? You're never fucking home."

He sighed. "I try. Work keeps me away."

"And is it work you enjoy?" I mocked, knowing full well Brodan *was running away from home, just like me. Hypocrite.*

"Arran ... this isn't you."

"Isn't it?" I grinned unhappily. "I'm the Adair fuckup, remember? This"—I gestured to myself—"plays right into my wheelhouse."

"You're not the Adair fuckup. And what happened isn't your fault."

Bile rose in my throat. "Shut up."

"No. I've shut up about it too long." Brodan turned to me. "You don't need to go home if you're not ready to. But you need to leave here. I've got a mate in Australia. He has a bar in Byron Bay. He's looking for a bartender."

"I'm already a bartender," I drawled.

"Kasem tells me you've been blowing off work for weeks. He never mentioned the drinking, though."

Indignation and shame roiled in my gut. "I don't drink. Tonight is special. It's one year tonight that it happened, don't you know?" I said with a casualness I mostly definitely didn't feel.

"Fuck." Brodan let out a ragged breath. "I didn't ... I knew it was a year, but I didn't realize tonight was … fuck, I'm sorry, Arran."

"It is what it is." I side-eyed him. "Can't believe Kasem called you."

"He's worried. He thinks you should move on from here."

Bloody hell. My friend had gone behind my back to my brother. Like I was five. I flinched, dropping my head as the shame overtook my indignation. It had to be bad for Kasem to have done that. And if I was honest with myself, I had selfishly left him in the lurch many times this past month.

Shit.

"Have you told Lachlan?"

"No," Brodan bit out. "I promised I would tell no one, and I'm keeping that promise."

Lifting my head, I stared out at the dark water again. I could hear Colin roaring my name in panic. Then silence. And then it was me calling for him.

So much silence. Just water crashing and silence.

I felt like I was losing my goddamn mind.

Staying was punishment.

Did I really deserve to leave it all behind?

"If you don't leave here, I'm terrified we're going to lose you," Brodan confessed hoarsely, "And Christ, Arran, hasn't this family lost enough?"

Tears thickened my throat as I forced myself to look at him. The sight of the glassy emotion in his eyes undid me. "I don't deserve to be here."

Brodan's jaw ticked. "It was an accident. Not your fault. And you don't deserve to wither away here in misery. Your family certainly doesn't deserve to get a phone call one day telling them their brother is dead."

A sob broke out of me before I could stop it, and I buried my head in my hands, half despair, half mortification.

I felt Brodan's warmth seconds before he pulled me against him.

"I've got you, Arr." He gripped me, his words gruff with his tears. "I've got you."

"I-I can't go home." I was a mess. There would be so many questions. I'd always vowed when I returned home, it would be as a man I was proud of. Now, it seemed like that would never happen.

"Then go to Byron Bay. Start over there. Get yourself together. Maybe talk to someone."

It sounded like an awful bloody plan.

But Brodan was right about one thing.

I was wasting away here.

If I wanted to move on, I couldn't stay. Only ten minutes before, I was certain I didn't care about moving on. Happy to live out a miserable fucking existence on my own. Seeing Brodan, however, changed everything. I couldn't do that to him. To my family. "I don't want anyone to know."

"You have to at least answer an email or text," he pressed. "Everyone is worried about you and asking me questions I can't answer."

"I'll ... I'll email or something. But can you ... can we just pretend I'm still here?"

"They won't think it unusual if you move somewhere else, Arran."

"I just ... let's just ..." I couldn't even explain why I didn't want them to know I was abandoning my life in Thailand. I was ashamed, but it wasn't as if they knew I had reason to be.

"I won't tell them," Brodan promised. "Just as long as you get on a plane with me in a few hours."

I pulled out of my brother's embrace, scrubbing aggressively at the wet on my cheeks. "I've got shit to do. Kasem, the bar, my place ..."

Brodan waved me off. "We can tie all of it up from a distance. We're going to head to your place, pack what you need, and go."

"Just like that?" I smirked unhappily. There was only a year between us in age, and among all our siblings, Bro and I were the *closest. We'd shared everything, even women. But he'd always been the more sensible of us, the one who stopped the fights I started, the calm who tempered my wildness.*

He was always my greatest defender, too, smoothing over the tension between me and Lachlan who acted more like a father to me than our dad ever had. I'd actually feared Lachlan's disappointment more than our dad's.

And it seemed I was always disappointing him.

I'd only disappointed Brodan once, but he'd gotten over that.

He was always picking up my pieces.

Even now.

It humbled me more than it ever had.

I probably never would have gotten up off that beach and walked away from that life if anyone but Brodan had asked.

Still, as I followed my brother, I glanced back toward the water and swore I heard Colin calling my name as I abandoned him once more.

"Arran?" Lachlan cut through the memories. His hand clamped onto my shoulder. "You've got me worried."

I blinked rapidly and shot him a smirk. "Not an unfamiliar feeling, I'm sure."

He sighed. "Aye, once upon a time, I worried constantly about you. But you've been different since you've been home. You're a man now. A man I'm proud to call my brother."

Emotion thickened my throat.

"But something has been bothering you these past few weeks, and tonight, you look as wrecked as I feel."

The truth, the confession, rose inside me as I looked into my brother's eyes. Everyone always said I was Lachlan's spitting image, just a younger version. Despite his own turmoil, he had always been our patriarch, even when Dad was alive.

Lachlan was our anchor. I wanted to tell him, but his words of pride made the confession stick inside me.

Looking away, I shook my head. "I'm okay."

I think I disappointed him with the lie we both knew I'd just told.

Yet we said no more.

Just passed that whisky between us until the world tilted back and forth like the bow of a ship on rough waters.

10

EREDINE

O nce I'd made it obvious to Jared McCulloch that I wasn't interested in anything but a dance, he left me with a regretful smile that lasted two point four seconds before he zeroed in on someone else.

That there was a player.

I looked around the packed hall, amazed that most of Ardnoch seemed to turn out for the anniversary ceilidh every year. This was a tight community, and overall a good one. The Highlands was one of the Whitest places I'd ever been, and Ardnoch was no exception. Suveer Siddiqui, who owned the Chocolate Box with his wife Moira, was here tonight with their two teenage children and some extended family. Chen and Wang Lei, who owned Ardnoch's Chinese restaurant, were also here. And me. That was it. Everyone else was White.

Of course, the village grew a little more diverse when the tourists arrived en masse during the summer months. But the glaring fact that there were only two non-White families living in Ardnoch unnerved me my first few months here. I'd found it isolating. The estate was a little better, now that Hollywood had made strides to become more inclusive, but it was still pretty White.

For a long time, I'd kept waiting for someone to point it out, make me feel like an outsider or less than, but eventually, I realized Ardnoch was filled with good people. If anyone was a racist asshole, they were keeping it to themselves. A few years ago at the anniversary ceilidh, a woman around my age whom I knew worked as a teacher at the primary school asked to touch my hair, but that was as bad as it had gotten for me here. Worse had happened in Inverness, but thankfully, I tended to stick around our neck of the woods.

Villagers smiled and nodded hello as they shuffled past, and I smiled back, trying my very best not to look like I was searching for Arran.

But I was. I'd been aware of his every movement, and he disappeared a while ago.

Then Robyn approached to ask if I'd seen Lachlan, and hearing the concern in her tone, I inquired of the rest of the family if anyone knew where the brothers had gone.

No one did.

Something was wrong with them. Arran had been off all week, and Lachlan had been so broody tonight, he reminded me of the pre-Robyn Lachlan.

"Not in the bar," Mac said as he and Thane approached us, looking harassed.

"Regan and I need to get the kids home," Thane said, brow furrowed. "Will you let us know when you find them?"

We agreed while Robyn and I exchanged a look. Hers was definitely more pissed off than mine. Thane and Regan left with the kids to wait in the car for Arran, and Mac offered to check out back. He gave Arro a quick kiss before he disappeared through the crowd.

Just as I saw Mac returning, head and shoulders above mostly everyone else here, Thane marched back into the hall. His expression was hard to decipher, but I think pissed was close to correct.

"They're across the street," he said in exasperation as Mac sidled up to Arro. "And they're absolutely wrecked, singing 'Flower of Scotland' at the top of their voices."

"Dear God," Robyn huffed, pushing past everyone to storm toward the exit.

We all hurried after her. I'd known something was wrong with those two. Worry made me quick in my high heels as I followed the Adairs outside. It was a still night but chilly enough that goose bumps prickled my skin as we hurried across the street, following the raucous clamor of male singing. They would've sounded fairly good had they not been slurring every other word.

Crap.

"Braveheart!" Lachlan yelled, pushing to his feet and almost landing back down on the bench where he and Arran sat. My attention flew to Arran who glowered, eyes half shut, up at Thane as he approached.

"Lachlan, lower the volume." Robyn hurried to his side to steady him.

He leaned heavily into her, and Mac rushed to hold Lachlan off.

But Lachlan brushed away his friend's grip and clasped Robyn's face in his hands, pressing his forehead to hers. She swayed with him, gripping his arms to center them both.

"Braveheart, I am so sorry," he said mournfully, drunkenly. "I am such a prick."

"Yeah, you can be," she agreed, though tenderly. "Let's get you home."

"You know I'm happy we're pregnant, right?"

97

We all tried to look anywhere but at the couple as their conversation turned private.

"Lachlan—"

"No, let me say this. I adore you and I adore this baby, and that's why I'm a prick."

I glanced back at Robyn and saw her lips twitching. "That's a weird reaction to loving someone," she teased.

"I can't lose you." He buried his head in her neck, and I ached for him. He murmured something else into her skin, and I shared a glance with Arro.

It was horrible to see Lachlan so vulnerable. He was always the one in charge, taking care of everyone and everything.

"You will not lose me. I'm the most stubborn person you've ever met, remember? And I have no intention of going anywhere."

He lifted his head, swaying harder. "Promise?"

"Yes."

"I love you so much, Braveheart," he said a little desperately, and then he wobbled into her and Mac pulled him back.

"C'mon, bud, let's get you home."

"We'll get Arran," Thane said, and we watched as Mac, Arro, and Robyn walked a wasted Lachlan to the parking lot on the other side of the building.

Then I turned to my other friend, who I was equally concerned about.

"Right, wee brother, let's go." Thane slid an arm under Arran and tried to pull him up.

But Arran used all his weight to stay down. "I likesh here," he slurred, even more unintelligible than Lachlan.

I lowered before him, drawing his gaze, and his expression softened but remained sad.

"Hello, gorgish," he said with a head wobble before patting the space beside him. "Sit wif me."

Giving him a coaxing smile, I took his hand in mine. "Why don't you come home and let me make you something to eat and get some water in you?"

He raised an eyebrow. "You'll come home wif me?"

"To take care of you, yes."

"Take care of me." His eyes closed abruptly, and he slumped.

I looked up at Thane. "Did he just fall asleep?"

Thane snorted and stood. "I don't know how we're going to fit everyone in the car."

I bit my lip. "I should have gone with Robyn."

"It's fine. I think it's good you're here. Just give me a second." With an abrupt nod, Thane jogged across the street and disappeared behind the town hall.

Arran slipped toward the empty side of the bench, so I hurried to sit beside him and hold him up. He immediately wrapped his arm around my waist and burrowed his head against my chest with a groan of pleasure.

He smelled pleasantly of cologne, but then he'd breathe and I could smell just how much whisky he'd consumed. A large bottle of Clynelish lay empty on the street beside the bench. I reminded myself to collect that before we got in the car.

Arran moaned and bussed his cheek against me.

My skin flushed hotter as his lips grazed my nipple. Dear Lord. Where was Thane?

Thankfully, I didn't have to endure Arran's cuddling much longer because Thane pulled up beside us. Regan was in the passenger seat, and Eilidh and Lewis were squished together in the back.

It looked like I was going to have to endure more Arran cuddles.

Endure probably wasn't the right word.

With some effort, Thane and I wrangled Arran into the car, and thank goodness he had decided not to attend the ceilidh as a true Scotsman because his kilt did not want to stay down. I got a flash of muscular thighs dusted with light golden hair, and despite the circumstances, my body reacted.

Ignoring my attraction, I concentrated on getting Arran into the car beside me without hitting his head. I concentrated on my worry for him.

Once we were in, I smiled reassuringly at the kids as I sat in the middle between them and their drunken uncle.

Lewis eyed Arran warily. "Is he okay?"

"He's fine, sweetie," Regan said, reassuring him. "Uncle Arran is just tired. He's had a long day."

Eilidh thankfully accepted this, yawned, and then rested her head against her brother. I melted as Lewis lifted his arm and let her snuggle into him, embracing her. They fought like cats and dogs sometimes, but there was no denying Lewis Adair adored his little sister.

Regan caught my expression in the rearview mirror and gave me a soft smile.

I returned it and then looked at Arran, whose head now rested against the window. It shocked me how desperately I wanted to know what was going on inside that mind of his, how much I wanted to soothe him.

"I want to stay," I insisted. Thane stood at the end of Arran's bed in the guest house. He'd helped Arran out of his clothing while I fixed some food, water, and aspirin in the kitchen in the main house. I'd returned to find Arran awake and throwing up in the bathroom.

"Are you sure?" Thane frowned.

"Yes. Go be with Regan and the kids. I'll look after him."

He still looked a little unsure, but at my unwavering stare, he finally nodded. "Just give me a shout if you need me."

"I will."

"Good night, Arran," Thane called to his brother.

Arran groaned in response from the bathroom.

"That's going to be one hell of a hangover." Thane patted me on the shoulder and exited, closing the annex door behind him.

"Is he gone?" Arran croaked.

"Yeah. Do you need help?"

The bathroom door opened, and Arran stepped out wearing only pajama bottoms, his face pasty and pale as he crawled onto the bed. "Just let me die."

Trying not to chuckle, I lifted the water and aspirin off the bedside table. "Here."

Arran reluctantly sat up to take the medicine but tried to shoo away the toast I'd prepared.

"Please," I insisted. "It'll make you feel better in the long run."

With another guttural sound, Arran leaned back against the headboard and raised a piece of toast to his mouth with a heavy arm.

I pulled a chair over from the mini dining area and watched him. He finally looked at me.

"Tell me what's wrong."

To my shock, his eyes turned glassy. "Just a shit night."

"Why?" I leaned over and pressed a hand to his arm. "Talk to me."

Something passed over his expression, something so sorrowful and grim, my pulse raced.

"I suppose if anyone should know who I really am, it's you," he muttered, before squeezing his eyes closed. "Fucking room won't stop spinning."

"Drink more water."

He took another gulp, and I went to the kitchen to refill his glass.

When I returned, he took the water from me but wrapped his fingers around mine to stop me from retreating. "I caused a friend's death, Ery. Four years ago tonight."

My heart plummeted at his confession.

11

ARRAN

K rabi Province, Thailand
Four Years Ago

"I THINK I'm going to ask Maranda to marry me." Colin grinned at me drunkenly as he staggered down the empty beach. The water lapped gently at the shore, the moonlight shimmering across the tranquil sea. It beckoned to my hot skin.

"Is that why you're blootered?" I mocked, swaying as I changed direction toward the shore.

Colin glanced over his shoulder and then spun around to follow. "I'm not drunk!"

I snorted. "If you say so."

"So, what do you think?"

"About?"

"Me marrying Maranda?"

I thought Maranda was a complicated lady. Adventurous and laid-back in some respects, but possessive and cloying with Colin. Our Thai friend Kasem owned a beach bar here, and we worked for him, even though it was illegal for foreigners to perform *manual labor in Thailand. Colin was originally from York and a bit of a wanderer like me. We'd met in Bangkok two years ago and traveled to Krabi together when Kasem, whom I'd met in Germany many moons before, contacted me about he owned a bar now and could use some part-time help. It turned into full time as we fell in love with the lifestyle. If anyone asked, Colin and I owned shares in Kasem's bar, and that was why we were allowed to work there. We knew one day, our luck might run out, but it would be fun until then.*

If Colin didn't marry Maranda first.

I couldn't imagine the woman who would make me want to settle down for good, but part of me hoped she existed somewhere.

But not a possessive lass like Maranda.

She'd arrived in Thailand from Dublin a year ago on a marine biology course, and she and Colin hit it off.

To each their own, I suppose. "If you love her, marry her," I answered simply.

"Yeah, yeah, that'sh what I thinks," he slurred.

"You're definitely more pissed than me. How much did you drink?"

"As much as you, so that means you're as drunk as me."

"I'm not drunk, and I will prove it."

"Oh, that breeze is good, mate. Hey, what are you doing?"

But I was already running into the ocean, trainers still on, mad fuck that I was. I laughed. "I bet I can hold my breath underwater for two minutes!" I yelled before I dove in. As I swam to the ocean bed, I could not see a bloody thing. Swimming along the bottom was amazing.

Just darkness and me.

Plant life brushed against me and fish swam by, and I felt connected to the world in a way I'd only experienced back home in Ardnoch. To my utter shock, I missed the place with a longing I'd never expected. Every trip home, however, was a reminder that I was someone different to my family than the man I believed I was. I couldn't get over the sense that they still saw me as the fuckup.

That was not who I wanted to be.

As the thought burned, I heard yelling above the surface.

How long had I been down here? It couldn't have been that long, or I'd be dead.

Pushing upward, I broke the surface—

"ARRAN!"

Fuck. I spun around, trying to follow Colin's panicked voice. I couldn't see him.

"I'm all right!" I yelled as I pushed toward the shore. "Colin!"

Splashing sounded in the distance.

I turned in the water, fear shooting through me. Colin wouldn't get in the water drunk. He was smarter than me, right?

But he would if he thought I was in trouble.

Shit.

He was definitely drunker than I was.

He probably had no concept of time right now or how long I'd actually been under.

"COLIN!" I roared, suddenly sober as I searched for any sign he was in the water.

I swam in the direction I thought I'd heard the splashing. Frantic, blood rushing in my ears, I strained to hear anything. Swimming under, I tried to see if he was in the water, but there was nothing. I kicked upward. "COLIN!"

Movement on the beach caught my eye, and I saw a couple hurrying toward the shore. "Are you okay?" the woman yelled.

"Have you seen my friend?" I called back. "I think he swam in, but he's drunk."

"There!" She pointed farther down the coastline. "We saw him run in shouting for someone."

Why the fuck didn't you go after him? *I thought wrathfully as I powered through the water.*

It was taking too long to find him.

Too long.

Every second counted.

Maybe he wasn't as drunk as I thought.

Maybe he was just fooling around. Getting me back for staying under too long.

Colin was always pulling shit like this that wasn't funny.

But then I saw him, bobbing to the surface.

Everything from that moment was a blur.

Dragging his heavy, limp body out of the water and onto the beach.

Using the CPR training I'd never used before.

But unlike the movies when the person inhales and chokes up water, Colin just laid there.

Heart silent in his chest.

"You have to stop. He's gone, my friend, he's gone." Kasem's familiar voice was in my ear, his arm around me holding me back from Colin.

There were people with us now.

I hadn't noticed.

Kasem was here.

I was here.

But because I'd taken a midnight fucking dive while Colin was drunk, he wasn't here.

He wasn't here.

12

EREDINE

"I don't know what I was thinking." Arran's words rasped like they were coated with sandpaper. Tears stung my eyes from the emotion bleeding from him. "I wasn't thinking. I was drunk. And I went into that water knowing Colin was even drunker than I was."

Compassion was a constant ache within me as I pressed a comforting hand to Arran's bare back. His skin was hot, probably from the alcohol. "It was an accident. You cannot blame yourself for someone else's actions."

Arran looked at me, and my stomach plummeted at the sight of tears in his eyes. Shocked, I flexed my hand on his back. "I knew better. You never go into the water when you've been drinking. He was wasted, Ery. He must have been confused about how long I was under and he dove in to save me ... and drowned." A low sob burst from him, and I watched helplessly as my seemingly happy-go-lucky friend began to cry.

"Arran." My lips trembled with tears, but I fought them to wrap my arms around him instead. Arran fell, his head buried against me as he cried. I soothed him, brushing my fingers through his hair, wondering what else I could do to help. He was carrying around so much misplaced guilt. My heart broke for him.

Eventually, he quieted and eased away. Arran scrubbed aggressively at his cheeks. "Fuck, I'm sorry," he said gruffly. "Just had too much to drink."

"It's okay. It's just me."

Our eyes met, his still red with emotion. "Just you," he murmured, his gaze dipping to my mouth.

My pulse leapt, and I tensed.

But Arran abruptly flopped onto his back, covered his eyes with a forearm, and groaned.

I kept my attention fixed firmly on his face because now was not the time for ogling. Getting to my feet, I patted his knee. "Don't fall asleep like that."

With a grunt of effort, Arran stood and then slid under the covers. I grabbed the edge of the duvet and pulled it up to his neck, and my friend caught my wrist before I could release it.

Those gorgeous blue eyes held me captive, filled with a dazzling vulnerability. "Only Brodan knows. I can't tell the rest of my family. It took me forever just to build up the courage to come home. They used to see me as such a fuckup, and this will ruin everything. And not being able to tell them ... I feel alone," he confessed. "I know I shouldn't ... but sometimes, I'm all alone, Ery."

This time, I couldn't stop my tears because I understood.

I understood completely.

I was alone too.

Surrounded by amazing, loving people.

And yet still so alone.

Arran's lids drooped as drunk tiredness overcame him, and his grip on me loosened, his eyes finally closing.

I didn't want to leave him alone.

Decision made, I checked to be sure the annex door was locked, kicked off my shoes, grabbed the decorative throw off the small couch, and rounded the other side of the bed. I reclined on top of the covers, snuggled under the light blanket, and turned on my side to watch Arran sleep.

"You're not alone," I promised.

As if he heard me, his lips curled at the corners in his sleep.

LIGHT PRODDED my eyes open and I wondered why. Had I forgotten to close my bedroom curtains last night? I blindly reached for my duvet to drag it up over my head but couldn't find it.

What?

My eyes flew open, and the bleary vision of a man's face met mine.

Fear shot through me, and I whimpered.

"Hey, hey, Ery, it's me. You're okay."

At the familiar sound of Arran, my pulse slowed, and I blinked a few more times to clear the sleep.

Sure enough, the man lying on his side before me, gazing at me in concern, was Arran Adair.

And just like that, last night flooded back.

"Oh. Hey."

His brows pinched together. "You all right?"

I nodded, a little embarrassed, and pushed into a sitting position. A dull throb pounded behind my eyes, probably from lack of rest. It had taken me a while to fall asleep because I'd been so worried about Arran. "What time is it?"

"I don't know. Haven't checked." He sat up, too, and yawned.

Keeping my eyes off his nakedness, which seemed so

much more intimate in the daylight, I asked, "How are you feeling?"

He raked his fingers through his hair as he winced. "Ashamed I got so drunk."

"Lachlan was even drunker than you, if that helps."

"Aye, what a right pair we make."

"Do you ... do you remember much about last night?" I wondered if he remembered his confession.

Arran held my gaze. "I remember everything. I told you about Colin and me ... had a bit of a breakdown about that. Sorry." He glanced away, embarrassed.

"You never need to apologize." I reached out to cover his hand with mine. "I hope you don't regret telling me. You know I will tell no one. It's not my story to tell."

He shook his head. "No, I don't regret it. And I trust you. I trust you with all my darkest secrets. But ..."

My heart lurched at "I trust you with all my darkest secrets," but the *but* gave me pause.

Arran's eyes narrowed. "Has it changed the way you see me?"

"Yes," I admitted.

He swallowed hard, pulling his hand out from under mine.

"No, Arran, not like that. In a good way."

Shock slackened his features. "In a good way? How is that possible?"

"Because I don't blame you for what happened, and you shouldn't either. But knowing that you do, that it made you fear coming home ... I admire you so much for facing those fears. I just wish you wouldn't blame yourself. It was a terrible accident. Now all you can do is be the man you want to be."

"I'm trying," he confessed hoarsely.

"You don't need to try. You're a good man. We wouldn't be friends otherwise."

Something bright gleamed in his expression, and he nodded. "Thank you."

I smiled but had to look away because holding his stare made breathing difficult.

"Do you think Thane might cook a fry-up? I'm starving," Arran suddenly announced, pushing out of the bed.

I shook my head, marveling at his steel stomach. If I'd have been that drunk, I'd be wrecked the next day. Then something occurred to me. "I probably should go, so no one gets the wrong idea."

Arran frowned as he strode toward the bathroom. "Don't be silly. They know I was useless to anyone last night. Come have breakfast."

My cheeks felt hot at the idea of Arran being the opposite of useless in that department. "Okay."

And then as I waited for him to freshen up, I heard his voice in my head over and over, telling me he trusted me.

He'd trusted me with information only Brodan knew.

Arran trusted me.

Something eased inside I didn't know needed easing. All this time, I was waiting to trust other people. It never occurred to me it might feel good to be trusted so completely in return.

13

EREDINE

It was rare when I didn't have something planned for my days off, and this Thursday was no exception. When I'd mentioned I missed my monthly hikes with Robyn and Arro, now that they were pregnant and unable to accompany me, Regan had offered to go in their stead.

Surprising, since Regan wasn't overly athletic, and she was also pretty busy with the kids and planning the double wedding for her and Thane, and Arro and Mac, this summer.

But I didn't turn her down. I loved hiking, being out in nature. It brought me calm, and when I was feeling overwhelmed, a hike always soothed me.

Currently, however, Arran occupied my thoughts. We'd gone running together almost every morning this week, as per usual, and I'd tried to be normal around him. Yet I felt different about him. I felt ... closer to him.

He trusted me, and I realized something amazing.

I trusted him in return.

That feeling of closeness had heightened my attraction to him.

If I was honest, I couldn't stop thinking about what it would be like to be with him. Intimately.

However, I also hadn't changed my mind about avoiding romantic relationships for the rest of eternity.

It was a clusterfuck of emotions.

"You're quiet," Regan observed about five minutes in. I'd chosen a trail fifteen minutes outside of Ardnoch, in an area called Ardgay, perfect for people who weren't avid hikers. It had well-constructed paths ambling through the forests, and you could either take the path to Loch Migdale or hike to the top to survey the views. I was leading Regan to the loch.

"Am I?" I threw over my shoulder.

"Yes. You've been kind of quiet all week, actually."

"Or my whole life," I joked.

"God, I thought Pilates would keep me in shape, but you're walking this trail like it's a straight path," Regan called, sounding slightly out of breath. "Arrgh!"

I whipped around at her sound of pain. "Are you okay?"

She was several steps down from me, grimacing, her hand on her lower back. "I'm fine, I'm fine." She winced again as she prodded a spot near her spine. "Just twisted my back last night, and it's acting up."

"We can turn around," I assured her.

"No, I'll be fine. I'm not ruining your hike."

This didn't really count as much of a hike but more a walk in the woods. Still, I'd take it. "You sure you're all right? How did you hurt it?" I turned to continue, but at her silence looked back over my shoulder.

She looked ... embarrassed. "Uh, you know." She shrugged and followed me again.

Realization dawned. "It's a sex injury?"

"Eredine!" Regan sounded surprised. Which kind of pissed me off. She'd have no problem telling Robyn it was a sex injury.

"Well?"

She huffed. "I just don't want to embarrass you."

I frowned and stopped to look at her again. "I'm not embarrassed."

Regan flushed. "I know, I just ... you don't talk about this stuff, so ..."

"I talk about it," I insisted belligerently. "We all talk about it."

"No, I just meant—"

"I've had sex, Regan. Plenty of sex. I'm not some shy, clueless virgin you have to be a prude around."

My friend blinked rapidly, clearly shocked.

Irritated, I turned and walked again. The steps led upward before they veered and started taking us back down toward the loch.

"I'm sorry." Regan caught up with me. It was a tight squeeze for us both, but she seemed determined to look me in the eye. "I'm sorry if I've made you feel that way."

I shrugged because I wasn't sure I hadn't overreacted. "So. Am I right? About your back?"

Regan gave a huff of laughter. "Yes. We tried this new position last night, but Thane has stamina, so I was in the same slightly twisted position a bit too long, and I've got a knot in my back the size of Scotland."

"Get him to massage it out. He put it there."

She laughed. "Yeah, I will."

We fell quiet again as I took the lead. Catching sight of a doe through the trees, I halted Regan with my finger pressed to my lips and then pointed so she could see the deer. Just as I did, a buck appeared beside the doe. Regan drew in a breath as we watched them forage.

Neither of us fumbled to find our phones to capture the moment. Instead, we stayed *in* the moment, enjoying it.

Silently, we moved on through the trail, trying not to

startle the deer. As we neared the loch, Regan spoke up. "Can I ask you a personal question?"

I instinctually tensed. Not a fan of personal questions. "You can ask." My tone implied I might not answer.

"How long has it been? Since you had sex?"

My cheeks heated as I snorted at the blunt query. "Nosy much?"

"Yes."

That made me laugh, and I shot her an affectionate smile.

Regan's shoulders seemed to drop as if she was tense over asking too.

"Let's put it this way," I answered. "I've only had sex with people I'm in a relationship with, and I haven't been in a relationship since before coming to Ardnoch eight years ago."

"That's a long time not to enjoy intimacy. Affection."

"I'm aware." I stomped down toward the loch, not needing her to point out something miserable about my life that I was fully aware of.

"I'm not judging."

"Really?"

Regan drew to a stop beside me on the banks of the loch. It wasn't a particularly sunny day; the water reflected the light gray clouds above our heads. But it lapped gently at the shore, and birds cawed and tweeted among the trees. I closed my eyes, listening.

But then Regan broke my meditative state. "Of course, I'm not judging you. You know I'm not that person. I'm just ... I don't ... I want you to have all the things. You deserve all the things."

I opened my eyes and met her worried gaze and softened. I knew Regan and all the Adairs cared about me, about my happiness. "Thank you."

"Have you ever considered casual sex? You know, just to take the edge off?"

"I can take the edge off on my own, thank you very much."

She laughed. "Good. I'm glad. You know, until Thane, I probably had better sex with myself, anyway."

I chuckled. "I'm so happy for you he came along, then."

"Yeah, me too. But I'm exaggerating. I had casual sex before Thane, and it was good. I mean, it wasn't the mind-blowing sex he and I have, but it was fun."

"Don't let him hear you say that," I joked.

"He knows he's the best I've ever had."

"I'm pleased for you. Truly." I was also envious as hell. "But your point?"

"My point is that you're a beautiful, smart, fun woman in her prime, and if you want to have sex with someone, you should absolutely have sex with them. Casual sex is not against the law."

"Regan, I know you mean well, but I *am* a grown-ass woman, and I know casual sex is not against the law or taboo or wrong. I just ... I need to trust the person I'm in bed with, and I would need to trust that person to not want to make it into something more than sex. That's an impossible combination."

"Not impossible." Regan stared at me with an unnerving, knowing look. "In fact, I'm certain we both know someone who fits the bill perfectly."

I shook my head as I realized what all this was about. Remembering she'd set it up so Arran and I babysat the kids together, I sighed. "Whatever you do, do not take up match-making. It's a disaster waiting to happen."

"I'm not playing matchmaker." She shrugged innocently. "I'm just putting thoughts out there. It's up to other people whether they listen to those thoughts."

"Yeah?" I smirked. "Well, why don't you close your eyes

and listen to what's around us right now? You'll thank me for it." I closed my eyes and hoped she'd follow my lead.

Thankfully, she did.

She'd said what she wanted to say, so she didn't mention it again.

Instead, we enjoyed the quiet of the loch. As we hiked back to the car later, she chatted away about wedding plans.

What I didn't tell her was that she got me thinking.

I'd already been obsessing over Arran.

Now ... I couldn't stop imagining what it might be like to be with him.

Just one night.

Scratch the itch and be done with it so I could stop driving myself crazy thinking about it.

As if Arran heard me, my phone beeped in the side pocket of my yoga pants as we reached my car.

Meet me for a late lunch at An Sealladh in half an hour?

AFTER I DROPPED Regan back at home, I drove to An Sealladh just in time to meet Arran for a late lunch. The restaurant parking lot was busy, and upon walking in, I found the place full of tourists.

Arran had texted he was already here under his surname, so I asked the hostess and she led me toward the front area that had the most spectacular views of the North Sea. An Sealladh was actually the first place I'd spent any real time with Arran. We'd gone to lunch with Arro, and he flirted outrageously with me, despite Arro's presence, and I actually enjoyed myself. Until later that day when we discovered someone had graffitied Arro's car, and that *someone* turned out to be her ex-boyfriend who was now in jail for trying to kill her.

The Adairs really had been through the wringer these past couple years.

I spotted Arran before he spotted me.

He was leaning back over his chair, talking to an adjacent table of women. The one closest to him put her hand on his shoulder and laughed loudly at whatever he said.

A white-hot heat licked up the back of my neck at the sight of her touching him, flirting with him.

Who the hell was she?

Part of me wanted to turn around and walk out, but a greater part wanted to stake a claim I had no right staking.

As if sensing me, Arran's gaze moved away from the table of what I assumed were tourists and found mine as I approached. He smiled as if truly happy to see me and then he said something to the women, gesturing in my direction, before he turned around in his seat.

The woman who touched him frowned at my approach and turned to her friends with a shrug of disappointment.

"Hey." I slid into the seat opposite him.

"Hi." Arran grinned. "I couldn't go the whole day without seeing you."

We hadn't run together this morning because of my plans with Regan. "I'm sure you can get through a day without seeing me."

"Can I?" His smile was flirtatious, his eyes roaming my face as if tabulating every tiny detail.

Then again, he had been flirting with a tourist before I showed up. "You looked like you were doing just fine without me."

His smile dropped, but the light in his eyes didn't dim. "Appearances can be deceiving."

Those words, his expression, the deep rumble of his voice … I felt it all between my legs, and my skin flushed hot.

This was getting ridiculous.

"Are you ready to order?" A server appeared at the table.

Arran didn't take his eyes off me. "Can you give us a few more minutes?"

"Of course." She walked away.

"So." Arran drummed his fingers on the menu in front of him. "What do you want?"

I swear to God I hadn't intended to say it.

To put it out there.

The words just erupted out of me as if they had a mind of their own.

"I want a night with you."

Arran's lips parted in shock, his nostrils flared. "Excuse me?"

My cheeks burned as I struggled in the quagmire I'd just created. I either forged ahead, faced my fears, and had a little adventure to break up the monotony of my life … or I backpedaled and lied.

I straightened my shoulders. "I want one night only of no-strings sex. With you."

Arran gaped like he'd never seen me before.

And I wanted the North Sea to come crashing through the restaurant to swallow me whole.

14

ARRAN

I shook my head, wondering if I'd heard right.

My pulse pounded in my ears as I asked, "You want one night only of no-strings sex? With me?"

Though I could tell from the strain in her eyes she was embarrassed, Ery set her delicate jaw with determination and nodded. "I do."

Holy shit.

I slumped back in my chair, not sure how to respond.

Because I'd been seconds from gathering the courage to ask Eredine out on a date. A real date.

And she only wanted one night of casual sex.

Disappointment churned in my gut, and I did my best to keep that emotion off my face. How could I possibly agree to that when I wanted more? Fuck, I might as well ask Ery to plunge a knife into my heart, right? Because there was no way I could come out of this unscathed.

Yet the thought of being with her made my hands itch to reach out and touch her already. It would be a sweet bloody torture, though, being with her, knowing it was only for one night.

"You're just staring and saying nothing." Ery fiddled with her paper napkin, tearing off wee bits at a time. She'd lowered her gaze, depriving me of those gorgeous hazel-green eyes. "Did I mess up? Have I ruined our friendship?"

Fumbling for a suitable response, it took me a few excruciating seconds to say, "No, of course not. But why? Why one night? Why me?"

Finally, she looked up. Her expression was stiff with discomfort. But unfortunately, that was the consequence of asking your friend to fuck you.

Holy shit.

She'd really done that.

This woman surprised the hell out of me.

The noise of fellow diners faded as I anxiously awaited her reply.

"I trust you," she said.

Joy filled me, a smile prodding my lips. I knew it was a huge deal to be given Eredine's trust. She didn't hand it over to many people, and I was honored she had done so to me. I only hoped I could be worthy of it. "Thank you. That means a lot. I trust you too."

She nodded. "I know. I realized that the other night."

I shrugged, awkward at the mention of my drunken melt-down last weekend. The truth was, however, that I'd felt unburdened, lighter somehow, after confessing everything to Eredine. Her understanding and compassion had blown away the dark cloud over my head. Another reason I'd been determined to ask her out on a date today.

Not for a one-night stand.

"And ...," Ery took a deep breath, "I'm attracted to you. Obviously."

This time I couldn't help my smug grin, and she huffed and rolled her eyes, making me laugh. "Well, we both know I'm very attracted to you."

Lips twitching with amusement, Ery nodded. "You've made that obvious."

I laughed, unabashed. I'd never been afraid of letting someone know when I was attracted to them. "So why just one night?"

Her amusement fled. "One, I'm pretty sure you're a casual-only kind of guy, and two, I don't want a relationship."

Casual-only kind of guy? Is that what I put across? "Ery—"

"I'm not cut out for a relationship, Arran. I can't give myself to someone fully like that. And the reason I propose just one night for us is because I value our friendship. There's no harm in scratching an itch, right? But if we were to prolong it, make it into something more, it would ruin us. And I can't live with that. I like having you in my life too much."

Fuck.

Dismay sat heavy in my gut because I heard the absolute sincerity and determination in Eredine's words. She was certain she didn't want to be in a relationship.

And I was certain that I did. With her. Only her. I wanted her to be with me, not just for one night. I didn't know if anything serious would come of us dating—I only knew I wanted to try.

"You're worried about our friendship," she assumed, her brow creased.

Deciding I wasn't enough of a masochist to put myself out there when I already knew the outcome wouldn't be in my favor, I lied and nodded. "Aye. I don't want to mess us up. But I … I am attracted to you. Very much. I know I haven't hidden that." I leaned forward. "Can I think about this?"

Abashed, her full lips pinched together as her gaze fled mine. "Sure."

"Ery—"

"No, I get it. It's fine." She pulled her menu toward her. "What looks good?"

Feeling guilty, I wanted to keep explaining, but I had a feeling she wouldn't thank me for it, so I pulled my menu toward me and made inane chitchat. The whole time, my pulse raced a little faster than normal.

MY PLOT of Adair land sat on the coast about two miles from Thane's and Lachlan's homes and half a mile from Arro and Mac's building plot. Pulling up to the chunk of gorgeous real estate, I grinned at the sight before me. Where once stood only foundations, now there was a structure, a wooden shell of the house. I could finally visualize what my large, three-bedroom home was going to look like. The site was abuzz with activity as I jumped out of my SUV and walked toward Thane.

My big brother smiled as I approached. "What do you think?"

"It's coming along fast now, eh?"

"It's getting there. C'mon, I'll show you what's been happening."

I'd taken the afternoon off from the Gloaming's renovations because Thane had offered to come out to my house site to update me on its progress. We tried not to get in the way as he showed me that electrical and plumbing was being fitted. Eventually, we made our way down to what would be my back garden overlooking the North Sea. It was spectacular.

"You'll love it," Thane promised. "Having this view every day is magic."

"I've always been envious of yours," I confessed. "I cannot believe I'll have it too. We had it from some rooms in the castle, but not like this. When you stand from your living room looking out, you almost feel you're floating on the sea. It's amazing. We're very lucky, brother."

"We are that. I'm honestly still in shock you're settling down, though. I half expected you to have packed up and left long ago."

I frowned. "And leave Lachlan to handle the Gloaming alone? I wouldn't do that. Not only have I invested my money in it, I wouldn't break a promise this big to Lachlan."

"No, I know that. I meant before that."

I sighed heavily, trying to cool my irritation. It wasn't Thane's fault he'd assumed I wouldn't stick around—it was mine. I'd left my family behind long ago. "I missed you all," I admitted. "I missed home."

Thane patted my back. "I'm glad. We missed you too. I don't know what the kids would do without you now. Lachlan's pissed off you've dethroned him as the favorite uncle."

I chuckled. "That's because I'm the cool uncle who gets them hyped up."

"Aye, don't I bloody know it."

Chuckling, I stepped closer to the water and then looked back at the house. I needed to bring Eredine out here so she could see for herself what it was on its way to becoming. The thought of her scored an ache in my chest.

That ache was the awful fucking discontentment of knowing Ery didn't want to date anyone, least of all me.

Though I suppose I should be flattered that she trusted me enough to want to scratch an itch.

Scratch an itch.

Bloody hell.

"What?" Thane scowled at the house and then back at me, and I realized I'd cursed out loud.

"Nothing." I shook my head and turned back to the water.

"Something's been bothering you lately. Is that something the reason you got drunk last weekend?"

"No. That was ... I was just getting drunk with Lachlan." Only the partial truth. Thankfully, Lachlan had finally had a conversation with Robyn after he'd gotten wasted at the ceilidh. She understood his fears, and he understood his fears couldn't suffocate her. He was trying. And Robyn was doing what she could to alleviate his worries without compromising her own happiness.

That was real love. What they had. Anyone could see it.

I never thought I'd envy my brothers for their romantic relationships.

Maybe I was getting sentimental in my old age. I snorted to myself.

"What now?" Thane frowned.

I heaved another heavy sigh and studied my big brother. He'd been married, widowed, and now was engaged after a somewhat scandalous affair with his much younger nanny and sister-in-law. Maybe his opinion wouldn't be a bad thing. "I have this friend."

Thane smirked because everyone knew what *I have this friend* was code for. "Okay ..."

"And my friend has this very good friend who he has feelings for. But she just asked him for no-strings sex, one night only, because she doesn't want to be in a serious relationship with anyone, and my friend doesn't know what to do about it. Does he have sex with her and hope it'll just naturally develop into something more, or does he tell her no, or does he just take what he can get and sleep with her once?"

My brother gaped at me.

"Well?" I scowled.

Thane cleared his expression. "Okay ... when you say *feelings*, do you mean your *friend* has serious feelings for this woman, or is it just an attraction?"

I looked away, uncomfortable with the depth of feelings I had for Ery, honestly not entirely sure what they meant. "He wants to date her to find out if it could be serious."

After a few seconds of silence that felt like forever, Thane said, "I'd need more background about your friend and his friend to give a truly insightful opinion ... but what I will say is that I'd worry about your friend getting hurt. He has to trust that his friend means it when she says she doesn't want a relationship, so he'd be risking a lot if he went into it, hoping he could convince her otherwise."

"So you would say no, then?"

"It depends. I knew deep down when I got into it with Regan that I was at risk of getting hurt, but I did it, anyway. It worked out for me, but it might not work out for your friend. Your friend should follow his gut, but be prepared for it ending badly if he goes for it."

That sounded fucking delightful.

And yet, as I got back into my car, I couldn't stop my mind from wandering, to imagining what it would be like to have Ery. To devour every inch of her. There had been so many moments between us I'd caught myself from reaching out to touch her, where I'd been seconds from saying "fuck it" and just kissing the hell out of her.

I could make it so good, she'd *need* a second night, and a third and a fourth ...

My hands tightened around the steering wheel as heat thrummed through me.

Aye, I think my mind had already been made up from the moment Eredine Willows asked me for one night only.

15
EREDINE

"Stupid, stupid, stupid," I muttered to myself for the millionth time as I lowered my e-reader and glared out my living room window. It was after six, and between the lunch I'd forced down with Arran and the butterflies fluttering in my stomach, the thought of preparing dinner nauseated me. I'd tried to read the latest Fern Michaels novel, but the conversation with Arran kept going around and around in my head. Obsessively.

I couldn't believe I'd walked into the restaurant and blurted that to him.

What had I been thinking?

You were thinking you were sick of people seeing you a certain way. Tired of your monotonous life, you embraced impulsivity.

"And look where that got you," I said, feeling the telltale sting in my nose warning of tears.

What if I'd chased Arran away? There had been something off about his reaction. Like ... he was disappointed in me for asking.

"What have I done?" I groaned and threw my head back on the couch. I had to think of a way to fix it. Maybe call him and ask if I could take it back? But could you take something like that back?

My phone vibrating on the coffee table drew my head back up, and I reached over, my heart leaping toward my throat when I saw it was Arran.

He was calling me. That was a good sign, right?

Blood rushing in my ears, I took a deep breath, trying to calm down before I answered and hit speaker. "Hey."

"Hi." His deep, warm voice soothed something in me. "So I've thought about it."

My pulse raced. "Yeah?"

"Aye." Arran's words sounded thick, smoky, when he continued, "I want a night with you too."

Oh.

Oh, okay.

What?

"You do?" I practically squeaked.

"You haven't changed your mind, have you?"

"No," I answered a little too eagerly.

"Good. I'll be over in an hour."

Surprise launched me off my couch. "You're ... I mean ... what ... we're ... tonight?"

He chuckled. "Well, you put the thought in my head, and now I can't stop thinking about you, so if you're on board, I want you tonight."

I'd need to shower and make sure my sheets were clean and that there was nothing lying around that would prick his curiosity about my past and I needed to shave. Yes, shave. I needed to shave. "An hour?" I calculated whether that was enough time. "Can we make it ninety minutes?"

Arran laughed softly again. "Ninety minutes. I'll see you soon."

He hung up before I could respond.

I stared stupefied around the house.

Arran was coming here in ninety minutes to have sex with me.

Sex with *me*.

Something low and deep clenched in my belly, and the excitement overwhelmed my shy nerves. I wanted this. It was out of character and impulsive, but I wanted it.

I wanted him.

One night only.

"Oh, Lordy." I let out a little laugh of surprise and then dashed toward my bedroom to shower.

FOR A SECOND, I could only gawk at Arran standing on my porch.

He looked delicious in a long-sleeved T-shirt and jeans, his hair freshly washed, the scent of something spicy with a hint of citrus lingering in the air around him. I wanted to nuzzle my face in his throat and inhale.

Instead, I got locked in his azure eyes, heartbeat thudding loudly.

"You look gorgeous," he said sincerely.

I hadn't known whether to wear regular clothes or something sexy that could be easily taken off, so I'd decided to go for it. It got hot in my lodge on summer nights because there was no AC, and I usually slept in silk nighties to keep cool.

I'd put on my nicest one, deciding against artifice with Arran.

I wanted to have sex with him, and I was dressed for that occasion.

His fiery gaze lowered down my body, lingering on my bare (and freshly shaved) legs. The way he studied me, the way his jaw clenched as desire flashed across his features, made my thighs squeeze. He noted it, his eyes flying back to meet mine. "Will you ask me inside?"

I smiled at his word choice. "I think I already did."

Surprise lit his eyes, and he chuckled. "That's very true."

We grinned at each other as I stepped back to let him in, and I realized, to my shock, that there was no awkwardness.

Closing and locking the door, I then reached for Arran's hand. "This way."

He slid his fingers through mine, and I shivered at the rough texture of his fingertips and palm against my skin. Holding his hand felt too good. Ignoring a brief flash of panic in the back of my mind, I squeezed his hand and led him into my small bedroom.

I let go and turned to face him by the end of the bed.

Arran's gaze was searching, and the intensity of his focus made my breath come sharp and fast.

He stepped toward me, and I trembled.

"You ready to do this?" Arran asked quietly, his brow pinched with concern as his hands settled on my waist.

A million thoughts raced through my head about this being a possible mistake, but my body throbbed with need. I zeroed in on that. Yes, this was happening really fast. But for once, I didn't want to be cautious or smart. I trusted Arran enough to share a moment of risk, of passion over sense. "Yes."

Arran's grip on my waist tightened as the heat in his blue eyes flamed brighter. He gave me what felt like a reassuring squeeze before his hands coasted down my hips and slipped under my nightie. I shivered at the soft caress of his fingertips on my belly.

"You have the softest skin," he whispered hoarsely. When he caressed a little higher, across my ribs, goose bumps prickled over my breasts, and they felt tight, desperately ready for his hands, his mouth.

"Arran ..."

He tickled his fingertips down my torso and down, down until his thumbs dug into the waistband of my underwear. He held my stare as he slowly tugged the lightweight lace over my hips. Then he guided them down, lowering to his haunches. I felt his hot breath on the silk of the nightie between my legs, and I shivered, the pulsing throb growing more insistent. Bracing a hand on his strong shoulder, I lifted one foot after the other so he could remove my panties.

When he curled his hands around my calves, looked up into my eyes, and caressed the backs of my legs, I swayed with absolute want. I knew it had been a long time since I'd been with a man, but I wasn't sure I'd ever felt this strong a pull toward anyone before.

A tugging sensation deep in my womb caused another rush of wet between my legs, and Arran's attention lowered there. His hands climbed higher before smoothing around my upper thighs. Gliding his thumbs toward my inner thighs, he pressed gently, and I automatically parted my legs for him.

My breathing grew louder, shallower, as Arran gently slid two thick fingers inside me. I gasped at the fullness.

"Ery," he groaned and rested his forehead against my right thigh. "You're so wet."

I flushed with embarrassment because I guessed that was what eight years of loneliness did to you. Or maybe it was just the Arran Adair effect.

Easing his fingers from me, Arran pushed my nightie up. "Hold it for me."

I clasped the fabric to my belly. And then Arran lifted my left leg over his shoulder, and I moaned as I realized his intent. Resting my free hand on his opposite shoulder for balance, I arched my back into him, and he made a guttural noise of desire seconds before his tongue touched my clit.

Need slammed through me, and I undulated against his mouth. His fingers dug into my thigh, and his groan vibrated through my core.

"Arran. Arran," I moaned.

He suckled my clit, pulling on it hard, and I panted as tension built deep inside, coiling like a spring. His tongue circled and then slid down in a voracious lick before pushing inside me.

"Yes!" I cried, thrusting against his mouth as I climbed higher and higher toward breaking apart completely. All my inhibitions had well and truly flown out the window as I gave myself over to *feeling*.

As if he felt how close I was, Arran returned to my clit and gently pushed two fingers inside me.

The tension was unbearable, and then suddenly it shattered, the release so epic and pleasurable, I shuddered against Arran's mouth for what seemed like forever.

He lowered my trembling leg, and I swayed against him as he stood. And it wasn't enough. As amazing as the orgasm was, it felt like I had a hundred more still locked inside. I wasn't done.

A thrilling feeling of power overwhelmed me as our eyes held. He smoldered, and his jaw set with a fierce need. I lifted my arms to help him pull my nightie over my head.

My chest heaved with my labored, excited breaths as Arran threw the silk to the floor and brought his hands to my shoulders. His eyes followed his fingertips as they trailed with excruciating slowness across my collarbone and down toward the rise of my breasts. I rarely wore a bra with the nightie, but something wicked in me had wanted to tease him, so I'd donned one of my sexiest white-lace bras.

My breasts were small and perky, and I'd grown to like them, but when I was younger, I'd been insecure about their size when an ex-boyfriend suggested a boob job. That was what living in LA brought you.

I had no insecurities about how Arran felt about my body, though, because he looked at me with a reverence no one ever had.

"You're so beautiful," he whispered, as if to prove my point, and goose bumps prickled in the wake of his touch. My nipples peaked against my bra with anticipation.

"Arran ..." My tone practically begged.

In answer to my needy plea, he gripped my hips and pulled me tight to him so I could feel his erection against my bare stomach.

Gently, he cupped my face in his hands. "Is kissing allowed?" he asked gruffly.

"You've already kissed me," I reminded him saucily.

He grinned. "Well, now, I feel like I kind of jumped the gun. I should have kissed you on the mouth first, and I'd really like to do that now."

I swear my lips plumped at the thought. "Then kiss me."

Arran made a sound low in the back of his throat and then his mouth was on mine as he kissed me so deeply, I could taste myself. Slow, sexy, and tender kisses that brought tears to my eyes. They made it feel like more than what this night was supposed to be. His kisses felt *right*. And I wanted more. So many more kisses from Arran Adair.

I curled my hands around his biceps to push him away. He breathed heavier, faster, searching my eyes, a frown appearing between his brows at whatever he saw there.

One of those voices in the back of my head whispered that going any further was a bad idea. Those kisses had not been casual.

And this was supposed to be casual.

One night only.

However, before I could decide what to do, Arran's hands

moved over my body. With light strokes, he learned every inch of me—my ribs, my waist, my stomach. Then his hands glided around to my ass, and he was kissing me again, deeper, hungrier kisses, and he drew me against his arousal. I thought it meant he was changing the vibe between us, pulling us back into that one-night-only place.

But as I stroked my hands down his arms, his kisses grew gentler. He nipped at my lower lip and then eased away to stare into my eyes as he glided his hands up my back to my bra strap. With a practiced dexterity, he unhooked my bra. I tried not to think about the other women from his past, and that soon became easy because of how he watched me.

Like I was the only woman in the world.

Arran nudged the straps down my arms, and it fell to the floor. His gaze slowly disconnected from mine, and I shivered as his eyes grew hooded. His hands tightened around my biceps while he feasted on the sight of my naked breasts. My nipples pebbled under his perusal, tight, needy buds that begged for his mouth.

"Fuck me," Arran groaned as he cupped them. "You're so gorgeous, I can barely stand it."

I moaned and arched into his touch. Ripples of desire undulated low in my belly as he played with my breasts, sculpting and kneading them, stroking and pinching my nipples. All the time, his eyes oscillated between my face and my breasts. I thrust into his touch, muttering my need for him.

"Do you know how long I've wanted this?" he asked hoarsely. "Fantasized about having you in my arms like this? It's fucking haunted me, Ery. And yet no fantasy could stand up to the reality of you. I need you." The words had barely broken past his lips when his mouth found mine. This kiss was rough, hard, desperate, and his groan filled me as he pinched my nipples between forefingers and thumbs.

I gasped, and his growl of satisfaction made me flush with pleasure. Feeling the fabric of his tee beneath my hands, I curled my fists into it and jerked my lips from his. "Take it off."

Arran let go of me, stepped back, and yanked his T-shirt up and off. As he threw it behind him and then worked on his boots and jeans, I reveled in the sight of him. I hadn't been able to ogle him the last time I'd seen him shirtless, but now I could enjoy the view.

He worked out regularly and had a gorgeous body, but it wasn't overly muscled. He was strong and masculine, athletic. Perfect. His thick thighs and muscular calves caused another hard flip in my lower belly. I moaned when he had to peel his boxer briefs over his erection, and when freed, he was so hard it strained toward his abs. He wanted me. Badly.

Every part of my body swelled toward him as I watched him pull a condom from his wallet and roll it over his erection. I licked my lips, desperate to feel the thickness of him inside me.

"Hurry."

In answer, Arran grasped me around the waist, but instead of guiding me down to the bed, he turned and sat on the edge. Then he guided me to straddle him, his arousal hot against my stomach.

Arran touched my chin, bringing my head up to lock our gazes. My fingers curled into the back of his shoulders as I took in his expression. There was so much emotion in his eyes. Lust, need … but something more too. I wasn't ready to contemplate what this meant.

"Arran?"

He slid his hand along my neck, tangling in my curls to grab a handful. Then he gently tugged my head back, arched my chest, and covered my right nipple with his mouth.

I gasped as sensation slammed through me, my hips automatically undulating as he sucked, laved, and nipped at me. Tension coiled between my legs, tightening and tightening as he moved between my breasts, his hot mouth, his tongue—

"Arran!" I was going to come again with only this.

Then he stopped, and I lifted my head to beg, to plead for him to keep touching me, but halted when he gripped my hips. Guiding me, he lifted me up, and I stared down at him, waiting as he took himself in hand.

Taking his cue, I lowered myself onto him, feeling the tip of him against my slick opening. Tingles cascaded down my spine and around my belly, deep between my legs.

Too long.

It had been too long.

That was what I kept telling myself. That was why I was so needy, so on the precipice of coming with just his tip in me. But I knew it was more.

It was him.

I wanted *him*.

Arran took hold of my hip with one hand and cupped my right breast with the other, and I gasped at the overwhelming thick sensation as I lowered onto him.

The coiling tension that had sprung so tight, so quickly, exploded with only his tip inside me.

I cried out and clung to his shoulders as my climax tore through me, my inner muscles rippling and tugging and drawing Arran in deeper. Shuddering, my hips jerking, my abs spasming, I wrapped my arms around Arran's neck to hold on as I shook through it. I rested my forehead against his.

As the last of the tremors passed through me, I became aware of Arran's bruising grip on my hips and the overwhelming fullness of him inside me. At some point during my orgasm, he'd plunged all the way in.

Oh, Lord.

Cheeks hot with embarrassment, I lifted my head to see his reaction, and the desire in his eyes made my inner muscles throb around him.

He grunted at the feeling. "Ery?"

Mortified, I whispered, "It's been a long time for me."

Arran's chest heaved a little. "That was ... fuck ... It took everything in me not to fucking unload watching you come on me." His countenance darkened. "But you better be ready to come again because we're not done, not by a long shot." Arran launched up off the bed and turned around to drop us on it. The motion drove him so deep inside me, it took my breath away.

Arran muttered a hoarse expletive as he hovered over me and then wrapped his hands around my wrists, pinning them to the bed on either side of my head.

He moved inside me with powerful thrusts, his eyes focused intensely on mine. Like he needed the eye contact. Like I needed it. And I hated to admit, but I did. I could never be in this moment with someone I didn't feel this connected to. That was the terrifying truth.

And I wanted to feel him everywhere; I wanted to grip his ass and feel it clench and release with each stroke, but he held me down.

I'd felt claustrophobic with an ex who liked to dominate in the bedroom. But with Arran, his holding me down so I could only take what he had to give, was strangely exciting.

The tension built again with every thick drag of him in and out. His features strained taut with lust, and with one more powerful glide in and out, I came again, shorter, sharper, but no less intense. With just one hard tug of my climax, Arran swelled inside me. He pressed my hands hard to the bed as he tensed between my legs and then—

"Eredine! Fuck! Eredine!" His hips jerked and shuddered against mine.

Eventually, he released my wrists and slumped over me, his face in my neck, and I wrapped my arms and legs around him, caressing his warm, damp skin.

Slowly, however, as his breathing eased and his whole body relaxed, the heaviness of his weight became too much. I couldn't breathe. And it wasn't because of his weight. I grew panicked as I realized ...

One night wasn't enough.

16

ARRAN

Not wanting to crush Ery, I rolled off and collapsed on my back, panting.

We'd just had sex, and it was phenomenal.

She tasted better than I could imagine. She felt better than any fantasy I'd had of her.

Turning my head to grin at her, I found her staring up at the ceiling.

"You should probably leave now, right?"

Scowling, I demanded, "Ery, look at me."

She reluctantly turned her head on the pillow. Confusion roiled in those beautiful eyes.

"You said one night only."

Eredine nodded. "Yup."

"The night isn't over, and I'm not done. I'm going to deal with this condom, and then I'm going to fuck you again. Sound good?"

She bit her lip as her nostrils flared with need. "Okay."

"Okay." I leaned over and kissed her in a manner that left no room for guessing what I planned next.

By the time I returned to the bedroom, Ery sat up against

the pillow, one long leg bent at the knee, her opposite arm flung over her head, her fingers playing with one of her curls.

I stood for a moment, frozen, as I took in the spectacular sight of a freshly fucked Eredine Willows relaxing naked on her bed. Blood rushed to my cock, and her eyes lowered as my semi went full mast. "Do you even know how beautiful you are?"

She gave me a pretty, almost shy smile. "You too."

I grinned at the thought of being called beautiful, but I'd take it. Swooping down to pick up my jeans, I pulled the packet of condoms out of the pocket, took one, threw the rest on the bedside table, and rolled one on. Ery watched my every move, and my skin was hot from her perusal.

Putting a knee to the bed, I climbed over her as I caressed my hand up her smooth leg, trailing my fingertips across her silky inner thigh as she spread her legs to accommodate me. Hovering over her, I reached for her mouth as she reached for mine, and kissed her as I slid two fingers inside her wet heat. Suddenly, the image of her filled to the brim with my cum made me harder than I thought possible. I kissed her deeper, hungrier, and she clung to me with a moan.

I didn't toy with her this time. Now that I knew moving inside Eredine was heaven, I wanted back in her too badly to wait. Removing my fingers, I braced my hands on either side of her shoulders and nudged between her legs. Releasing her from the kiss, I stared into her eyes, seeing the rivers of greenish gold that made her hazel eyes seem green in certain lights, and I pushed inside her.

Eredine brought her hips up around my waist and slid her hands down my back to grip my arse as I thrust. Her lips parted on a high gasp, and I felt the sound throb in my dick at the same time her fingers clenched into my arse cheeks. Fuck yes.

I pulled my hips back, a teasingly slow withdrawal, and

then groaned as her tight heat squeezed me when I pushed back in.

"Faster," Eredine whispered against my mouth. "Harder."

I smirked and didn't pick up my pace, even though every nerve ending was screaming at me to fuck her. But I didn't want to be just a one-night stand. I wanted to devastate and satisfy her in equal measure.

Gripping her thigh, I yanked her hips higher, changing the angle of my thrusts, as Eredine released her hold on me and slid farther down the bed. "Oh, Lord," she panted as I dragged out of her painfully, pleasurably, slowly, until only my tip was inside. Her hands fluttered near her face, eyes sparkling with passion, and everything about her transfixed me as I drove back in. I found her clit with my thumb as I moved, and her eyes widened as she tilted her chin back and whimpered.

Fuck, yes.

I circled her clit harder.

"Arran." She gripped my waist now, fingers biting into me. "Harder. Faster."

Knowing I was at the breaking point, I increased my thrusts, fucking into her, her small but beautiful tits trembling with my every drive. Her whimpers grew into moans and needy pants, making me harder. So fucking hard.

"Is this what you want?" I panted as I braced over her, hips snapping as the need to come overtook everything.

"Yes!" Her nails dug into my back. "Arran ... ahhhhh!" She threw her head back on a cry of pleasure as I felt her inner muscles throb around me in waves of orgasm.

"FUCK!" I roared as the power of it tore through me, my hips jerking against her as I ground my cock into her, wanting to feel every single lingering tug of her climax.

The only thing that could have made it better was coming inside Ery instead of a condom.

I fell over her, my lips against her damp skin as I breathed heavily into her neck and shuddered, my cock pulsing inside her.

Finally, I lifted my head to meet her stunned gaze.

I might have thought that coming harder than I'd ever come in my life would mean I wanted to roll off Ery and sleep.

It didn't.

I was addicted.

"Give me a minute," I murmured, "and then we're going to do that again."

Her eyes widened. "Again?"

"Oh, aye. There's more where that came from, Eredine Willows." I crushed my mouth over hers, kissing her deep but slow, languid. She throbbed around me, and I grunted into the kiss. Oh, aye. We were definitely not done.

IT WAS AROUND two in the morning when I finally dressed to leave Eredine.

She'd donned her sexy silk nightie to say goodbye at the door.

We'd had sex two more times and done plenty of sucking and licking of every inch of each other. It was the most hedonistic night of my life, and I loved how my reserved Ery wasn't so reserved once she realized how much her touch excited me.

"Well ..." She bit her lip, looking uncertain as we stood in the doorway. "Thanks for a ..." She laughed softly. "It was wonderful."

I smiled. "It was. It was amazing. Some itch we scratched."

She laughed again, but then her expression turned serious. "I ... I don't want anyone to know we did this."

Disappointment churned in my gut at what that meant, but I nodded. "It's our secret."

But did she really expect us to continue on as if nothing had happened between us when I'd just experienced the best sex of my life? There was a connection here that went beyond the physical. And I knew I wasn't alone in that.

"Good night, then." She reached for the door and opened it.

I stared at the porch for a second, my heart thudding. I wanted to demand more, but I was afraid it would push Eredine away entirely. So instead, I pulled her to me and kissed her like we'd never kiss each other again. By the time I released her, we were both panting. "Are we still on for our run tomorrow, or is that too early now?"

She shook her head. "We can run."

"All right ... good night," I said, my words hoarse. Because I would have given anything for her to invite me back into her bed, to give me the pleasure of waking up next to her.

Something I couldn't decipher crossed Ery's expression, but it was fleeting, and whatever it had been made her face close down. "Good night." She stepped out of my embrace.

And so I left her there.

I got in my car and drove in the wee hours back to Cael-more, trying to figure out how I could change Eredine Willows's mind. Because our night together had blown *my* mind beyond anything I'd expected, and now, I was afraid there could never be a woman who matched her.

She'd fucking ruined me.

17

EREDINE

Rather than go on a run with Arran, all I really wanted to do was run *away* from Arran. He'd left in the early hours, and I could not sleep for a while after his departure. Images of him, of what I'd just experienced with him, played over and over in my mind, and I couldn't believe it, but I felt insatiable.

He'd satisfied me so well that I needed more.

Arran Adair was the best, most giving lover I'd ever had, and like a greedy, starving woman, that one bite had made me hunger for it all.

It had been a little more than a bite. Our night together had been an unrelenting display of passion. Once I'd said good night to him and locked up, I'd returned to my bedroom only to find it was heavy with the scent of sex. I'd cracked open a window, but that didn't help with my bedding. Arran's cologne was all over it.

I'd finally drifted to sleep with the smell of him in my head.

That I woke up exhausted, restless, and needy made me

panic. One night with Arran was supposed to scratch the itch. It wasn't supposed to make the itch spread.

Okay, bad analogy.

The point was, I couldn't get him out of my head. As I showered that morning, my body felt overly sensitive, and I longed for him to be here with me, his soapy hands gliding over my slender curves.

Damn it.

This was not good.

I'd messed up.

I'd underestimated Arran and myself.

The desire to run away from this reality was great, but I would not do that to my friend. We had a deal, and it was contingent on our night together not messing up our friendship. Sure, it would be weird at first the morning after we'd learned every inch of each other's bodies, but time would take care of the weirdness.

I'd fallen asleep without taking care of my hair, so it was a wild mess. Wrangling my curls into two buns at the base of my neck using a ton of pins, I then dressed in workout gear. I was just slipping into my sneakers when my phone buzzed on the vanity.

Arran's name was on the text notification. My pulse raced, a small smile prodding my lips, and I tapped on it.

Ery, I can't make our run this morning. I have to be at the Gloaming first thing to accept a delivery. Talk soon.

My stomach roiled as I tapped out a simple "OK" and sent it. Was Arran blowing me off?

Anger and hurt churned inside me as I grabbed my keys, opting to run, anyway. My first class at the estate wasn't until eleven, so I had plenty of time. During the drive to the beach, I clenched the steering wheel so hard, it was a wonder it didn't crack in my hands.

Was he truly blowing me off?

I'd trusted Arran, and now he was making it weird between us.

Of course, there might actually be a delivery at the Gloaming, but the timing was suspect.

Asshole.

Ugh, why did men always inevitably have to be such men?

MY CLASSES WENT FINE. Contrary to what Michelle and Natalia said about the other guests being wary of me since Iris Benning's expulsion, I'd had no comments or strangeness from club members. I did have one actor who'd recently started taking my Pilates classes who had taken Pilates in LA for years and kept trying to take over the instruction. I'd learned to be patient with know-it-alls like him and just smile and continue talking to everyone else. It was irritating but nothing I couldn't handle, and according to Michelle, his visit would be brief, as he rarely stayed at the estate. Which was true for quite a few members. They were too busy to visit, but they wanted the prestige of being able to tell people they were Ardnoch members.

Still, despite the ease of my workday, by the time I drove up to Thane and Regan's at six thirty, I was exhausted from last night's lack of sleep. Just as Regan had promised, Arran's vehicle wasn't there. He was mysteriously busy. And that was why I'd offered to watch Eilidh and Lewis on a Friday night while Thane and Regan attended parents' evening, followed by a late dinner. I knew the kids would have already eaten, so I could only hope there were leftovers since I'd come straight from work and was starving. I'd changed into loose sweatpants and a T-shirt after showering at my studio, but I hadn't had time to grab dinner.

Hurrying up the front steps, I let myself in because Regan

had admonished me too many times for knocking. She said I was family, and their home was my home.

It was sweet, but I still felt strange just walking in. "Hey, it's me!" I called as I stepped inside.

"In here!" Regan called back.

I followed her voice into the main kitchen/dining/living space and found her standing at the counter while Thane stood at her back, clasping a necklace around his fiancée's throat.

"Ery!" Eilidh yelled, and I turned just in time for her to dive at me. She was getting too tall to haul into my arms now, so I cuddled her as she wrapped her small arms tightly around my waist.

"Hey, cutie pie."

She grinned up at me. "Mum and Dad are going to talk to my teacher about how awesome I am."

Her parents chuckled, as did I. "I'm sure they are." I looked to where Lewis sat on the couch watching TV and waved. "Hey, buddy. You doing okay?"

"We had pizza," he informed me. "We left you some."

"Thanks. I'm starving."

"We're watching a film about a giant snowman. I can't pronounce the title, which is stupid because it's a kids' film and we should be able to pronounce it," Eilidh said with a curl to her upper lip.

I struggled not to laugh again. "That's very true."

"Thank you again for doing this. We'd have asked Lachlan and Robyn, but they've gone to Glasgow for the weekend, and Arran is busy at the Gloaming." Regan wore an apologetic look.

"It's fine. You know I love watching the kids."

"I know, but ..." Regan shared a glance with Thane. "We feel like we're leaning on you too much."

"Don't be silly. If I didn't want to do it, I wouldn't," I promised. I owed them this.

Thane gave me a gruff nod. "Thank you, Eredine. We really do appreciate it."

"Of course." I was uncomfortable with their thanks, considering I'd allowed the kids to be traumatized when Regan's stalker knocked me unconscious. It had taken a lot to get me to look after them again, but once I did, determination replaced my fear. I'd never let that happen to them now. If I was the one babysitting, then I had some control over the situation.

I could protect them next time.

Not that I wanted there to be a next time.

"Shouldn't you get going?"

Regan and Thane left a few minutes later. I grabbed a couple slices of cold pizza and a bottle of water and returned to join the kids on the massive sectional. I sat next to Eilidh, who snuggled into my side. "What are we watching?"

"The snowman thing."

I'd just finished my last slice and was actually enjoying the beautiful animation set in China when I was startled by the sound of the exterior laundry door opening.

"It's me!" Arran called.

Suddenly, the pizza felt like a lump in my gut. My stare was trained on the doorway into the laundry room, and I swear the breath stuck in my throat as Arran stepped through it.

He'd taken off his boots and jacket and strode in wearing jeans and a long-sleeved Henley that did wonderful things for his arms.

Images of last night flashed across my mind, and my cheeks burned.

"Uncle Arran, we're watching a movie," Eilidh announced from her place by my side.

"I can see that." He smiled indulgently at her as he moved toward us, and then his gaze met mine.

Knowing sparked between us, and I honestly didn't think I could speak.

"Ery." He nodded.

Forcing out a *hey*, I turned back to the screen since it was apparently impossible to talk to him if I was looking at him. "I thought you were working."

"I got home earlier than expected. Anything to eat?"

Regan and Thane had ordered more food than any one family needed. "There's cold pizza on the counter." I still didn't look at him, my eyes glued to the TV screen.

"That'll do."

A few minutes later, Arran joined us on the sectional.

On my other side.

So close, his arm brushed mine every time he lifted a slice to his mouth. The scent of his cologne was a trigger, and I felt that low, deep, swooping want.

Oh, Lord. This was ridiculous.

I tried to shimmy a little away from him without being too obvious, turning in toward Eilidh, but all that did was turn my ass in Arran's direction, and I swear I felt his burning gaze on it.

That only reminded me of him crawling down my body as I laid flat on my stomach last night, feeling his sexy kisses map my curves. When he'd kissed my ass cheeks and then gently bit one, I'd been surprised by how erotic it was.

Now my breathing seemed too shallow, too loud, as my skin tingled. Every inch of my body felt too sensitive, and all Arran had done was sit next to me.

This was insane!

"Excuse me, cutie," I murmured to Eilidh. "I need to use the restroom."

"Okay." She slid away and I shot up off the couch, hurrying toward the front to the downstairs bathroom.

Once inside, I turned on the cold tap and held my wrists under it. Granny taught me that trick. It was a way to cool or calm down, depending on the situation, without ruining your makeup by splashing your face.

I jumped in surprise as the door opened and Arran walked in, closing it behind him.

Whirling around from the sink, I glowered. "What are you doing? You can't follow me in here while the kids are right outside."

He scowled as he bridged the distance between us, forcing me to lean into the sink as he pressed the entire length of his body against mine.

"Arran," I whispered.

"I didn't blow you off this morning, by the way," he surprised me by saying as he searched my face.

"What?"

His frown deepened. "I deduced from your very terse and uncharacteristic 'OK' that you thought I was blowing you off. I wasn't. My contractor called at five in the morning to tell me the windows we've been waiting on were being delivered at six a.m. I had to get out there to accept the delivery. I wasn't blowing you off."

Oh.

Okay.

"I believe you."

The crease between his brows disappeared, and he smirked. "Good." Then, before I could even compute what was happening, his mouth was on mine, his arms around me, and I was plastered to his body as he devoured me.

Need bloomed between my thighs as I matched his voracious kiss. I wanted to unzip his jeans and yank down my sweatpants and feel him thick and deep inside me more than I'd ever wanted anything.

As he groaned into my mouth, I almost lost all reason.

Until the faint sound of music from the television infiltrated my senses.

I yanked my mouth from Arran's and gaped at him. "What was that?" I pushed against his chest now, and he reluctantly released me.

Skirting around him, toward the door, I stared warily at him. Mostly because I'd met no one who had the power to fry my brain with lust like he did.

"I want you again, Ery," Arran said gruffly, his eyes hot with desire.

I wanted him too.

There was no denying that.

I'd barely thought of anything else but him all day. The need to talk to someone about it was surprising, too, but I couldn't confess this to the people I trusted because the people I trusted were Arran's family. It was too convoluted. And it had to remain a secret. The more times we gave into our attraction, the harder it would be to keep it a secret.

"We can't." I reached for the door handle. "It'll just complicate things."

"Ery—"

"No. I'm going back out to the kids, and when you appear, you're going to tell them you have things to do and you'll leave."

His eyes flashed with anger. "So I can't even spend time with you now? That wasn't the deal."

Remorse flooded me. "I don't mean it like that. I just mean ... maybe we need a little time to readjust to friendship only. Tonight isn't that night, Arran, clearly. So please, just let me look after the kids alone. We'll go for our run tomorrow.

It should feel normal between us in that setting. Familiar. Routine."

Arran's expression darkened, and the fun-loving guy I knew so well disappeared as he sneered and said, "If that's what you choose to believe. Fine."

"Arran—"

"No, no. We'll go for a run tomorrow, and we'll miraculously forget that last night we had mind-blowing sex that makes me hard every time I think about it."

My body responded instantly to his words, tight nipples, dampness between my legs. His nostrils flared as if he sensed my physical reaction. He probably did.

"It's too complicated," I repeated weakly and then fled the bathroom.

A few minutes later, Arran appeared in the living room to tell the kids he had work to do. They complained, and he winced with guilt, which made me, in turn, feel remorseful. He didn't look at me again before he left the house.

And I worried about that all night.

Maybe he wouldn't bother showing up tomorrow.

18

EREDINE

I'd woken up an hour before my alarm, worrying that Arran might not show. Ignoring my feelings about that potential outcome, I spent the extra hour getting ready, so I had time for a protein shake and an attempt to read some chapters of my latest book.

My gaze kept flicking to my phone, however, and now and then, I'd wake the screen to check the clock. That tick became more frequent the closer to six thirty it got.

Then my pulse leapt at the sound of a car engine in the distance. I wanted to jump up and peer out my window. Instead, I opened the house security app on my phone and tapped the front porch camera.

Arran's SUV appeared out of the trees a few seconds later and stopped behind my car.

Relief, excitement, trepidation, worry ... a gamut of emotions coursed through me at the sight of Arran Adair jumping out of his vehicle. Closing the app, I got up off the couch just as he approached the front door and rang the bell.

Taking a deep breath, I moved to the door calmly and

cursed the slight tremble of thrill in my belly as I pulled it open.

He stood before me in his regular workout uniform of fitted T-shirt, sweatpants, and running shoes. And my senses immediately overwhelmed me as I recalled the feel of his hard pecs brushing against my breasts, the taste of his damp, hot skin on my lips, the smell of his cologne mingled with the scent of sex.

I remembered the way he'd held my gaze as he moved inside me and how it had felt more right to be connected to him than any boyfriend from my past.

It was terrifying.

A giant red flag.

Yet whatever Arran saw on my expression, it made him charge into the house, slam the door closed behind him, and lift me like I weighed nothing onto my dining table.

In shock, I moved to push against his chest, and he wrapped his hands around my wrists and held them to him instead. His azure eyes blazed.

"You want a workout this morning, Ery?" he asked gruffly. "We don't need to leave the house for that."

"Arran—" I cut off as he released me, but only to whip off his T-shirt.

His chest rose and fell a little faster as he gripped my thighs and spread me as he pulled me into him.

I gasped, resting my hands on his yummy pecs for balance. "Arran?"

He searched my face. "Tell me you don't want this. Tell me you haven't been thinking about this every second of every hour since the wee hours of Friday morning."

At the feel of his arousal pressed to my core, all rational thinking fled me. I wanted to feel. I wanted more. Because the truth was, my night with Arran was the first time in eight years that I'd felt fully awake. Alive.

In answer, I reached for the short hem of my sports tank and pulled it off, throwing it over Arran's shoulder. His gaze dipped to my bare breasts for a few hot seconds and then returned to my eyes.

Then his mouth crashed down on my mine in a hungry, sexy-as-hell kiss. I slid my arms around his back, my fingers digging into his warm muscles as he devoured me. His fingertips trailed over the tops of my thighs as he moved between my legs.

Soon the kiss was out of control, wild and hurried, as he dug into the waistband of my yoga pants. Following his lead, I lifted my ass up off the table to aid him in yanking them down. Arran pulled off my sneakers and then the yoga pants were gone and I was in nothing but my teeny-tiny undies. Arran caressed my legs all the way back up, pushing between them again as he studied every inch of me with that smoldering expression that made my belly clench deep with want.

"Arran," I whispered.

His eyes traveled up my naked breasts to my face, and he confessed hoarsely, "Every time I see you, you're more beautiful than the last time. How is that possible?"

An aching flare of emotion resonated inside me. I didn't want to deal with it. Instead, I reached for him, caressing every ripple and hard muscle of his torso. Arran's hands settled on my waist, his eyes low-lidded as he let me touch him. Then, just as I dipped to cup him, he wrapped his hand around my nape and kissed me again.

Then his lips were gone.

"Arran," I protested, but he gave a slight shake of his head before he tugged me gently, my ass almost hanging off the table. Then he lowered his face between my legs, and my head fell back in a groan as he pressed soft, teasing kisses along my inner right thigh. I jerked at the touch of his mouth against my sex. He blew the cotton of my underwear against me, and I shuddered.

"You're ready for me, Ery, aren't you?" His voice was thick as he curled a finger around the material, brushing me. "Do you want my mouth?"

"What do you think?" I huffed, pushing my hips toward him.

I felt his chuckle against my skin. "I remember you being a little more patient the other night."

"Then you remembered wrong." I opened my eyes. "Please."

His expression turned tender. "Fuck," he whispered. "For the rest of my life, all you'll have to do is say that word, and I'll be putty in your hands."

My heart lurched. "Arran—oh!" I fell back on my hands as he roughly ripped my underwear down my legs. I barely had time to think before Arran was pressing my thighs apart again.

Then his mouth was finally on me.

"Oh, Lord," I whimpered, leaning back as he licked at me, his tongue flicking and tormenting my clit. "Arran, please."

I could feel it building, my muscles trembling and tightening.

And then two fingers pushed inside me.

He sucked and licked and slid his fingers in and out. I was heading for the cliff's edge. I stiffened and then fell over, crying out his name as my inner muscles clamped around his fingers in a hard climax.

Arran stood, only to lean down into me, wrapping his arms around my waist so he could gather me against him. I lifted my legs around his hips and clung to him as he kissed me, the taste of me on his tongue, moving against mine in hard, quick strokes. The kiss was so desperate it almost brought tears to my eyes.

Breaking the kiss, Arran's hot lips trailed down my neck. I arched my back, wanting his mouth on me everywhere.

The heat of insatiability set the languid aftermath of my climax alight as Arran cupped and stroked and kissed my breasts, learning every inch of them all over again. He then closed his mouth around my nipple and tugged, sucked, and licked it until it was so swollen, it was tender. He moved to the other until my legs were climbing his hips. I writhed against his erection, desperate for him to take me.

"I need you," I moaned. "Arran, I need you."

He kissed me, fierce, hungry, one hand under my ass urging me up against him as he ground between my legs, the friction of his sweatpants over my sex building me toward climax again. I gasped into his kiss as his other hand moved to my hair. I could tell he wanted to release it from the pins, but there were too many holding my curls, and I was too impatient to wait.

Apparently, so was Arran.

My eyes opened as he released me to grab a condom out of his wallet and then push down his sweatpants and boxer briefs. He hurriedly, almost comically, kicked off his sneakers, his cock hard. In seconds, he sheathed himself and then he was hot and throbbing and ready for me.

I looked down, feeling a sudden roar of fire lick up from my heels, shooting through my whole body at the sight of him. He wasn't overly long, but he was thick, and I remembered the delicious fullness of him inside me. I needed him like I needed oxygen.

I licked my lips.

"Fuck, Ery," Arran breathed against my mouth as he pressed his forehead to mine.

I kissed him, my tongue flicking against his lips. I took the steely heat of him in my hands and squeezed, and Arran kissed me harder, gasping and panting, as I stroked him with one hand and dug my fingers into his ass with the other, urging him to me.

I guided his tip to my entrance and smoothed my hand up his rigid stomach.

With our lips still touching, our eyes met and held.

Arran gripped my hips and pushed inside.

My eyes fluttered closed at the satisfying burn that quickly gave way to an exciting fullness.

"Ery, open your eyes," he demanded.

I did, holding his ardent gaze.

"Keep your eyes open." He thrust deeper. "Keep your eyes on me."

He tilted my hips as he slid in and out of me slowly. I trembled against him as he took pleasure in taking his time, and I marveled at how safe I felt with him. I was more vulnerable than a person could be, and yet with him, I felt not just protected but ... free.

I fought hard against a sudden onslaught of tears and closed my eyes against them.

"Ery. Your eyes. Please," he begged, his deep voice strained with desire.

My eyes flew open for him.

"There you are. You feel amazing," he huffed against my lips, a small, amazed smile curling his mouth.

I moved against his thrusts. "You feel wonderful too."

"Ery." His grip tightened, his eyes blazing into mine. "Eredine."

"Arran," I whimpered back as he thrust at just the right angle to brush my clit with his movements.

"Fuck." He pumped harder, faster.

It built again, and I shuddered against him in little jerks.

"Come for me," he commanded, gruff with need. "Come around me."

That soft demand, just as it had been before, was my trigger.

I cried out his name, my fingers digging into his shoulders as I clenched around his driving cock, and I lost his eyes as I threw my head back in euphoria.

As I pulsed around him, Arran held me as his rhythm increased. A few seconds later, his face pressed against my neck, he stiffened, and groaned my name. His hips jerked against mine, and I felt the throb of his release inside me.

I held on to him as we tried to catch our breaths. My skin was slick against his, my breasts crushed into his pecs, and we were as close to each other as we could get. I squeezed my thighs around his hips, reveling in this delicious aftermath.

Don't panic, I coached myself. *You're still in control. You can have this with him and have it not be complicated. This is Arran. You can trust him to keep it uncomplicated.*

Before I could voice the reminder of what this was between us, he swept me into his arms and carried me into the bedroom.

He laid me gently, almost reverently, down on my bed. I opened my mouth to speak, but he beat me to it. "While I grab the condoms from the dining table, why don't you take your hair down?"

My skin flushed at his intentions. "Arran, is this a good idea?"

His eyes narrowed. "I don't want to stop. Do you? And be honest."

I took a deep breath, not wanting to hurt his feelings, but wanting to give him the honesty he'd asked for. "I don't want to stop, but I still don't want a relationship, so where does that leave us?"

Arran contemplated me a few seconds before he offered, "I propose a casual affair. No one needs to know. We stop when one or both of us decide we're done. No promises, no commitment. But we only agree to it if we promise to remain friends after. I don't want to lose you. And no seeing anyone else while we're doing this."

My breathing grew shallow at the idea of losing Arran's friendship. But I also knew I wasn't done craving this closeness between us. It was exhilarating, and I was addicted to this new sensation. It was like I'd been living with all my senses turned down to fifty percent. Arran had come along and turned the dial until I was feeling and smelling and hearing and tasting and seeing everything at a level I'd forgotten existed.

I didn't want to lose that either.

As for the latter rule, that wouldn't be a problem for me.

I nodded. "Okay. Let's agree to that."

Arran's expression darkened with satisfaction. "Hair down," he repeated. "I'll be back in a few seconds."

"It'll take me more than a few seconds," I grumbled, sitting up. "I'll just leave it up so we can get to the good times faster."

"Please." He smoldered at me.

I flushed under the heat of his stare but rolled my eyes. "Fine."

Sure enough, when he returned, I was still sitting on the edge of the bed pulling out pins.

Arran laughed and sat beside me to help. I caught our reflection in the vanity mirror, and a smile tugged at my lips at the sight of us completely naked, taking hairpins out of my hair.

"By the time we're done here, my balls will be blue," Arran said teasingly.

"I told you. But you're the one who insisted."

"I love your hair." He pressed a kiss to my lips and then whispered in my ear, "I love it wrapped around my fist as I fuck you."

My breathing stuttered as I met his eyes in the mirror. No one had ever talked to me so crudely in the bedroom as Arran. Yet, surprisingly, it worked. It worked big-time. I guessed because it didn't seem crude, it just seemed intense and visceral. He chuckled as I hurried to release my hair, and once that last pin was out, I lunged, taking him to his back.

Arran's laughter filled my bedroom, but as my lips found every line and curve on his body, his laughter turned to desperate groans.

And we were lost inside each other.

Anyone might have called the cell phones we'd left out in the living room, but we'd never know. We only stopped to use the bathroom and grab snacks.

For the first time in my life, I spent an entire day and night in bed, sometimes talking about our lives without delving too deeply, but mostly savoring each other's bodies and competing to give the other the most orgasms.

It was surreal.

It was mind-blowing.

It was a day I'll never, ever forget.

19

ARRAN

Arriving at the Gloaming around seven thirty, eight o'clock every morning meant that me and the workers could secure parking in the large Castle Street lot. By ten, however, all those spaces would be filled with cars and camper vans. That was what happened every year as soon as Ardnoch hit the summer months, and it was now June.

After a morning run with Ery, followed by a quickie in her shower, I left for work. Keeping our casual sex arrangement secret this past month hadn't proven too difficult, to be fair, considering how much time we'd spent together before.

What was proving difficult was keeping *feelings* out of it. I knew going in it would likely become an issue for me as time went on. I wanted to know about her past. I wanted to know what she was hiding from.

That Lachlan knew and I didn't was a thorn in my bloody side.

I wanted Eredine to trust me with this.

And I was pissed off and frustrated she wouldn't. Yet, I couldn't show her that was how I felt because that wasn't our deal.

The deal was great sex for however long we wanted.

Neither of us was showing signs of growing bored either.

I just hoped the moments we stole together made her happy enough ... that maybe I was becoming essential to her. That maybe she thought of me at least once every hour, like I thought of her.

My biggest distractions from Eredine were the Gloaming and my house. The Gloaming renovations were well underway. The bar and restaurant were now open again at night and making us some money. We'd kept on most of Gordon's staff and had been paying them while we were closed, which was eating into profits, so it was good to have them back and working. Eventually, when the bar and restaurant reopened during the day, I'd serve as the day manager, and we'd keep Bobby, who'd worked as Gordon's right-hand man for years. We'd finally given Bobby his due and made him the restaurant and bar evening manager.

The biggest renovation was the addition of en suite bathrooms in every guest room. It had taken some planning to fit them in, and now the plumbing was giving me a headache. Needing a breather from the organized chaos, I slipped out of the Gloaming around noonish to grab a coffee from Flora's and sandwich from Morag's Deli.

Ardnoch was always busy at the weekends with tourists, but you could rely on quieter streets during most weekdays in winter months. Summer meant there were people every-bloody-where hoping to bump into a celebrity on the loose from my brother's estate, like they were zoo animals. Yes, I was grateful for the tourists. They frequented the Gloaming and soon they'd book our rooms. But the hustle and bustle on the streets, taking up all the tables in the cafés, and making an obstacle course of Castle Street, was jarring. I'd never really had the chance to experience Ardnoch like this until now, though I'd stayed in much more crowded places in my life.

As I approached Flora's to grab a to-go cup, I slowed at the sight of Monroe Sinclair standing outside talking to a young woman I didn't recognize. The tension in Roe's body caught my attention, the way her eyes darted around, as if she wanted to escape.

She'd been successfully avoiding me for a month, which probably meant she wanted nothing to do with me, but Roe would always be my friend, and right now, I didn't like the vibe of whatever was going on.

I picked up my pace. "Roe!" I called just before I reached her.

Roe started, her gray eyes wide as she looked up at me. "Arran, hi."

"You all right?" I looked at the unfamiliar woman and noted how she held her phone out between her and Roe. A quick glance at the screen revealed a recording app.

What the hell?

I narrowed my eyes on the young blond who didn't look a day over twenty.

She tilted her head as she looked back at me. Something flickered behind her eyes before recognition suddenly lit them. "Are you an Adair?" she asked in a North American accent. "You look like Lachlan Adair."

"Who is asking?"

The blond beamed and announced, "I'm Harriet Blume, a celebrity journalist."

"You barely look old enough to have graduated from high school," I said, my back up even more to discover she was a journo. Lachlan had told me over the years that Ardnoch attracted paparazzi and journalists during the summer. Paps hoped to snap a photo or two of members who dared venture into the village.

However, most of the celebrity gossips learned, after a few years of trying, that they couldn't get the locals to talk about whatever went on at Ardnoch Estate. One, because anyone who didn't work on the estate had no clue what went on; and two, because they were loyal to the village and to Lachlan. Many people owned businesses on Castle Street, the four streets that made up the village center, and down the many quaint lanes that connected those streets. Ardnoch relied on tourism, and its tourism had increased tenfold since my brother transformed Ardnoch Castle. The estate remained popular for its privacy, and the villagers understood that.

No one talked shit about the estate to tourists, let alone journos and paps.

Harriet tittered as if I were flirting by commenting on her youth. "Oh, that's sweet. I'm twenty-one. But I'm not a graduate. No, I started interviewing celebrities on my social media platform. I have five million followers."

Bloody Nora. "Is that so?"

"Aye," Monroe finally spoke as she gave me a meaningful look. "Harriet here was looking for some—I think the word she used was *dirt*—on Ardnoch Estate and/or the Adair family."

"Did I say that?" Harriet's fake grin faltered. "I'm not sure I said it like that."

"I'm certain you did." Monroe gave her a false smile.

I glanced at Harriet's phone. "Are you recording this?"

"Yeah, so?" She shrugged.

Instead of answering, I took Monroe by the shoulders and guided her away from the girl.

"Hey, where are you going? I have questions."

I looked over my shoulder at her. "Ms. Blume, we don't take kindly to journalists harassing our residents or tourists. I'm afraid you've wasted your plane fare."

"Are you an Adair?" she called after me.

I ignored her, cursing under my breath, and then Monroe stopped us a few feet past Flora's. "You all right?"

She tucked her hair behind her ear. "I had to book the morning off school to take Mum to a doctor's appointment and thought I'd just drop her at home and then grab a coffee before heading to school for the afternoon. I didn't expect to get accosted by an aggressively happy and nosy girl shoving a phone in my face and asking me what dirt I could dish on your family."

I glanced back down the street to see Harriet had disappeared among the crowds. Those same tourists walked by Roe and me as we huddled against the side of the building that housed Flora's. "Hopefully, she'll be gone soon."

"This place is different," Roe said quietly, almost mournfully.

I sighed. "You mean, since Lachlan opened the estate?"

Roe looked at me but didn't hold my gaze. "I've only been home a few times over the last eighteen years. Only once since Lachlan opened Ardnoch as a members-only club, and it was in winter, so I didn't see this. Ardnoch was always a busy wee place in the summer, but not like this. It didn't attract paparazzi, for a start."

"It's a pain in the arse, I know. But the village is financially thriving from it."

"I know." She nodded. "I just ... I'm ... I've missed the quiet this past week. They seemed to converge on the village in a sudden swarm."

"I'm surprised you've noticed. I haven't seen you in weeks."

Roe looked up at me now, guilt in her expression. "I'm sorry for running away last time I saw you."

"Things don't have to be awkward between us, Roe. I'm not angry about the past. Brodan and I are good. We've been good for years. It's *in* the past. I hope we can move on from it and be friends."

Her expression softened. "I'd like that."

"Good. Now, tell me how you're doing? Really?"

"I'm fine." She shrugged, but I saw exhaustion in her eyes. "I like my job. Mum broke her hip about six months ago. She didn't tell me. I got a phone call from her neighbor about how much she was struggling with recuperation. She also mentioned the job at the primary school, and so it seemed like the right thing to do, the right timing. I came back to help with her recovery."

I didn't know all the details, but I knew their relationship hadn't been easy when we were younger. "How is that?"

Roe looked away. "She's doing well enough that I can move out. Gordon's renting me a caravan in his park down by the beach."

Irritated by the thought of Roe in a caravan, I scowled. "You can't stay in a caravan permanently. It's bloody freezing down there in the winter."

"It's just until something affordable comes available. Rent is much higher here than it used to be."

Because of Ardnoch Estate.

Fuck.

My mind raced. Surely, we knew someone who could offer Roe a nice apartment or cottage for a decent rental cost? I'd look into it.

"I can see that Adair mind racing, but I don't need help, Arran. In fact, I won't accept it if you try." Roe laid a hand on my arm. "I'm fine. I promise."

Aye, we'd see. I sighed. "You'll come to me if you need anything. Promise?"

She smiled that pretty smile and reached up on her tiptoes to draw me down to a hug. Memories flooded me. She and Brodan walking together on the estate. Or hanging out down by the beach, when we were kids, and me and Arro would chase after them. The many, many times we played hide-and-seek in our old drafty castle. So many years of friendship.

I squeezed her tight. "It's good to have you back." I pressed a kiss to the top of her head and looked up as I released her, only to find Eredine standing in the middle of the pavement staring blankly at us.

"Ery." I stepped back from Monroe, who turned to look at Eredine.

"Hi." She gave Ery a small wave.

Ery remained expressionless as her gaze moved to Roe. "Hi." Her tone was flat.

Roe blushed. "Okay. I better get going, or I'll be late for school." She looked up at me with a tender smile. "See you around, Arran."

"You will," I promised her.

She chuckled, nodded, and gave us another wave before hurrying away, forgoing the coffee she'd originally set out for before Harriet Blume accosted her.

Approaching Eredine, I noted the way she stiffened as I got closer.

Was she ... jealous?

"Hey. What are you doing here?"

She wouldn't meet my gaze, and I cursed as a tourist couple knocked my shoulder hard trying to get past us. I gestured toward the side of the building, out of people's way. Ery walked over to join me.

"I thought I'd grab a sandwich from Morag's," she answered flatly, her eyes darting up and down Castle Street. "I forgot it would be like this."

I frowned. "Look at me."

She lifted her gaze to mine. Carefully blank.

I sighed. "Please don't tell me you think something is going on between Monroe and me? It was just a hug."

"It was an awfully long, intimate hug." Ery shrugged like it was no big deal when her tight tone suggested the opposite.

"She's an old friend."

"Who you've had sex with." She shrugged with fake breeziness. "It's no surprise if there are still feelings there."

"There are none," I snapped, my frustration with our situation taking hold. "That was over a long time ago."

She shrugged again. "It's nothing to me if it wasn't over. We're just casual. But we promised no other lovers while we're sleeping together, so just give me the memo—hey!" she cried out as I grabbed her hand and hauled her after me down the street. "Arran," she hissed.

I didn't stop. Not until I'd pulled her down the alley between Flora's and the outdoor clothing store. Then I only stopped once we were far enough down it to hide in shadows from Castle Street. I pressed Ery up against Flora's, bracing my hands on either side of her head, and crushed her lips beneath mine.

At first, she was resistant, but I kissed Ery like I'd never get the chance to kiss her again, breathing in the scent of vanilla and jasmine that would forever remind me of her. I felt her hands grip my waist as I lifted Ery's thigh to press in between her legs, letting her feel how hard I was for her. All it took was a kiss to get me like this, and a woman hadn't been able to control my body like that since I was a teen.

I nibbled at her mouth before slowing to brush my lips over hers. Then I murmured against them, "You never need to be jealous of anyone, Ery. You're all I think about." I met her desire-laden gaze. "Every fucking hour of the day."

Uncertainty filled her eyes. "Arran—"

I kissed her again, harder, cutting off words I was pretty sure I didn't want to hear.

A throat cleared, cutting through the fog of need.

I tensed at the same time Ery did.

Fuck.

Breaking our kiss and lowering her leg, I kept my body pressed protectively to hers as I turned to greet the throat clearer.

Dread filled me as the intruder was revealed.

Jared fucking McCulloch, of all people.

He smirked at us and waved an empty to-go cup from Flora's. "Just thought I'd save myself a trip and toss my cup in Flora's rubbish." He gestured to the commercial rubbish bin beyond us. "Sorry for interrupting."

No, he wasn't.

Then something flickered across his expression I didn't like as he looked at Ery. "I always knew there was a wildcat buried beneath the shyness. Pity I didn't get there first."

That fucking prick! I lunged at him but was surprised by the strength of Ery's hold as she held me back. "Don't!" she cried. "Not worth it."

Jared looked delighted by my reaction. "Good," he said cryptically.

What the fuck?

"Jared." Eredine stepped around me. "Please don't mention this to anyone. We don't want people to know."

Hurt lit through me that secrecy was her first concern.

As for Jared, his chin jerked back as if surprised. And then his gaze flashed to mine, his expression hardening. He made a huffing sound before he looked back at Ery. "It's none of my business, so I'll keep my mouth shut." He threw the empty cup with perfect aim into the bin, and then said, "But you deserve a man who is proud you want to be with him, Eredine." He cut me one last dark look and then strode out of the alley.

Frustration and anger churned in my gut. I felt like I

might break out of my skin. Ery turned to look at me, trepidation on her face.

For a reason.

I needed to get away from her before I exploded.

"Arran." She reached for me, but I jerked away.

Of course, people would draw conclusions—either that I was a player messing around with a good woman, or worse, I was a privileged White prick who wanted to sleep with a Black woman but didn't want anyone else to know about it.

That was what Jared McCulloch thought, right?

"Arran—"

"Do you know what this makes me look like?" I bit out.

"It's not my fault if he draws a conclusion like that. It's 2022, Arran, not 1950. I mean, Heaven forbid, *I* would be the one pulling the strings here. Not the guy. Not the White guy."

"Pulling the strings?"

She blanched. "I didn't mean it—"

"I have to go." I marched past her, my hands clenching into restless fists at my sides.

"Arran!"

I couldn't do this anymore, I realized. I couldn't pretend I didn't want more from her, from us. And I certainly fucking hated the conclusions people might draw if they knew we'd been hiding our relationship.

20

EREDINE

We hadn't spoken in two days.

As angry as I was with Arran, I hated I hadn't heard from him. I thought for sure he might come and apologize for being pissed about the conclusions Jared obviously drew in Flora's alley. And then I could apologize for my seething jealousy at the sight of Arran hugging Monroe Sinclair in the middle of the village. It hadn't looked like just a friendly hug. He had this tender expression on his face as he kissed the top of her head that had sparked my possessiveness.

It wasn't my right to feel territorial. We had a deal. A deal mostly driven by me.

But I hated the history between him and Roe. I couldn't help it.

To say my stomach was in knots as I pulled up outside Thane and Regan's was an understatement. They were hosting family dinner, and while Arran and I had already made it through one so far without revealing what we were up to, I wasn't prepared for this scenario. How did I pretend

I wasn't equal parts furious and scared he didn't want to be with me anymore? Anytime I thought about what it would be like to not have permission to reach out and touch him, to kiss him, to feel him ... it was like a sharp knife scoring right through me.

Oh, Lord. I'd really screwed up getting into this with him.

The Adair family were as rambunctious as ever as I walked into my friends' house, Eilidh running to greet me, while Lewis argued with his dad about a video game. The adults all laughed and talked over one another as they set the table. Arran stood next to Arro, and whatever he said made her burst into laughter and shove him gently. He chuckled, delighted by her response, and my heart swelled.

Damn it.

As if he sensed me observing him, Arran looked across the room, and his amusement died.

Double damn it.

"Ery, I want to show you the swimsuit Mum bought me."

"After dinner, Eils." Regan came over to hug me. "Hey, come in, come in. How are you?"

"I'm good. How are you?"

We chitchatted as she led me over to everyone else, and I tried my best not to look at Arran. Robyn and Arro were comically growing their bellies in sync. They literally had what looked like almost the same size bump, which I knew had to be freaking out Mac and Lachlan.

"I'll be the size of a house for the wedding next month," Arro groaned after I told her how beautiful she and Robyn looked.

And they did. Arro's morning sickness had abated, and she was feeling a lot better these days, which had also relaxed Mac a bit. Robyn was taking her pregnancy in enviable stride.

"You're stunning," Mac assured his fiancée as he came up behind her and placed his hands on her belly. She leaned back into him as he kissed the side of her face, and I felt another irritating pang flare inside me.

My curiosity took over, a mind of its own, as I watched Arran cross the room to intervene in the argument between Lewis and Thane. Once it was over, Arran looked over his shoulder at me.

I couldn't read his expression.

Lowering my eyes, I turned to answer Robyn as she asked me what I thought of the novel we were reading for book club this month. I welcomed the distraction.

EILIDH DRAGGED me outside before dinner to play with the miniature badminton set her parents bought last week. While my cutie pie was a beautiful dancer, not too shabby at soccer, and a fast runner, badminton wasn't her game. But Eilidh persevered valiantly, determined to hit the shuttlecock.

We hadn't been out there long when Arran appeared on the deck. My stomach flipped with an amalgam of emotions.

"Sweetheart," Arran called to his niece as he descended the steps. "Your mum wants you inside. You promised to help her with the mash."

Eilidh happily threw her racket on the ground and ran past him, calling over her shoulder, "Play with Ery, Uncle Arran. She needs practice!"

Laughter burst between my lips, and Arran's eyes twinkled as he approached me.

"Don't worry, I've been forced to play with her all week, so I know who really requires the practice."

I didn't need the reminder that he was good with his niece and nephew.

The memory of our last encounter came to mind instead, and my anger returned. Moving past him to collect the racket, he clasped my arm, halting me.

I glanced hurriedly up at the house and then back to him. "Let go."

Arran scowled but released me. "I wanted to apologize for being pissed at you about Jared's reaction. You're right. His assumptions are not on you for deciding to keep us a secret, and I feel like a shit for saying it was. I'm sorry."

Tension eased inside me. "Thank you for saying so. Apology accepted. And I'm so—"

"Ery, I can't do this anymore," he cut me off.

Panic replaced my earlier tension. "What?"

His blue eyes clouded with a mix of tenderness and frustration. "I didn't mean to do this here … I just … I want more. I want a relationship with you, but you won't give me that. And I don't want to hide what I feel from *you*, let alone anyone else. I have real feelings for you, Eredine. This isn't just sex." He ran a hand through his hair and let out a huff of sad laughter. "If I'm honest, it never was."

I didn't know what to say.

A huge part of me wanted to grab and kiss him and promise him I'd give us a real shot if it meant not losing him. But the past had its claws clamped around my ankles, and I couldn't move toward him. I couldn't even speak.

Disappointment gleamed in his eyes. "Right. I guess we're done, then."

He moved to walk away, and I forced out the words, "Arran, I …" But then I didn't know what I wanted to say. It was awful.

"It's fine." He couldn't meet my gaze. "We'll go on as

before. I might need some time, but we'll find our rhythm as friends again, Ery. We promised each other that, and I intend to keep that promise."

Friends.

I watched him hurry into the house, tears burning my eyes, and I turned away, sucking in a deep inhale of sea air to fight back my panic.

"YOU OKAY?" Regan asked at my side as conversation flowed around us at the dinner table.

By sheer force of will, I'd returned to the house and sat my ass down at the table. I couldn't look at Arran. It hurt too freaking much.

He'd turned everything upside down. Until him, I was certain I could never be in a relationship again. But this last month with him had been like a relationship. And it had felt great. Better than great. I'd felt alive and not alone for the first time in eight years.

I wanted to give myself to him, but I wasn't sure I'd ever be able to give him the whole of me, and that wasn't fair to Arran.

Yet the panic rising within terrified me. I'd never felt that about anyone. In the past, long before Ardnoch, I'd been broken up with. The rejection had stung; it had hurt. But I'd never felt such overwhelming dread.

Never mind that Arran would eventually meet someone and, as his friend, I'd have to endure watching that.

"Ery?"

I unclenched my jaw and looked at Regan.

She'd asked me a question, hadn't she? "I'm fine. I didn't get much sleep last night, so I'm a little spacey."

She studied my face for a second. "Okay."

I wasn't sure she believed me.

Glancing down at my plate, I tried to concentrate on the two different conversations happening at the table—one between Thane, Eilidh, and Lewis about a camping trip their father had promised to take them on during the summer holidays, and the other among everyone else about the renovations on the Gloaming's guest rooms.

Then Arro cut through the noise by calling down the table, "Arran, I meant to say, Mac and I bumped into Lisa Duncan yesterday in Inverness. She's moved back to the Highlands."

Lisa Duncan?

My gaze moved to Arran, but so had everyone else's, so their curiosity camouflaged mine.

"Who is Lisa Duncan?" Eilidh asked.

Her uncle shot her a smirk. "An old friend."

Arro snorted. "Um, just about the only girl your uncle ever liked who showed no interest back. Until now."

My heart lurched.

Arran raised an eyebrow. "Excuse me?"

"She gave me her number to pass along. Apparently, she's single and has changed her mind about you."

"That's odd, considering she hasn't seen him in years," Regan huffed. "If she didn't want him then, why now? Could it be because two of his brothers are famous?"

Lachlan choked on a sip of water while Arran feigned hurt as he sat back, clutching his chest. "Regan, you think so little of my charms?"

She rolled her eyes. "I think it's weird that a woman who hasn't spoken to you in years would give her number to your sister."

"You're such a momma bear," Robyn teased. "You do know Arran is ten years older than you, right?"

Regan glowered at her sister. "Men can be stupid when it comes to women."

The men at the table looked affronted.

Arro shook her head at Mac and joked, "History does not lend itself to you in an argument against her accusation."

Before he could retort, Regan pointed her fork at Thane. "Nor you."

"You're being harsh," Robyn opined. "They all got there in the end."

"You would say that since you were equally stupid about Lachlan," her sister goaded.

Robyn wagged a finger at her. "Don't call a pregnant woman stupid. That's stupid."

I wanted to enjoy their easy banter, but my pulse raced at the thought of Arran taking this Lisa woman's number.

"So, do you want her number?" Arro asked her brother. "I assume you do, considering the lack of choice in Ardnoch."

"How long has it been?" Lachlan grinned devilishly at Arran.

"How long has what been?" Lewis frowned.

Robyn nudged an elbow into her husband's side and gave him a warning look.

His lips twitched, but sufficiently chastened, he told his nephew, "Since your uncle went on a date."

Lewis wrinkled his nose. "Ugh."

"You'll change your tune soon enough."

Thane looked at Lachlan. "Leave him be. If I have my way, he'll change his tune when he's ninety."

"I thought fathers were only supposed to be overprotective of their daughters when it came to romance?" Arro chuckled.

"This is Thane," Arran said. "I remember many a time when he coc—" He blanched, remembering the kids. "I mean, stopped me from dating a pretty girl."

Thane snorted. "Only the ones whose dads or brothers or *boyfriends* would've killed you."

Arran flicked me a quick look before staring down at his plate. "I wasn't that bad."

"So? Lisa?" Arro insisted.

"Aye, whatever," Arran agreed.

The conversation turned to the double wedding next month, but I barely heard a word of it. Instead, my ears burned with rushing blood, my pulse wouldn't slow, and a mixture of anger and hurt and jealousy choked me.

Aye, whatever.

As I was about to get into my car later that evening, I heard the side entrance door closing. Something overtook me. Perhaps it was my panic, maybe even a little desperation (though my pride refused to dwell on that), but suddenly, I was moving around the house toward the guest annex.

Sure enough, there he was, striding from the main house toward the annex entry.

"Arran," I called quietly, hurrying after him.

He spun, his brows raised at the sight of me.

Thankfully, he started walking to bridge the distance between us.

I just wanted to throw myself into his arms.

I wanted to cry.

And part of me resented him for making me feel too much.

Shooting a quick look at the house to make sure we had privacy, I stopped before him, pretty sure everything was in my eyes.

"Are you really going on a date with that woman?" was

179

the first thing out of my mouth. I squeezed my eyes closed briefly in embarrassment.

Arran's expression was careful as he searched my face. "No. Regan is right. Lisa didn't want me our entire senior year, so what's changed, other than my famous brothers? But I would have been within my right to date her. Right?"

That hurt.

And angered me.

"Yeah. But then I wonder how you'd feel if I started dating Jared right away."

The muscle in his jaw flexed as his eyes flashed hotly. "You know how I'd feel. And why him, specifically? Do you have a thing for him?"

Ugh. Men. "No. I just plucked him out as an example. But it's good to know you'd be jealous too."

"Of course I would," he hissed. "I'm the one who admitted to feeling more for you. Remember?"

"Arran." I reached out to touch him but then lowered my hand when I realized I didn't have that right. Not yet. "I'm not good at … I'm a very private person."

"I know that."

"I … it hurt, okay? The thought of you with her, or anyone. It hurts."

"Ery." He stepped toward me, hope gleaming in his eyes.

He stopped with a glower after I raised my hands. "I …" Here goes nothing. "I want to try something real with you, too, but, Arran, I can't make any promises. I can't promise you I'll be everything you need me to be. I can't."

He gripped my biceps, pulling me into him, his voice low and passionate as he replied, "No one can make promises going into a relationship, Ery. It's a gamble everyone takes, not knowing if or when it will end. How much it'll hurt. But it's a risk worth taking when you feel this way." He gave me a little shake with a tender smile. "Do you know how rare it is to have this connection? I've never felt anything like it."

"Me neither," I whispered.

Arran kissed me then, deep and hungering, and I fell into it, relief and pleasure melting away the panic that had clung to me for the last few hours.

When he released me, he said, "But I won't keep this a secret. I want to date you, and I want everyone to know."

My pulse skittered at the thought of everyone throwing their opinions into the mix. Of having them watch us interact. Yet, I knew Arran was right. We couldn't stay in the shadows if we wanted to make a real go of it. "Okay," I agreed.

"But first, before we tell everyone and invite our family into our relationship—because you know that'll happen with those nosy buggers—I want to take you on a proper date. Tomorrow night. North Star."

North Star was a fancy restaurant a few miles up the coast. This just got real! "All right."

He grinned hugely. "Aye?"

I laughed at his giddiness. "Yes."

He kissed me again, one quick kiss after the other, as if he couldn't get enough. "I'll pick you up at seven."

"I'll be there." I reluctantly stepped out of his hold. "I better go."

Arran beamed boyishly. "See you soon, gorgeous."

"See you soon." I turned on my heel to walk away but couldn't resist looking over my shoulder before I disappeared around the corner. Arran was still there, watching me with that flirty smile curling his mouth. I laughed under my breath and gave him a little wave before I walked out of sight.

Excitement, fear, thrill, affection, desire, worry, hope—it all bubbled inside me as I drove home to my woodsy haven.

My haven. Arran should know that was what my lodge was to me. And he should know why.

But I didn't think I could bring the pain and darkness of that life into my new one.

Which meant there would forever be a part of me I couldn't give him, and I didn't know how long Arran could handle that. Was he an all-or-nothing kind of guy?

I guessed I'd soon find out.

21

EREDINE

I couldn't remember the last time I'd made out in a car. It had to have been in high school. I smiled at the thought as Arran swept me up in his intoxicating kisses. He pulled back to murmur, "What's the smile for?"

I shrugged, a little giddy. "This is nice. Making out in your car."

He grinned. "It's very nice."

"With a view like that too." I gestured out the windshield to the North Sea. Moonlight glimmered across the water beyond the cliff we'd parked on.

The entire night had been surreal. Arran picked me up wearing a suit that fitted him to perfection. I wore a purple dress with a conservative neck- and hemlines, but it was sleeveless and contouring, so still pretty sexy. My four-inch heels made me the same height as him. He'd kissed me so hungrily at the door, I'd had to reapply my lipstick and use a cleansing wipe to wash the plum-colored stain off his lips.

We'd kissed every inch of the lip color off after an amazing seafood dinner at North Star. If anyone we knew from the village was there, we didn't see them. Then again, we weren't looking, so completely into each other. Arran talked about the Gloaming and some of his travels; I chatted about work, his family, and life in LA, without delving too deeply. He seemed to sense my reluctance to go there and swiftly changed the subject.

He also flirted outrageously with me, but Arran Adair had been doing that from the moment we met.

He stroked a thumb across my mouth. "That view out there doesn't compare to the one I have in here."

I rolled my eyes, chuckling at the overt flattery, but secretly, I loved it.

Arran smiled but continued, "I'm serious. When I saw you at Lachlan's wedding last year, it was like waking up after years of being asleep. I'd never seen anyone so stunning in my whole life."

My cheeks grew heated at the compliment and also at the reminder of the wedding, because I hadn't been paying attention to Arran that night. I'd been too preoccupied with Brodan. That felt wrong now. Guilt rode my shoulders, even though my crush on Brodan had been obliterated by my feelings for Arran.

Deflecting, I said lightly, "We met before the wedding. You do remember that, right? Several times."

He chuckled. "I do. But I … I'm ashamed to admit I was in my own wee world for far too long. I couldn't see a damn thing in front of me. If I had, if I'd seen you then like I should have, I don't think I would have left again."

His confession made my breath catch. Like his words last night, it suggested a depth of feeling that both exhilarated and terrified me. "Arran," I whispered, reaching for another kiss.

After a while, we drew apart, and he leaned his forehead against mine.

I felt closer to him at that moment than I'd felt to anyone in a long time.

"I was thinking ..." Arran finally broke the sweet silence as he pulled back a little. "We should tell people separately that we're dating."

My belly flipped at the thought of everyone knowing. "What do you mean?"

"I'll tell my brothers. You tell Arro, Regan, and Robyn."

Nodding, I chewed on my bottom lip as a riot of nerves flooded me.

Arran gently released my lip from my teeth with his thumb. "What is going on in that gorgeous head?"

I released a heavy sigh. "What if ... what if they're not happy about it? What if they interfere?"

"Well, I think we can say with absolute certainty that Regan will be happy, since she's been trying to make this happen for months."

I chuckled because I was pretty sure he was right.

"And I love my family, Eredine, but we're none of their business. We're telling them because we don't want to hide this, but that isn't an open invitation for them to stick their noses into our relationship."

I snorted. "Arran, we're talking about the Adairs here. Noses *will* be stuck in our business."

"Then they'll just need to back off. And I'll make that clear. They can stick their noses in once you and I are settled into this. But for now, we need time to figure this out together without their input."

"I respect their opinion," I said. Because it was true. It would bother me if one or more of them didn't think this was a good idea.

Arran frowned. "More than you respect what's between us?"

"Of course not," I hurried to assure him. "It's just … don't pretend like it's not complicated."

"It isn't complicated. Lachlan had an affair with his best friend's daughter who is ten years his junior. In turn, that best friend fell in love with our sister who is thirteen years younger than him. And Thane started sleeping with Robyn's twenty-five-year-old sister behind everyone's backs. Not one of them has the right to judge us for our innocuous decision to date."

I laughed, and then couldn't stop, and soon Arran joined me. Finally, the amusement slowed, and I wiped tears of hilarity from my eyes. "Oh, man, when you say it like that"—I grinned at him—"you Adairs are a bunch of deviants."

"Except me. There are only four years between you and me, and that is perfectly acceptable."

"True." I chuckled again, shaking my head. "Lord, this family has turned Ardnoch into a soap opera."

He reached for my hand, tangling his fingers through mine. "The heart wants what it wants. And the Adair men seem to have a penchant for American women."

The heart wants what it wants. Such a painful truth. If I wasn't currently listening to mine, I'd be tucked away in bed with no fear of anything ever changing in my life. While my days had become stagnant until Arran, they had also been safe.

I was gambling with that safety by giving into my heart.

But looking into his beautiful blue eyes as he played with my fingers, sensation shivering up my arms and to other more pleasant places, I couldn't imagine life without him now.

And wasn't that utterly terrifying?

WE'D MOVED this month's book club meeting to Tuesday evening because Regan and Arro had wedding stuff to do on the weekend. This meant I had less time to think about telling them about Arran, which was both good and bad.

What I wasn't expecting was to find Mac at book club—Arro hadn't mentioned that. I'd thought he'd be with the guys because Arran had asked Lachlan to come over to Thane's while we were at Arro's, so he could tell them about us.

Now I'd have to tell Mac, and he was very protective of me, so I didn't know how this would go down.

"I'm not a huge thriller reader," Regan said as we settled in Arro's living room. "But I gotta say, this one kept me glued. I finished it in a few nights."

"I don't know." Robyn waved her copy at us. "The cop stuff was a bit off."

"Agreed." Mac grinned at her. "But I imagine only a police officer would be bothered by the inaccuracies."

And since they were both ex-cops, that made sense.

"Let's keep things positive and start with the good stuff," Arro suggested, holding out a tray of snacks. Everyone else took a cookie to eat with the tea she'd served, but I waved her off nervously.

Mac took the tray from Arro and steered her into a seat, but she trained her eyes on me. "You okay, Ery?"

My stomach rolled, and I had to take a deep breath. Sitting up straight, I looked at my friends and gave them a tight smile. "I wanted to ... well, I wanted to bring up something before we got started."

Every single one of them sat forward, completely alert.

"I, um ..." I tried to remember what I'd gone over with Arran last night. He'd dropped me off at the lodge without coming in, teasing about wanting it to be like a proper first date. But before that, we'd decided we wouldn't give everyone too much detail about how long we'd been seeing each other or how it had only been casual at first. "Arran and I are dating."

Stunned silence greeted me.

I looked to Mac, who was frowning.

"Our friendship," I hurried on, "has been important to me, and, um, to Arran, but we realized it's more than that. So we've decided to date. Each other. *Just* each other. We're seeing just each other, no one else. Not that I was, anyway." I laughed nervously. "But Arran is just seeing me. There's no one … yeah, we're dating." I clamped my mouth shut to stop the nervous rambling.

Arro's expression was careful as she processed. Robyn chuckled, and Regan practically bounced with glee on the couch, her hands clasped together over her breast.

Mac … Mac had moved on to scowling.

Arro, following my gaze to her fiancé, sighed at his expression. "Mackennon, you know I was the first person to warn Arran off Ery last year."

She was?

"But he's different now. He's different with her. I think this could be a good thing."

He raised an eyebrow at her. "So now you trust your brother with Eredine?"

"Aye, I do."

Mac scoffed. "He's a player."

"No, he *was*. I have to have faith that he's become a mature thirty-six-year-old man who respects his family enough not to fool around with and potentially hurt someone we love. I didn't give him his due all those months ago, but now I want to. I need to."

Relief flooded me at her defense of her brother.

But her fiancé was still frowning as he turned back to me. "You're happy?"

I smiled at his question. "I am."

"Then that's all that matters."

Robyn snorted, smirking at her father. "You're going to threaten to kill him if he hurts her, aren't you?"

Mac took a noncommittal sip of his tea, but both his fiancée and daughter laughed, so I guessed that meant he *was* going to threaten Arran's life.

And I thought about this with positivity.

Because it meant Mac cared about my well-being.

They all did.

"I'm happy for you." Regan reached out to squeeze my arm. "I saw sparks between you from the very beginning and was hoping this would happen. You're so good for him."

Just like that, the sweet relief I'd felt from their reaction, from Mac's protectiveness, died a sudden death.

Because I wasn't the one they needed to worry about.

Arran was.

He was the one in danger of being hurt here.

He'd already confessed the darkest part of his past to me.

And yet ... he didn't even know my real name.

I doubted I'd ever be able to tell him.

Right then, it hit me in a way I hadn't allowed before. If things went south with us ... I could lose the Adairs.

I could lose everything.

189

22

ARRAN

As soon as Thane returned from upstairs where he'd left the kids to do their homework, I commandeered the conversation. "So I need to tell you something."

Lachlan sat on a stool at the island, nursing a beer, while I stood on the other side of it, nursing mine. Thane slid onto the stool next to our brother and said, "We assumed so, since you asked Lachlan to be here."

I had requested the men to gather at Thane's, but Mac hadn't shown, and Lachlan told me he was at Arro's book club, which meant it was up to Eredine to tell him. I hoped to Christ that went well.

I looked between my brothers. "Let me preface this by saying that I respect this family, and I would never go into anything lightly that would affect them or someone they loved."

"This sounds ominous," Lachlan replied dryly.

"I'm seeing Ery," I blurted out, and then took a long chug of beer.

Thane smirked knowingly.

190

Lachlan ... well, he glowered at me like he wanted to take my head off my shoulders. "Explain," he bit out.

Not particularly relishing the fatherly tone he'd used many a time when I was younger, I pulled back my shoulders and tried to keep the defiance from my tone. "I care about her. As more than a friend. She feels the same way. So we're dating. And it's serious. For me, anyway."

At that, my eldest brother's expression softened, but I saw the worry in his eyes. "Is it serious for Eredine?"

"I think so. I hope so." I shrugged, running a hand through my hair. "She gives me what she can of herself, but I know there's a lot she's hiding. And she specifically didn't make any promises of being able to give me more."

"And you can handle that?" Thane frowned.

"I have hope she'll come to trust me enough." I shot a look at Lachlan. "It isn't exactly fun to know your brother probably knows more about the woman in your bed than you do."

He sighed. "I understand. That would stick in my craw too. But it can't be helped. I won't tell you anything she doesn't want you to know."

"Just tell me if ... is she safe?" And I realized as soon as the words fell from my mouth that the worry for her well-being had been weighing on me.

Lachlan nodded. "I've made sure of it."

Which meant there was something to keep her safe from.

Fuck.

"Give her time," Thane offered. "She'll tell you when she's ready."

"Do you know?" I asked sharply.

"No. I don't believe anyone but Lachlan and Mac have been entrusted with Eredine's history."

That relieved me. It would be utter shit if I were the only one in our family who didn't know.

"You really do care about her, don't you?" Lachlan mused.

I swallowed hard against the rising emotions. "More than any woman I've ever known."

"Good." He clinked his beer against mine. "Just be there for her. Let things play out naturally."

"Thanks," I murmured.

"I hate to bring it up, but ... you should call Brodan," Thane said, expression grim. "I don't know what happened between him and Ery—"

"Nothing happened," I replied. "I've already asked."

My brothers shared a look before Lachlan shrugged. "We all saw there was something between them, even if nothing technically happened. And considering your history, you need to call Brodan. You need to be the one to tell him. Don't let him find out from someone else."

"If he wanted her, he should have stayed," I argued, hating that this conversation was bringing up the old guilt about Monroe and transferring it to my relationship with Ery. "She's a human being. Not some fucking toy he had dibs on."

"For fuck's sake, we know that," Thane grumbled. "But he's your brother, and he had feelings for Eredine, so be a grown-up and call him."

MOST OF MY calls to Brodan lately had been going to voice mail, so I was certain it would this time as I stood on Thane's back lawn staring out at the water that glittered beneath the waning sun.

Four rings in and the line clicked on. "Hey, what's up?" Brodan answered.

Things had been tense between us ever since I'd told him Monroe had come home.

I had a feeling this conversation would do very little to defuse the tension. "Eh, aye, I'm good," I wavered. "You?"

"Fucking exhausted," he said, sounding it.

Worry cut through everything else. "You've been working nonstop, Bro. Surely, you've made enough money to take a breather?"

"There's nothing to take a breather for."

Hurt, I snapped, "Uh, your family?"

"Shit," Brodan huffed. "I'm sorry. I didn't mean ... I'm just tired. I didn't mean ... I'll think about taking a break, but the schedule is packed for now."

"You are coming home for the wedding in a few weeks, right?"

There was a hesitation.

Anger flared through me. "Bro, take it from me ... if you don't come home for your brother's and sister's weddings, you'll hurt them beyond anything you can repair."

Brodan cleared his throat. "I'll be there. I'll make it happen."

"Good."

"Did you just call to lecture me?"

Swallowing hard, I shook my head, even though he couldn't see me. "No. I called to tell you something."

My tone must have alerted him because he sounded frantic. "Is everyone all right? Has something happened?"

"No, everyone is fine," I assured him. "I just ... Considering everything ..." I took a deep breath again. "Bro ... I've started seeing Eredine. We're in a relationship."

Silence greeted me on the other end of the line.

"Brodan?"

"Right," he bit out tersely. "Good for you. They're calling me back to set. I need to go." He hung up before I could say another word.

"Fuck!" I threw my phone in the grass and glared up at the darkening sky.

"I take it that went well, then?"

193

I turned to find Thane standing on his deck, frowning.

"I refuse to feel guilty," I growled. "She's been here for eight fucking years, and if he wanted to be with her, he should have made his move. I wanted her, and I made my move. I won't give her up for him."

"I know, I know." Thane nodded, stepping down toward me. "And you're right. Brodan used to drop back home, shower Ery with attention, and then fuck off, only to be photographed with some actress or model a few days later. You have nothing to feel guilty about. But you do, anyway, don't you?"

"It's not guilt." I shook my head. "Not for this. I just ..." I eyed my big brother. "A few weeks ago, I told him Monroe was back, and he couldn't get off the phone fast enough. Things have been strained between us since. I'm worried that this, on top of that, will take him back to that place we worked really hard to get out of. I miss him as it is. I don't want to push him even farther away."

Thane clamped a hand on my shoulder. "Something has been eating Brodan for a while now. Something he won't talk about. And that's not on you. Or me or Eredine or Monroe. You can't live your life tiptoeing around him. He hasn't exactly been there for us this past year, so we're living our lives the way we want until he's ready to come back to us."

Except that wasn't true.

Brodan had been there for me when no one else had.

But Thane didn't know that because I was still too ashamed to tell him and Lachlan about Thailand.

Brodan hadn't condemned me. Neither had Ery. I should tell Thane now, for Brodan's sake, but the night had already been so heavy with confessions. And I still wasn't sure I was ready to disappoint my elder brothers when we'd made such strides toward them seeing me as a responsible man.

Nodding, I allowed Thane to lead me back into the house

to finish my beer. An hour later, Regan and Robyn returned and enjoyed teasing me about Ery. But they also seemed happy, so that was a relief. Moreover, they said Arro, of all people, had defended me to a concerned Mac. Arro. Ironic, since last year she'd vehemently told me to back off Ery. I smiled at the thought, glad my sister saw me for who I was now.

I bid them all good night and returned to my annex, hoping to catch Ery on the phone before bed to see how she was feeling about everything.

Remembering I'd thrown my phone in the back garden, I walked around the side of the house to retrieve it.

As I strolled to the annex again, I tapped the screen and then halted at the notification banner.

I had a new email.

Tapping it open, trepidation filled me.

Don't worry. I'm still here. I haven't forgotten about you.

Pulse racing, I let myself into the guest house and locked the door behind me.

Why did emails that had once seemed like a silly prank now feel fucking sinister?

I hadn't stopped long enough to wonder about how they kept ending up in my main inbox. I'd relegated each one to spam, but they came from a different email address every time.

That didn't feel like the kind of time someone would spend on a prank.

Had I been burying my head in the sand?

Did this feel more like an obsession than a prank?

But who the hell would have it out for me?

Sinking onto the bed, I stared at the wall, pissed off as I considered the best approach to this. After everything our family had been through, the right thing to do would be to alert them and have Lachlan's security team look into it.

I just didn't want to bring this up a few weeks from the weddings.

Or freak Eredine out.

Shit.

I laid back on the bed and scrubbed my hands down my face.

I had no clue what to do, especially if I was just overreacting now that I had Ery's safety playing on my mind.

23

ARRAN

I hopped over the fence between Thane's and Lachlan's back gardens, the rain pelting my skin like it was comprised of stones instead of water. The roar of the crashing North Sea bellowed from below as the waves pounded the cliff's edge. Heavy clouds hung above, so dark you might mistake it for late evening rather than midday.

Hurrying up the back deck of Lachlan's house, I was already soaked by the time the overhang offered protection.

Fucking great.

I peered into the house and saw Lachlan sitting at his dining table, frowning at the laptop in front of him. "Lachlan!" I hammered on the bifold door.

His head jerked up, surprise lighting his face before he hurried from the table to cross the room. A few seconds later, I was inside, dripping all over his wood floors.

"What the hell are you doing?" he demanded. "Wait there and I'll get a towel."

My clothes were stuck to me, and I shivered as I waited for him to return from the bathroom. Chucking the towel at

197

me as he approached, I scrubbed it over my head and face. "Where's Robyn?"

"In her darkroom. Probably waiting out the rain like a sane person. You want to tell me what was so important that you couldn't wait a couple hours until dinner?"

My first week with Ery as an official couple had been rocky. She'd been distant, and I was less than loquacious because I was worried about the bloody emails. That she was on her period meant we couldn't even connect physically, and I was more than a wee bit panicked that we were circling the drain before we'd really even started.

One thing I had made my mind up about, though, was the emails.

I couldn't have them hanging over my head.

It wasn't just about my safety anymore. Involving myself in Ery's life meant I was responsible for her well-being too.

"What I'm about to tell you ... I need it to stay between us."

Lachlan's brows pinched. "Should I be worried?"

"First, I need you to promise."

"Of course. I promise."

I sighed. "I've been getting these emails. They come from different addresses every few months."

Concern strained my brother's features. "What kind of emails?"

"Strange emails. Usually just one or two lines. I thought they were from some random arsehole pranking my email address, but then I got another one this week, and with Ery ..."

"What do the emails say?"

"All along the similar line. That this person hasn't forgotten me. But there's ... it's hard to explain, but there's a threatening edge to them. I don't know. I've stupidly been deleting them, but I kept the one I got this week."

My brother nodded. "Okay, I'll have my team trace it. They'll need access to your email."

I stared at him, gratitude filling me. He didn't even question if I was overreacting. He trusted my gut. "All right."

His eyes narrowed. "Do you have any idea who might be behind them?"

"None at all."

Lachlan scrubbed a hand over his face. "We've already had one copycat of Lucy's case. I hope we're not dealing with someone who's become obsessed with us and that whole thing."

Lucy's obsession with my brother may have kicked into high gear two years ago, but the high-profile trial was only last year. While talk and speculation still circulated about it, it hadn't affected Brodan's career in Hollywood.

"Fuck." Lachlan sighed. "And I just got word from one of the club members that there's a script circulating about Lucy's life, including her stalking me."

Disgust filled me. "Someone wants to make a movie about one of the worst things that's ever happened to you?"

"Looks like." He seemed suddenly exhausted. "Everything's fodder in Hollywood. No one's safe from it."

"I'm sorry." I clamped a hand on his shoulder. "I wish they'd just let you move on."

"Och, it could be worse. We live *here*. We can still have a life, normality here. That's something."

I nodded, because it was true. Ardnoch was a strange beast. It didn't offer complete privacy, but it offered more than most places. Its remoteness and the security on the estate are what drew members in the first place.

"It doesn't feel like the emails are related to Lucy. I think if they were, the sender would've alluded to it, you know?"

"Can I see the one you have?"

I pulled my phone out of the wet back pocket of my jeans and found the email for him.

He bent his head to look, his jaw muscles ticking with anger. "Fuck." He looked up at me, annoyed. "I really wish you hadn't deleted the others."

I shrugged. "I thought it was just someone being a prick. But if any more come in, I'll keep them. And like I said, this is just between us."

"Aye, agreed. No use worrying everybody about something that might mean nothing."

"We do seem to be danger magnets."

Lachlan's focus drifted by me to the grim day beyond his windowpanes. "Sometimes I think there's some grand fate out there obsessed with the balance of things."

"How do you mean?"

He looked at me. "Our mother dies before her time, then Aunt Imogen, our father, then Thane's wife. But we're blessed with wealth and some fame ... more than that, someone sent me Robyn." A depth of emotion I was only beginning to understand burned in Lachlan's eyes. "I'd live in hell if it was the only place I could be with her. And Thane feels the same about Regan, Arro for Mac ... maybe one day you for ..." A small smile played on his lips.

"It's an anomaly. To have a family where so many of us are lucky to have found that one person who gives life meaning. Maybe that's why bad things keep happening to us because we have more than our fair share of bounty. Balance." He shrugged.

I contemplated his words and asked quietly, "Do you really believe that?"

"I'd rather believe that than what I used to believe."

Understanding dawned. "That the Adair men are cursed to lose the women they love."

A bleakness filled my brother's expression for a second

before determination replaced it. "I refuse to go back to that fear. It infects everything. If I let it, it would take me from Robyn, anyway."

"We're not cursed, Lachlan," I assured him. "And I don't know if I believe in some grander fate and balance ... Bad things happen to people every day, and some people never get a fighting chance. Life is shit from the moment they're born, and it doesn't let up until they die. That hasn't been the way for us. We've had bad times, but so much good too. I think that's normal."

My brother snorted. "You think stalkers, murderers, and psychotic exes are normal?"

I chuckled. "So we attract some crazies."

"Aye, that's an understatement." He exhaled slowly. "I'll be in touch about my team looking into the email, but we'll keep it between us and hope it's nothing. Now get back and get dried before you catch a chill, or you'll be useless to your new girlfriend."

Reaching for the door, I glanced over my shoulder. "Is a woman your *girlfriend* when you're in your thirties?"

"I don't know. I proposed to Robyn before we really had that conversation, and she was my fiancée from that point on."

"You wasted no time there." I pulled open the door, the sound of the storm crashing inside. "See you in a bit!"

"Arran!" he called out as I hurried onto the deck.

I looked back at him. "Aye?"

"When you know, you know. And there is no point wasting time," he offered, his expression serious. "Trust that feeling."

EREDINE

THE DREARY DAY mirrored my mood perfectly. As I approached Caelmore, the dark clouds finally moved on, and light, golden rays streamed through breaks in the gray puffs left behind. For days, I'd had my own personal storm hanging over me, but the nearer I drew to Arran and the chance to figure things out, the better I felt. I wanted to talk to Arran alone as soon as I got there, so I'd texted him before I left for Sunday lunch with the Adairs to ask him to meet me in the annex.

He must have heard my car pull up—he stood waiting in the guest house's front doorway. His brow furrowed, and he looked a little tense.

"Everything okay?" he asked.

I gave him a small smile as I brushed past, my skin tingling where our arms touched. We hadn't had sex in a week because I was on my period, but it ended last night, so I was looking forward to reconnecting. What was more important at this point was to make sure we were okay. I'd been a little in my head after I realized how much I was jeopardizing if this didn't work out, and it had taken me the rest of the week to conclude that my fears were irrational. Not because this might not work out with Arran. Of course, it might not. But because I knew neither Lachlan nor Arro would let me fall outside the family fold, no matter what.

And once I realized that, I was unnerved that Arran had also been very distant this week.

I wanted to know why.

Usually, I let people be. If they had a problem and wanted to talk about it, I was happy to be a soft shoulder or a listening ear. Rarely did I coax problems out of people, because that would be hypocritical.

Today I was going to be a hypocrite.

I turned near the foot of his bed as Arran closed the door behind us. "You've been quiet all week. I know I've been quiet, too, but it was because I was in my own head about everyone knowing we're dating. So I'm sorry, but why were you in your head?"

Arran's lips twitched at my rambling, and he approached slowly. His eyes roamed my face in a manner that made me feel more beautiful than I'd ever felt in my life. He looked at me like I was the best thing he'd ever seen. It was over-whelming and thrilling.

Reaching out, he slid his arms around my waist and pulled me to him until our chests touched, my mouth inches from his. "I was in my head because you were in your head. I was worried you were having second thoughts."

That was what I'd assumed, and I hated it. "I'm sorry. You know … you're the one Adair who bulldozed into my life and pushed me to be social with you. Everyone else tiptoed around on eggshells, afraid to push me. I like that you push me, challenge me. Don't stop now that we're in a relation-ship. I hate to tell you this," I said wryly, "but sometimes your girl needs a giant shove."

Arran grinned, his arm squeezing me in reflex. "My girl?"

My cheeks heated. "Well, I am. Right?"

"Oh, aye," he replied hoarsely and dipped his head to touch his lips to mine.

What started out as a shivery brush of mouth against mouth turned hungry in an instant, and Arran shuffled us back toward the bed.

I broke the kiss on a gasp. "Dinner," I reminded him.

"Is your period finished?" he asked, staring at my mouth like a starving man.

"Yes."

"Then dinner can wait." He threw us on the bed, and my laughter was soon swallowed by his kisses.

"So, is this how it's going to be from now on?" Regan asked quietly at my side as I helped her in the kitchen.

The rest of the family was already around the dining table. "Huh?"

She grinned at me, flashing her adorable dimples. "Thane saw you pull up to the house when he was in the office. You went to Arran's, and both of you arrived not only just barely in time for dinner, but you have a sex glow."

I almost dropped the wine bottle in my hand. "What?"

Regan chuckled evilly. "You have a sex glow. Your skin is glowing and you're all dreamy."

I gaped at her, horrified. "Do you think anyone else knows?"

"Pretty much all the adults." She shrugged casually and picked up the carved roasted chicken to take over to the table.

Oh, Lord. Now I really was one of them. I couldn't count how many times the others had been teased for disappearing at a party or turning up late to an event and all of us knowing why ... because of the sex glow.

Now I was in that club.

While embarrassment heated my cheeks, I also felt a thrill of belonging. And not just belonging, but ... like life was finally happening to me instead of around me.

Once all the food was on the table, I took my seat next to Arran who reflexively leaned in to give me a quick kiss on the lips.

"Uncle Arran!"

Everyone turned toward the squeal to find Eilidh gaping at us from across the table.

Her brother sat next to her, his mouth hanging open.

"You kissed Ery!" Eilidh's eyes were so big, they were beyond comical.

"Eils, lower your voice, please," Thane said beside her, though amusement curled his lips.

"I'm sorry," she said, deliberately softer and slower. "But Uncle Arran just kissed Aunty Eredine."

My heart lurched in my chest.

She'd never called me *aunty* before.

I melted in my seat, blinking back tears. Happy tears.

"Well …" Arran cleared his throat as he slid an arm around my shoulders. "Eilidh, Lewis, Aunty Eredine and I are dating. Do you understand what that means?"

"Of course, we're not five." Eilidh rolled her very grown-up seven-year-old eyes.

I struggled not to laugh.

"Are you getting married too?" Lewis wrinkled his nose.

Arran almost choked. "Um … we're not quite there yet, pal."

There *yet*? Wow. Okay.

"Good." Lewis shot his soon-to-be stepmom a weary look. "Weddings are boring."

Regan met Thane's gaze. "I guess I've been talking about the wedding too much."

Her fiancé grinned.

"Weddings are not boring," Eilidh disagreed, throwing her brother a scowl. "I get to wear a pretty dress."

"So do I," Lewis huffed.

"A kilt is not a dress," Thane, Lachlan, Mac, and Arran said in unison.

I snorted with laughter as Lewis made a face and replied, "Aw right, keep your hair on."

And just like that, Arran and I were forgotten, the kids accepting our relationship without another word.

I didn't know what I'd expected at dinner as an outed

couple—perhaps constant questioning looks or to feel Lachlan's concerned gaze on me? But there was none of that. Our friends seemed to have processed and accepted us too.

Eventually, I relaxed and just enjoyed the wonderful, warm banter of the Adairs who, in losing so much, had learned that nothing mattered more than family.

I was proud to be counted among them.

24
ARRAN

T wo weeks of bliss.

That's what this is, I thought, as Eredine rode me in bed that morning.

To have her like this, without the shadow of secrecy hanging over us, was everything I'd wanted for months. And it was better than I could have imagined. Even the sex was better now that I didn't have to hide how I felt about her.

I groaned, my hands flexing on her waist as I tried to hold back long enough for her to come first. It wasn't easy when she was so warm and tight, each lift of her hips a searing drag of her pussy up my cock. Her nipples were tight on her perky tits, and her face was flushed. Her lips parted to release her gasps and pants. All of that, with her dark curls tumbling down her back, was too much beauty to behold.

"Fuck, I'm going to come," I grunted. I slipped my hand between us and slid my thumb against her clit, circling it roughly, desperate for her to climax first.

And come she did.

Her hips juddered, her belly flexing as I felt her inner muscles throb around me.

"Fuck!" I threw my head back as I let go, white lights of pleasure blinding me.

Ery collapsed over me, her face in my neck as she shuddered, her hair tickling my skin wherever it touched.

I found the strength to wrap my arms around her, loving the feel of her dewy skin pressed to mine. Bliss.

Bloody wonderful bliss.

After a while of holding each other, Ery finally lifted her head to smile at me. I loved her smile. It was sweet and sexy and shy and mischievous all at once, and I had no idea how she achieved that feat. But achieve she did. Ery gave me a light kiss and moaned as she lifted herself off me. Christ, I wanted her again. The woman made me insatiable.

"Want a coffee before we shower?" she asked as she got out of bed and slipped on her robe.

"Sure."

As Ery left the room, I moved into her bathroom, trying not to touch the dress hanging on the door for the double wedding. It was sealed in a protective bag, but I wasn't allowed to see it. She was a bridesmaid for Regan and Arro and wanted to surprise me.

Considering I'd become infatuated with her after seeing her in another bridesmaid dress at another wedding, I couldn't even imagine how I'd feel now that we were together.

I whistled, feeling so fucking content I almost sickened myself. Things were going great. Renovations at the Gloaming were nearing completion. Money was flowing again from the restaurant and bar at night. My Caelmore house was in the second-fix stages, and Ery and I had gone public.

The only shadow on the edges was that Lachlan's team couldn't trace the origin of the email, which meant whoever sent them really knew what they were doing. Still, I hadn't received any more, and there was no certainty that it still wasn't a prank. Lachlan had passed it along to an ethical hacker friend, and we were waiting to see if she'd have better luck.

Despite that hanging over me, things were good. They were great. Better than.

Dealing with the condom, I searched the bathroom for towels for our shower and found none.

While Ery was quite happy for me to roam around her main living space, she was a little cagey about her bedroom for some reason. But we'd been sleeping together for six weeks and dating for two, so I didn't suppose she'd mind if I looked in her linen closet for a couple of towels.

She had a double closet for her clothes, and a single closet beside it. I looked in there and sure enough, folded linens sat on the upper shelves. Pulling out a couple of towels, the bottom of the closet caught my attention. It was stacked with boxes and what appeared to be an old trunk. The trunk wasn't latched correctly and sitting on top were a pair of worn ballet shoes, wrapped tightly together by their pink ribbons.

Curiosity overtook my common sense, and I picked them up, pulling them out of the closet to see them in the light.

"What are you doing?" Ery's shrill demand filled the room.

She stood in the bedroom's doorway, holding two full coffee mugs, her features strained and wan, her eyes round with what I could only interpret as fear.

Confused, I waved the shoes at her. "What are these?"

Suddenly, she dumped the mugs on her vanity, coffee spilling out of them, and then she practically launched herself across the room to rip the shoes from my hands. "What the hell are you doing?"

Shocked because I'd never heard her raise her voice like

that, I held up my hands, trying to appease her. She was shaking. Fuck. "Ery, I'm sorry. I was just looking for towels." I pointed to the towels at my feet.

"You had no right!"

"Ery—"

"Get out." She grabbed my jeans off her vanity stool and threw them at me.

Stunned, I fumbled to catch them. "Eredine!"

"I thought I could trust you, but as soon as my back is turned, you snoop!" She threw my T-shirt next. "Get out!"

"Ery—"

"Get out!" she shrieked, stumbling into the corner like a frightened animal.

Horrified, beyond confused, I hurried into my clothes. "I don't ... What's going on here?"

"I knew this would happen," Eredine whispered, not looking at me, her knuckles pale from holding the dance shoes so tightly.

"What would happen?" I snapped impatiently. "I have no fucking idea what just happened."

Finally, she looked at me, expression stark. "I can't do this with you."

Fear sliced through me. "Can't do this?"

She shook her head. "I can't do this. We're ... over."

Anger cut through my fear. "Because I opened a fucking closet door?"

She flinched. "It wasn't your door to open." Then something occurred to her, something that made her look nauseated. "What else did you see?"

What the hell was going on here? "Nothing. Just a trunk. But I didn't open it, and unless you've got body parts in it, I don't see what the big damn deal is."

She didn't laugh at my joke.

Instead, tears filled her eyes. "Just go, Arran."

"Not without a reason. You can't end this without a reason."

"Yes, I can." Her tears slipped free. "It's called free will."

Panicking now, I tried to step toward her, but she looked so afraid of me, I stopped. And did that not hurt worse than anything? "You don't trust me."

Ery didn't say a word.

"Jesus Christ!" I bit out, grabbing my shirt and yanking it on. "Aye, I guess if you don't trust me, this was never going to work, was it?" Stuffing my feet into my shoes, I rounded the bed to grab my phone off the charger. "Keep your secrets, woman," I spat angrily as I stormed across her bedroom toward the door. "I hope they're worth a lifetime of loneliness." Slamming the bedroom door behind me, I marched out of her house and got into my car.

My hands shook as I pulled on my seat belt.

Feeling sick, I sucked in a breath and sped out of there, wondering how it was possible to go from utter bliss to the worst bloody nightmare within minutes.

25

EREDINE

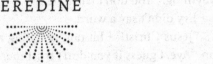

I think I was in a state of shock.

My reaction to Arran finding my pointe shoes had stunned even me.

Once he was gone and the emptiness of the lodge crowded in, I came out of that feral state of fear and realized I'd reacted on instinct.

And so I hadn't reacted to Arran as an individual—as a person I trusted—I'd just reacted.

I'd broken up with him.

For the past twenty-four hours, I'd vacillated between hating myself for that impulsive decision and reminding myself that maybe it was for the best. If this was still my response to the past, then maybe my gut was telling me I didn't trust Arran.

Or maybe it was just fear.

I didn't know.

I was a mess.

Arro called, and then Regan and Robyn and even Lachlan, but I ignored them.

I couldn't sleep, I couldn't eat, so I just sat on my couch

and stared numbly at the TV, not even paying attention to what was on.

It really shouldn't have been a surprise, then, to hear the gentle hum of a car engine.

Damn it.

I wanted to be alone to wallow in the horribleness of yesterday morning.

And panic flittered across my chest every time I thought of Arran.

Part of me wanted it to be him pulling up to the house, but I think I knew it wasn't. Footsteps sounded on my porch. And then Arro peered into the living room.

Reluctantly, I got up and opened the door for her.

Her gaze swept over my bedraggled appearance, sympathy in her eyes.

She knew.

I guessed that was what all the calling was about.

Without a word, I slumped back toward the couch and threw myself on it.

Arro sat at the other end and placed her bag on the floor. "We're worried about you," she said.

"Sorry," I mumbled, staring at the TV.

My friend reached for the remote on the coffee table and switched off the screen, forcing my attention to her.

"Why are you here, Arro?"

"Because my brother turned up at our place last night, shaken, distraught, and confused. He's now nursing the world's worst hangover after decimating a bottle of Mac's favorite whisky."

Guilt suffused me. And worry. "Is he okay?"

Her gaze narrowed. "No, he's not okay. Are you okay?"

Tears burned my eyes, and I shook my head.

Arro's expression softened. "Ery, you don't need to tell me anything. My friendship is not contingent upon me knowing

213

your deepest, darkest secrets, though I hope you know you can trust me. But ... romantic relationships are different. Even if you don't want to tell Arran some things ... flying off the handle at him for opening a closet and then breaking up with him ... It just means this was never supposed to work out between you."

I wanted to protest. She didn't know what it was like between me and Arran. She didn't know how it felt to be in his arms or to talk with each other about our days before we fell asleep. Did she even know what a big deal it was for me to have him sleep over almost every night? "That's not fair."

She reached out to pat my knee, and part of me wanted to push her hand off. "You don't trust him, Ery. If you did, you would have explained why him opening a closet door disturbed you."

"It's not about trust," I blurted out in my need to defend my feelings for him.

"Then what's it about?"

"Fear," I whispered.

Concern puckered her brow. "Of Arran?"

"No. No, of course not." I sat up. "I ... I've been afraid for a really long time. Sometimes I forget about it. But then things will bring it back to the fore, like Lucy and Fergus trashing my studio, Austin attacking me ... but after a while, I'd forget again. And with Arran"—the tears escaped fast and free—"I really thought maybe I could be unafraid now. But it's always there, Arro. Like a demon on my back. And yesterday, I wasn't me. I was my fear. I treated him so badly. I ... I don't deserve him."

"Hush." Arro pulled me into her arms, holding me tight as I shuddered through my tears. "No more talk of deserving. You need to talk to Arran. Tell him this."

I shook my head. "He's better off without me. Trust me."

"Ery—"

I pulled out of her hold, brushing away my tears. "No. Yesterday just proved that I'm an emotional wreck. Your family has been through enough. Arran doesn't need to take on my baggage."

"That's up to him to decide. And cutting him out without giving him the chance to decide for himself is wrong. Mac did that to me for so many years, and it broke my heart, Ery. Please don't do that to my brother."

A painful ache of guilt and remorse scored through me. It was only last year that Arro shared with me everything she and Mac had been through. I'd felt her pain that day and wished so much I could take it away.

I didn't want to be the person who caused someone else that kind of pain.

But fear didn't just go away with a snap of your fingers. "I'll think about it."

My friend nodded. "That's all I ask."

26

EREDINE

"Well, well, well," Anne-Marie said as I sat down at
our regular Monday table in the staff lunchroom.

I raised an eyebrow, exhausted, and in no mood for their
usual banter. "Well, well, well what?"

Jacinda frowned. "Are you okay? You looked tired."

Gee, thanks. I shrugged.

"The well, well, well was for after all your protesting
about just being friends, it comes to my attention that you're
dating Arran Adair."

His name cut through me like a knife, and I tried not to
wince as I speared a fork into my salad. "What?"

Silence overtook the table, and then Michelle spoke.
"People have seen you in the village together. Kissing and all
that."

I shrugged again because I couldn't bring myself to tell
them I'd broken up with him.

"Trouble in paradise already?" Natalia asked softly.

"I don't want to talk about it."

More silence, and then Michelle huffed, "Men are
bastards."

A rumble of agreement rounded the table. I lifted my eyes now, realizing they thought whatever was going on was Arran's fault. "He didn't do anything."

"Then what's the problem?" Anne-Marie waved her fork at me a little impatiently. "You're dating one of the few sexy, eligible men in Ardnoch, you lucky cow."

"We're just in a tiff," I lied. "Of my making."

"Apologize," Jacinda said, as if it were that easy. At my annoyed look, she chuckled. "You know, in the many years I've worked here, I don't think I've ever seen you in a bad mood. You must be in love."

I sucked in a sharp breath at the thought.

No.

I wasn't in love with Arran.

I couldn't be.

Surely, you had to have shared everything about each other for love to be a possibility?

And yet, that constant knot in my gut would not go away.

"It's really hard to make yourself vulnerable to someone, isn't it?" Natalia said, her expression introspective. "To have them know that their mood affects yours, their actions determine your day, their nearness affects your contentment. So much power to give one person. In the wrong hands, they could play you until you're broken." Her gaze was sympathetic. "But we're all a wee bit broken, anyway, so maybe it's worth the risk. Who knows? The right person might even heal some of the cracks."

Her uncharacteristically wise words settled over me—I think all of us at that table, in fact—and a sense of calm moved through me.

I knew Arran. While I couldn't predict what would happen in our relationship down the line, I knew him enough to know he was worth the risk. And yes, I was terrified of opening that closet and letting all those demons loose again ... but maybe they were doing me just as much damage staying hidden.

There was only one scenario, however, where they'd definitely result in me losing Arran.

And I was more afraid of that now than I was of the demons.

As the ladies fell into conversation, I pulled out my phone and typed a text.

I understand if u don't want to talk to me, but I'd really like the chance to explain some things. Will u meet me at my place tonight? 7pm?

Taking a deep breath, I sent it.

I HADN'T HEARD from Arran before my next class started, and it took everything within me to focus on the yoga session when my attention kept drifting to my changing/shower room where my phone was situated.

The butterflies in my belly were raging by the time class ended and the last person left the studio. Hurrying into my private space, I grabbed my phone off the vanity, and relief flooded me. I shook as I swiped up the notification with Arran's name on it.

I'll be there.

Okay, it wasn't a warm, fuzzy response, but he would be there. He was attempting to be there. Maybe we had a chance.

That was when it hit me what I had to do tonight.

Nausea rose up in me, and a tightness crawled over my chest.

A panic attack.

I slid to the floor, back to the wall, as I flushed hot from head to toe, my cheeks tingling as the tightness increased.

Coaxing myself through it, I concentrated on correct breathing, reminding myself I was just having a panic attack, that I could control this.

Eventually, the tightness dissipated, and I was left exhausted by the adrenaline dump.

Thankfully, that had been the day's last class.

So I sat for a while, trying to gather myself. Trying not to let the panic overwhelm my resolve to tell Arran the truth. Eventually, I eased onto shaky legs and grabbed my stuff to get out of there. Perhaps a little nap before Arran arrived would help me feel strong enough to face the past.

ARRAN

I AM A GLUTTON FOR PUNISHMENT, I thought as I pulled into Eredine's driveway. I'd spent the weekend and today convincing myself that after her treatment, the woman wasn't worth the hassle. That I should forget about her and move on.

Yet I couldn't erase the image of her trembling in the corner of her bedroom like a frightened animal. I knew for Lachlan to be protecting Ery that whatever happened to her was bad. But I wasn't sure I was prepared for how bad.

And it killed me she was dealing with something big on her own.

However, it also brutally fucking hurt that she didn't trust me enough to share it. That instead, she threw me out of her bedroom, her life, like I was nothing but a stranger.

Aye, that cut like a bastard.

Worse was the way my bloody heart jumped in my throat

when I got her text this afternoon. The impulse to text back immediately was strong, but I gave myself time to think about it.

And ultimately decided I needed to give her this chance.

If it was more surface, shallow excuses, then no matter how I felt about her, I knew I had to walk. I couldn't find myself in another situation where she lost her mind at me for God knows what.

I still didn't understand why finding the dance shoes was such a big deal.

Tonight I hoped to find out.

Or we were over.

Maybe that made me an arsehole, but I couldn't have a halfhearted relationship with Eredine. For the first time in my life, I wanted everything with a woman, but not just any woman. Her. Only her. I couldn't settle for less. It wasn't in my nature.

The lodge door opened as I got out of my SUV. She stood in the doorway in shorts and a tank, and I cursed the muggy summer temperatures because Eredine Willows's gorgeous long legs were my Achilles' heel. Fine. All of Eredine Willows was my Achilles' heel.

Dragging my gaze to her face, my pulse picked up speed.

Worry strained her features, her pretty eyes wide as she stepped back to let me in without a word.

"You look like you're going to be sick," I commented as I walked into her living space. "Am I really that bad?"

"Arran."

I turned to look at her as she closed the door.

"No banter, okay?"

I might have been irritated by that if she didn't look seconds from bursting into tears. My fingers curled into fists to stop from reaching for her. "What's going on?"

"Will you follow me, please?"

Confused, I could only nod.

Ery walked toward the rear of the lodge, and I wanted to protest. The last time I'd been in her bedroom wasn't a scene I cared to repeat. My eyes wandered over her slender back, her round arse, to her long, shapely legs. Her hair swayed across the top of said round arse. Even now, when I was hurt and angry, I wanted this woman more than I'd ever wanted anyone. Not even as a constantly hard teen had I felt this pull toward someone.

I wanted to resent her for it.

She led me into her bedroom, and as I walked in and opened my mouth to object, my attention snagged on the familiar trunk. It was now sitting on her bed, the dance shoes laid on top.

I swallowed hard and looked at her as she turned to me, expression reading as panic. "What's this?"

As if her legs couldn't hold her any longer, Eredine practically fell to the edge of the bed.

"Eredine?"

She shook her head. "Maya," she said softly. "My real name is Maya Washington."

Shock humbled me, and I stumbled for the vanity table stool. Elbows braced on my knees, I scrubbed my hands over my face as I tried to process her confession.

Not that I hadn't always known Eredine Willows wasn't her real name. But I think part of me thought she'd never tell me her birth name.

I needed to know more.

Taking my hands from my face, I said, "I'm listening."

27

EREDINE

I'd imagined telling someone my story, but I was only ever able to do that knowing I'd never really go through with it in real life. Now I had to dig deep, I had to brace myself, not knowing what would happen if I shared my past with Arran. I'd looked in the trunk on my bed a million times over the past eight years, but that was to remember my childhood, the life before everything went to shit.

I rarely let myself think of the events—of the person, rather—who destroyed my life, who severed a piece of my soul.

But I was realizing, perhaps for the first time, that maybe keeping the truth hidden to protect my safety was too heavy a price ... because it gave *him* power over me.

"Ery? I mean, Maya—"

I waved a hand at Arran, giving him a sad smile. "I'm Eredine now, Arran. Maya Washington ceased to exist a long time ago."

"Can you ... will you tell me why?"

I nodded. "That's why I asked you to come. I'm sorry about how I treated you on Saturday. Sorrier than I can say.

It wasn't about you. My instincts took over, and I wasn't thinking rationally."

Arran nodded, his expression soft, concerned.

"I never want to treat you like that again. I'm sorry."

"Ery, I accept your apology. And I'm sorry for snooping."

Tears burned my eyes at his grace. "You weren't snooping. You're my boyfriend. You should be able to look for a damn towel without getting thrown out."

His lips twitched with amusement, but his eyes were still filled with wariness.

Preparing myself to unleash the truth, I sucked in a breath and exhaled slowly, my lips trembling. I could already feel the tears, and I really wanted to get through this without becoming hysterical. It had just been such a long time since I told my story.

"Can I get you anything?" Arran asked. "A glass of water?"

Lord, he was the sweetest man. "I'm all right. Thanks. Do you need anything?"

He smiled tenderly. "Just you, gorgeous."

I ached at his words.

Band-Aid.

Rip it off like a Band-Aid.

"I had a sister who died," I told him, fighting back the emotion. "Kia. She was my twin."

Shock slackened his features. "Ery," he whispered, sounding heartbroken for me.

And that there, knowing how much he cared, gave me strength to continue. I lifted the lid off the trunk and moved aside some trinkets to take out the photo album. Handing it over to him, I said, "We were born in Chicago. Raised by our mom."

Arran flipped open the album and looked through the baby pictures of me and Kia. We grew into teenagers in that photo album.

"We didn't know who our father was. I don't remember Mama talking about him, and then she ... she died when we were only six. Crossed a busy street without looking. I only have vague memories of her now."

His gaze lifted from the album. "I'm so sorry."

Remembering what happened to his mom, I shrugged sadly. "You and I have something in common, I guess."

"I wish it wasn't that," he whispered.

"Me too."

"Who's this?" He raised the album and pointed.

"Granny." I smiled. I couldn't help but feel happy and sad when I thought of her. "She'd moved out of Chicago before we were born. Her sister had money, and she left Granny her place in LA when she died. Granny had a difficult relationship with Mama, so she put distance between them. But when Mama died, Granny came and took us back with her."

"So you grew up in Los Angeles?"

"Yeah. It was a good life with Granny. She was strict but kind. She raised us with respect and affection, and I often wondered if Mama was really the problem in their relationship because *I* loved my grandmother. She was my hero. I would have done anything for her. Kia too. Even though she and I were different in so many ways, our love for Granny was immeasurable." Thoughts of my sister and grandmother opened gaping, raw cracks inside me. I rubbed the spot on my chest where it hurt the most, moisture blinding my vision momentarily.

"It feels like they were part of a past life. Kia. Granny. When Granny died, I felt like I lost my anchor. When Kia died, it changed me fundamentally." My tears slipped down my cheeks, and Arran's eyes grew bright with his own. "It was like someone stole a piece of me. Like I wasn't whole anymore."

"Ery ..."

224

I waved him off because if he touched me, I'd break.

"I was the shy one. Quiet, you know. Kia was outgoing and social and all my friends were Kia's friends. Not that I needed them. She was my best friend. Plus, Granny always told me I had a sixth sense about people, ever since I was a child. As I got older, I thought she was right. I could tell if someone was playing me false or if they weren't being their authentic self with me, and I didn't like it. Granny told me to always trust that feeling, and I did. Only a few times in my life had it ever failed me. Lucy was one of those times. She was a damn fine actress.

"Anyway, Kia didn't have that sixth sense as Granny called it. She'd make friends with anyone, and I wanted to protect her from that, but I was also jealous she could just throw herself into friendships so easily." I reached for the pointe shoes. "Granny signed us both up for dance classes when we moved to LA as a distraction from losing Mama. Tap, ballet, street. I fell in love with ballet and Kia with street. I was so cripplingly shy, though, and some days I wanted to quit because I didn't like the attention, even though I loved dancing."

My hands tightened around my shoes. "Kia pushed me. She kept me dancing. And over the years, I got over most of my shyness. When I was nineteen, I was offered a spot with a touring dance company. It was the first time Kia and I had been apart. I hated it so much, but she kept telling me it was for the best and that she enjoyed her independence, so I didn't want to seem weak by telling her I was miserable.

"I stayed with the company, and Kia started posting street dance videos to YouTube under the stage name Cadenza. It didn't take her long to blow up. She had millions of followers," I said with pride. "Talented, funny, beautiful. I always knew she would shine like that. *She* loved the attention."

Arran glanced down at the photo album, his fingers

brushing a photograph of Kia and me at our high school prom. "What happened to her, Ery?"

I took a shuddering breath. "First ... Granny passed." My voice cracked. "I'd been with the dance company for a year, and I felt so guilty that I'd missed out on that time with her. Kia was on the verge of signing a TV contract to host a new dance competition show. But when Granny died, Kia fell apart. I always thought it would be me, that my twin was the strong one, but she couldn't handle the grief. She decided to stick with her YouTube channel and turned down the TV show. She was making a lot of money through sponsors and ads. But I think she made that decision because she knew she was spiraling, and she didn't want to be responsible to other people.

"As soon as I realized how bad the drinking, drugs, and partying was, I quit the tour and went home to LA to try to get her back on track. I moved into Granny's with her and got a job with a local theater.

"There were so many arguments, so many ugly words hurled at each other that I wish had never happened." I shrugged sadly. "But I didn't give up. I stayed and pushed, endured every time she told me she hated me, until finally, I thought we were making progress. She stopped drinking and taking drugs. But ... instead, she fell into the most toxic relationship she could find."

Hatred threatened to consume me as I met Arran's gaze, and he flinched at whatever he saw in my eyes.

"His name is Ezra Jefferson. He tracked her down after watching her videos, and she thought that was sweet." I scoffed harshly. "I told her it was creepy, that there was something off about him, but he swept her up in all his money and attention. They fought a lot, but it was a few months into their relationship when I started to notice the bruises. I tried to confront her about it, but she'd get so defensive and angry. One night I was sick at work, and they sent me home early. I walked in on them physically fighting, and she was giving as good as she was getting. I was horrified."

"Fuck," Arran said hoarsely. "That sounds beyond toxic."

"I think she just wanted to feel anything but grief." I shrugged, renewed tears soaking my cheeks. "I'm not making excuses for her. It took her a really long time to see how bad it was between her and Ezra. She just couldn't see it." I swiped at my tears. "They were dating for about nine months, and I got in between them during an argument, and Ezra punched me."

Arran's body jerked, fury filling his expression.

"That's what broke her," I whispered. "Seeing me hurt. It finally got through to her, so I would take that punch over and over again to get that result ..." I struggled to get my next words out. "I ... He wouldn't let her go. He started stalking her, sending her gifts with threatening notes. We tried the cops ... but here's the kicker, Arran ... he's the son of a Supreme Court justice."

As if he knew where this was going, his face paled. He shook his head in horror.

I nodded through my tears. "I found her." Images of that night, the memories, flooded me, crushing my chest with their heaviness. I sobbed, and then Arran was holding me to him as I tried to cry through the pressure of such anguish.

After a while, Arran's hushed words of comfort seeped in. My breathing calmed, and I kept my head on his chest, his shirt soaked with my tears.

Once I could speak again, I lifted my head but kept my fingers tangled with his. "He ..."

"You don't have to tell me the details if you don't want to," Arran whispered, brushing the tears from my cheeks.

"I need you to know. I need you to know how bad it was so you can understand why I am the way I am."

He nodded, a muscle ticking in his jaw. "All right."

"He …" I tried to step out of that life and back into this one because it provided the distance that allowed me to live with the past. "He raped and strangled her."

Arran made a hoarse, wounded sound, and I gripped his hands tighter.

"But he got away with it. They found his DNA on her, but they said because they were in a relationship, it only proved that she'd slept with him at some point before her attack."

"What the fuck?"

I nodded, wanting to be numb to the injustice. "The house was wrecked, so his defense concluded that someone else had broken in and raped and killed her. Our reports to the cops had magically disappeared, and there was no record of her filing any complaints against him. Friends lied and said they were still dating. It didn't even go to trial, Arran," I said, my rage bubbling up from where I kept it locked tight.

Arran shook his head. "How? Fucking how?"

"I didn't have time to be angry. A lot of people in our community were angry, and there were protests. Once upon a time, all you had to do was google my sister's name and you'd find articles all over the internet about it. But to protect me, Lachlan employed someone to run a program that finds any mention of me or my sister. Then his hacker took the pages down. For a few years, there were articles, conspiracy theories, that it was Jefferson's family wiping the internet clean of it, thus proving his guilt. But there haven't been any in a long time. People just eventually forgot."

Arran's chest rose fast and shallow. "Lachlan's doing that because Jefferson came after *you*, didn't he?"

I nodded. "That's why I didn't have time to be angry. He started stalking me. And I was too afraid to go to the police because there didn't seem to be any point. He made problems for me with the company I danced for, and I lost my job. He wanted me to have nowhere else to turn but him."

"All because you looked like Kia?"

"Yes. It wasn't about *me*. He didn't see me. He just saw her and this twisted idea that he had a chance to make her his again. I'd gotten work at a hotel gym as a Pilates instructor. I did a lot of Pilates while training as a dancer, so when I couldn't get work dancing, I started instructing.

"One night I was afraid to go home, so I slept in the locker room. That morning I was leaving before the gym opened, and Ezra had tracked me down. You know, he was so convinced of his invincibility that he didn't care about the cameras in the gym. He snapped quicker with me than he did my sister." I still remembered the terror, the brutal burn in the wake of each punch. The feel of his fingers curling around the waistband of my yoga pants.

I shuddered. "I don't know what would have happened if Mac and Lachlan hadn't shown up early thinking the gym would be open. They were in LA to recruit members for the club. They got him off me and got me away from him, and I don't know why … I just told them everything. It all spilled out. Lachlan kept me safe in his hotel suite while he checked out my story." A sob burst from me as I relived the profound relief of that moment. "He believed me."

Arran cursed under his breath and pulled me into him again.

"I'd been so alone in it for months. Even with the people who believed, so many voices still called me a liar. And here was this Hollywood actor, of all people, who took me seriously. Of course, he'd seen firsthand what Ezra was capable of. But he didn't know me." I looked up at Arran. "I was a total stranger, and he jumped right in to help. He paid for a new identity for me. He gave me a fresh start. And he helped me sell Granny's house so I could pay him back. I've never met anyone like your family, Arran."

He squeezed me closer, his voice hoarse as he said, "I've never been prouder of you. Lachlan might have helped, but you were the one who had the courage to start over somewhere new. That must have been terrifying, but you did it."

I looked at him, sad, a little defeated. "I ran. I hid. I didn't get justice for my sister. I'm not who I used to be without her. For a while, I didn't know who I was at all. It took me a few years, but I finally know who I am without my twin sister. And I'm broken, Arran. This new me is broken in ways I don't know can ever be fixed. I want to be with you. But I don't know if I can ever be what you'll need me to be."

Clasping my face in his hands, Arran looked deep in my eyes. "Now you listen to me, Eredine Willows. You did all you could to protect Kia. To get justice for her. Sometimes corruption wins, and it's fucking awful, and I can't even imagine the depth of your anger ... but the very fact that you live each day treating everyone with patience and kindness and gentleness ... I have never met anyone as strong or as good as you. And I won't let you feel guilty for doing something I know, without even having known her, that your sister would have wanted you to do. You lived, Ery. You're living. And maybe this new you is broken, but we're all a little broken. I just need you to be you. I'm not going anywhere."

Gratitude for this man sank heavily into my bones, and I wrapped my arms around him, breathing him in, feeling his tight embrace and hoping that his compassion could bring me a whisper of peace.

2 8

ARRAN

M uch to my relief, Eredine slept through the night. I worried that after everything she'd confessed, the darkness of her past would keep her awake. Instead, she curled up in my arms, and though she stirred a few times during the night, I managed to soothe her back to sleep.

Around six o'clock when we were usually up and preparing for our run, I called my brother, and quietly, so as not to wake Eredine, explained what had happened. That she'd told me everything. I told him Ery wouldn't be in to work that day and neither would I, and he understood. He asked if she was okay, and I told him I'd make sure of it.

After we finished, I nestled next to the woman at my side who elicited feelings I honestly never thought myself capable of. Not once did it cross my mind to be afraid of her baggage, to worry if I had the emotional capacity to support her. I only cared about protecting her from any more hurt. About making sure I was there for her in case opening that trunk had opened old wounds.

Exhausted, Ery slept right through until around eleven a.m. She woke groggy and in a panic that she'd missed work

231

until I told her I'd called Lachlan and he'd given her the day off.

We made breakfast, talking softly, the shift between us noticeable. It wasn't a bad shift. The opposite. There was something deeper between us that hadn't been there before. Like we'd been attached by a string since the moment we met, and that string had pulled us closer and closer over the weeks until there was barely space between us.

"Do you feel like getting out of the house for a while?" I asked as we ate.

Eredine shook her head, her curls wild this morning. "Everywhere will be packed with tourists."

It was true. Even the trails were busier during the summer months.

"Stay here, then?"

She considered that. "We could go for a drive up the coast."

"A drive it is, then. I'll need to stop at my place to get a change of clothes."

"Why don't you do that after breakfast while I shower?" Ery tugged on a curl. "I didn't prep my hair last night, so I'll need to figure out something to do with it."

"Prep your hair?" I gave her a teasing smile.

"Hey"—she pointed a fork at me—"you have no idea the amount of product and energy that goes into caring for curls."

"I do. I've watched you." I grinned, feeling smug that I knew Ery's haircare routine because I'd been there to see it in action. It was something no one else knew about her, an intimacy between just us. Among other things.

"So. You get ready while I get ready, yes?"

Unease shifted through me. "I'll wait with you and then you can come with me, and we'll set off from my place."

She lifted her gaze to meet mine. "I'm okay, Arran. You can leave me alone for an hour. I won't break down."

"*I'm* not okay," I told her honestly. "I need to be with you right now. As long as that's all right with you."

Ery reached across the dining table and covered my hand with hers. "That's all right with me."

WE WERE ABOUT HALF an hour into our leisurely drive around the coast, the Range Rover's AC blasting, our sunshades down, sunglasses on, as the humid, sunny weather of the past week continued. It had been an unseasonably warm summer so far. "Did you ever find out anything about your father once you moved to LA with your granny?" I asked.

If Eredine was startled by the question, she didn't show it. "No. Kia and I asked, of course. But Granny said she didn't know who he was, and we believed her. I often wondered if it was partly the cause of the rift between her and my mom."

"Does it bother you? Not knowing?"

"It used to when we were younger. Especially because we literally had no leads on who he was. We used to wonder about him, what his job was, if he was successful or poor, or, or, or. The ors and what-ifs went on and on. All we knew was that he gave us our eyes. Granny and Mama both had beautiful dark brown eyes."

I heard the smile in her voice when she said, "When I was thirteen, I bought a pair of dark brown contacts because I wanted eyes like Granny." She laughed. "But they were these cheap, nasty things, and they irritated my eyes so much, Granny ended up taking me to the eye doctor for drops. She told me that God had seen fit to give me hazel eyes, and every inch of my body was a gift I ought to be grateful for.

She was always reminding us to be grateful for the blessings we had and not to mope over the things we didn't."

"So that's where you get your strength," I mused.

Ery sighed. "I'm not as strong as she was. I've moped for eight years."

"No, you haven't," I said sternly. "Ery, you've kept it hidden out of fear of Jefferson finding you. That's not the same as moping over it. Considering what you've been through, you're a goddamn miracle." I glanced at her and saw the soft smile on her lips. I wanted to kiss her. Later.

Looking back at the road, I asked, "Did you have many relationships in LA?"

"Romantic, you mean?"

"Aye."

"Hmm. I'll tell you, if you tell me."

I shot her another quick look and saw the teasing quirk at the corners of her mouth. Chuckling, I shook my head. "There's nothing to tell."

"Oh, come on. I can't be the first woman you've wanted a relationship with."

Embarrassment crept up the back of my neck in a hot flush.

"Arran?"

"You're the first woman I've wanted a relationship with," I confessed.

She was silent a moment, and then, "There weren't even longer affairs?"

"Aye, but do you really want to know about those?"

"I just … I want to know if there has been anyone who felt like *more* than a one-night stand in your life?"

I shrugged. "There were casual relationships while I was in Thailand and Australia, but they didn't last longer than a month or two. The only one-night stand I've ever had where she meant more was Monroe, but not for romantic reasons," I hurried to assure her. "She was my friend."

"And Brodan's."

I felt that same remorseful ache anytime I thought of Roe and Brodan. "I used to call them Roe and Bro." The memories made me smile. "Drove them crazy ... though secretly, I think they liked it."

"It's cute."

I shot her another look. "I told Brodan about you and me. I didn't want him to be blindsided at the wedding."

"I'm sure it doesn't even matter to him."

"It matters. He hung up on me, and things have been tense with us since."

Ery sucked in a breath. "I ... I can't imagine that's about me, Arran. Your brother ..."

"My brother?"

"Well, he flirted with me a lot and was very attentive whenever he was home, but as soon as he left, I'd see him in photographs online with a woman on his arm. His feelings for me couldn't have been deep."

"That was my argument when I pursued you. That I wanted you more, and if he'd wanted you, he should have stayed."

"Exactly."

"But I'm worried that it just reminds him of what happened with Roe."

"Does he know she's back?"

"Aye, I told him. He couldn't get off the phone fast enough."

"Wow."

I looked at her. "What?"

"Come on ... it sounds to me like he's still holding on to that. No one holds on to something that happened eighteen years ago unless it left a mark."

"My thoughts exactly. It'll be interesting to see how it plays out when he gets home."

"Do you think he'll see her?"

"It's a small village." I smirked. "And stop trying to distract me. I asked about your relationships back in LA." At her silence, I said, "Only if you want to. If it's too much—"

"No, it's not. All this time since we started seeing each other, I was terrified that if I opened the door to my past, somehow it would swallow me up in this black hole. And it's the opposite, Arran. I feel lighter than I've felt in years. So thank you."

"You don't need to thank me for that. The gratitude is mine."

"Then we'll both be grateful."

"All right." I smiled. "I can live with that."

"As for relationships, I've had a few. You're the first guy I ever propositioned for a one-night stand."

I shook my head. "I don't know if I should be honored or offended."

"You shouldn't be offended, you moron," she teased. "I wanted you so badly, I asked for a one-night stand. Me. Miss Haven't Had a Relationship in Eight Years."

"Now I'm offended by the moron comment."

"You are not. I've said worse to you before we were even friends, and you weren't offended in the least. In fact, I think it turned you on."

Shoulders shaking with laughter, I admitted, "You're absolutely right."

"Sick man." Ery chuckled.

"Nah, just high on you."

"Charmer."

"Stop distracting me, woman, and tell me about these men who came before me."

"You're really not bothered by it?"

My hands tightened on the wheel. "I suppose not because they're in your past, but I guess it'll depend on what you share."

"Okay, well, I had a first love, which I think differs from other kinds of love. It was almost like puppy love. His name was Michael. We were fourteen when we started dating—high school sweethearts. He was on the football team and won a scholarship. He was quiet, but not in a shy way. He was beautiful. And kind. He didn't pressure me for sex, and somehow that made me want him more, so he was my first. I got lucky with Michael. Kia had one bad relationship after another, but Michael was one of the good ones. I think even Kia had a crush on him."

Something a lot like jealousy gripped me at the affectionate tone when she spoke of this guy. "What happened?"

"We broke up when he went off to college."

"That was it?"

"That was it. And then I had a few relationships over the years, but none stuck and none were memorable, to be honest. I started seeing a mechanic a few months before my sister's death. I'd taken my beat-up car to his garage, and Nick was very charming. Kind of like you, actually."

There was that jealousy again. "Like me?"

"You know, overtly flirtatious, gregarious, the opposite of me."

"Right."

"I thought there might be something there. Potential. And while sex had been okay for me in the past, it was good with him."

Yeah, maybe I couldn't handle this. I grunted in response.

"Arran." Ery slid her hand across my thigh and squeezed. I looked over at her, and she'd shoved her sunglasses into her hair so I could see the warmth in her beautiful eyes. Unfortunately, the road called my gaze away from hers. "That night with you, and every night since, has been the best sex of my life. And what I felt for Nick doesn't come close to what I feel for you."

The knot inside me relaxed, and I shot her a wry smile. "Guess I get jealous too."

"I don't think either of us needs to be jealous anymore, do you?"

"No," I replied hoarsely. "I only want you."

"And I only want you."

I covered her hand on my thigh and threaded our fingers together. For a while, we drove like that, in perfect, comfortable silence, finally certain of each other.

29

EREDINE

I strolled into Flora's later that week, still in workout gear since I had a class later in the afternoon, and smirked at the sight of Arro guarding the small bistro table by the window. She glowered at the counter. The café was packed, and a few people waited at the counter, eagle eyes on the table, as if willing her to leave. Arro's hand was settled on her small bump as if to emphasize the point that these people really didn't want to mess with her right now.

Her entire face lit up when she saw me, and she relaxed as I sat across from her. "How did you secure this?"

"Mac did. He was driving through on his way to Inverness and stopped by for a quick kiss." She beamed, smug that she had a guy who would stop mid journey for a kiss from his fiancée. "He was pissed off I was standing while waiting for a table, so as soon as one became available, he eyed those people currently eyeing me in a way that said, 'You wouldn't dare deny my pregnant fiancée a table.' And of course, they wouldn't with a six-foot-four Scotsman scowling down at them. He basically used his intimidating presence to grab the next available table."

Chuckling, I shook my head. "You do realize there is nothing in the world you won't get if you want it. He'll make sure of that."

Her smile turned secretive and so full of happiness, I ached with the same emotion for her. "Aye, I know."

"Ladies, ladies." Flora appeared, looking harassed. She glanced over her shoulder at the rest of the café and then bent toward us to mutter, "I know these summer months keep me open, but sometimes I wish the tourists would just go away, you know."

"Oh, I know." Arro shot another annoyed look at the threesome still staring at us, as if trying to creep us out enough that we'd give up our table. "Sometimes I could kill Lachlan for making this place a destination spot."

"Och, I wouldn't go that far," Flora tutted. "We're all very grateful for the business. It's just ... *trying* sometimes. Now, what can I get you?"

We ordered sandwiches and tea, and the words were barely out of our mouths before Flora was hurrying off to serve the next person. I wondered where her extra staff was today. But only for a millisecond because Arro asked, "So ... how are things with you and Arran?"

"You haven't spoken to him?"

"Some texts, but he was a little vague and a wee bit absentminded."

"I'm sorry. That's probably my fault. He's been at my place after work all week."

"So, it's going well, then?" She leaned forward, her stunning pale-blue eyes glittering with hope. Only she and Brodan had eyes that striking shade of blue. Lachlan and Arran had eyes the color of the sky on a sunny day. Thane was the odd one out with his lovely gray blue. Arran's were my favorite. He had a laughing gleam in his that always made me smile. "Ery?"

"What? Sorry? I was woolgathering."

Her lips twitched. "I take it things are going well, then, between you and Arran? You fixed your issues?"

I leaned in so I could lower my voice. "I told him about my past."

Arro gaped at me, clearly stunned.

"You told him? You really told him ... everything?"

Suddenly, I wondered if she'd be hurt that I told Arran when I hadn't told her. But now that I knew talking about it wasn't nearly as scary as I'd expected, I wanted Arro to know. She was my best friend. While I'd had nightmares the past few nights, ones Arran held me through, I think telling Arro the story would be easier now that I'd ripped off the Band-Aid.

"I told him everything," I confirmed.

"How are you?" My friend covered my hand with hers, giving it a squeeze. "Are you doing okay after all that?"

Of course, Arro's first thought would be of my emotional well-being and not that I had shared my past with Arran before her. That wasn't who she was. I nodded. "It ... I feel freed by it, Arro."

She squeezed my hand again, eyes bright with emotion. "I'm so glad."

I covered her hand with my other. "I don't want too many people to know, for my own safety, but I will tell you. I want to tell you." I glanced around the café. "Just not here."

"You know you don't have to. There's no pressure."

"I know. But you're my best friend, and I want you to know."

Tears welled in Arro's eyes. "Oh, goodness." She pulled her hand from mine to reach for a napkin. "This baby has turned me into a watering pot."

"Excuses, excuses," I teased.

She gave a huff of laughter as she dabbed at the corners of

her eyes. "I know. I'm just so happy for you. You're my best friend too."

"So, we'll take some time to talk later, yeah?"

"Absolutely. Name the date and time."

Flora returned to our table at that moment with our sandwiches and tea. My stomach grumbled at the sight. Ever since telling Arran the truth, I had more of an appetite. I was just about to say so when Arro said, "Oh my God, is that Monroe?"

I looked up to see Arro peering out the café's front window. Her gaze was fixed on a familiar, tiny, gorgeous redhead standing outside Morag's, rifling through her purse for something.

"That *is* Monroe," Arro surmised. "She hasn't changed a bit."

We watched her stride down the street and out of sight.

"You haven't spoken to her yet?" I asked before taking a bite.

Arro shook her head, still staring out toward the street. "I haven't been in the village much lately, and I don't have her number. I kept waiting to bump into her. I'll need to make more of an effort." Her eyes came to mine and narrowed at whatever she saw in my expression. "Oh, Christ. Arran told you, didn't he?"

I shrugged. "Maybe."

"You can't be jealous of Roe, Ery." Arro frowned. "It was a mistake between them. A huge mistake that ruined all of our friendships with her."

"I can't help it." I made a face. "I've never been possessive over someone before, but when I think about her with Arran, it bugs me. He's told me he doesn't care about her that way, and I believe him, but they have a history and … I don't know why I feel jealous. I told him we have nothing to be jealous over. We trust each other."

Arro snorted. "Jealousy doesn't disappear because you trust your partner. Jealousy is an unfavorable aspect of human nature. We're territorial creatures. That's a fact. I still want to pop people's heads off when they flirt with Mac. Even more so now." She touched her belly. "That's normal, I think. The problems arise when you mistrust your partner out of jealousy. That's not the same thing as someone flirting with your man or knowing they've had sex with him in the past."

That made me feel a little better. "Okay. Well, I guess that explains my irrational feelings about Monroe. Especially as Arran's convinced Brodan was the one who had romantic feelings for her."

A sadness flittered across Arro's pretty face. "I suspect Arran's correct. God knows why Brodan didn't make a move there if he cared so much for Roe." Realization dawned in her eyes. "Brodan's coming home for our wedding. He might bump into her. He knows she's here, right?"

"Arran told him."

Arro nodded, expression thoughtful. "I wonder how he'll feel about it."

"It would be nice if he had another reason to stay in Ardnoch," I mused. "Instead of traveling the world, avoiding his family for reasons unknown."

She chuckled. "Don't tell me you're trying to play matchmaker?"

"No. And might not have to if we tell Regan." I grinned.

Arro laughed. "That is very true. She was trying to get you and Arran together all along. And I think secretly she wanted Mac and me together too. She's a bit of a romantic, that one."

"A bit?" I scoffed. "Try a huge romantic. Speaking of, how are the wedding plans coming along?" We were only ten days out from the big day.

With a grimace, Arro confessed, "I've really just left it up to Regan. I'd feel bad about that if she didn't seem to thrive on the planning. Mac and I have weighed in with some decisions, but we really just said, 'Here's the money, do as you wish with it.' Not that it's going to be a big to-do like Robyn and Lachlan's wedding. It's fairly simple. And Mac and I don't really care, to be honest, as long as we're surrounded by family. We just want to be married already."

The double wedding ceremony was to be held on the land the Adair family owned in Caelmore, situated between Thane's and Lachlan's residences and Arro's and Arran's almost completed homes. On the cliff, overlooking the North Sea. And the newly renovated Gloaming would play host to the reception after. The banquet hall normally used for the anniversary ceilidh every year was being transformed for the two couples' reception.

"I think it's going to be perfect," I told her truthfully.

We talked a little more about what Regan had organized, and I marveled at her ability to juggle that, her studies for her business degree, and being a full-time mom to Eilidh and Lewis. She was the youngest adult in our little clan, but you wouldn't know it. Regan had a maturity far beyond her years, which was why the thirteen-year age gap between her and Thane wasn't a big deal.

When Regan had first appeared in Ardnoch, I'd been surprised to learn she was nothing like rumor had it. I'd expected a spoiled, immature, flighty princess, and instead I met a sunny, kind, loyal young woman desperate to mend her relationship with her big sister. No one had expected her and Thane to fall in love after he asked her to be the children's nanny, but fall in love they did. And I'd watched Thane, whom I knew fairly well from babysitting the kids over the years, lose the shroud of sadness that had encased him for years. I witnessed his transformation into this new person. Because Regan made him happy.

That was the kind of love I'd always wanted.

Transformative.

My breath caught at the thought because ... I had changed. I was more open. And more content than I could remember being in years.

Did that mean I was in love?

Thankfully, before I could fall down that rabbit hole, Arro distracted me with wedding, work, and pregnancy talk. Soon enough, though, it was time for me to get back to the estate and Arro back to work. We paid up, called goodbye to Flora, and as I held the door open for Arro, she stepped outside and tensed.

Alert, I hurried to her side. "What is it?"

Arro's gaze was firmly fixed down the busy street. "Do you see her? That social media gossip bitch. The young blond on the phone."

I raised an eyebrow at Arro for calling anyone a bitch. It wasn't really her style.

She sighed. "Sorry. This pregnancy is making me salty, as Eilidh would say. I don't know where she picks that stuff up."

My lips twitched as I tried to spot the influencer she was talking about. And there. Outside the sportswear store owned by Zuzanna and Prentice. "Why is she still here?"

"Because she's as scummy as the paparazzi." Arro curled her lip in distaste. "Lachlan is aware of her. The local police have warned her after a few residents complained she was trying to harass them for information about our family and the estate members."

I turned Arro away. "Just ignore her. She's not worth your energy."

"Ery! Arro!"

My heart leapt at the familiar voice as we looked up

across the street toward the Gloaming. Arran checked the street was clear and then jogged across, smiling at us. Anticipation and giddiness filled me at the mere sight of him.

Arro snorted at my side. "You've got it bad."

"Pot, kettle," I reminded her before turning to Arran, and just in time.

He grinned as he bridged the distance between us and then I was swept in his arms and he kissed the life out of me right in the middle of the street.

I couldn't help the little moan that escaped me, and I wound my arms around his neck to hold on. He held tighter and lifted me off the ground to increase the depth of the kiss.

"Ahem. AHEM."

At Arro's exaggerated throat clearing, Arran released me with a chuckle and lowered me to the ground. His hand settled on my hip, keeping me pulled to his side. "Oh, hello, wee sister. Just noticed you there," he teased.

Arro rolled her eyes. "Enough of the PDA, Arr. You're thirty-six, not sixteen."

"Tell that to my libido," he deadpanned.

I bit back my laughter as Arro made a comical gagging noise. "Okay, you're provoking my morning sickness, so I'm going back to work."

"First." Arran released me to step toward his sister and place a hand on her belly. "How is my niece or nephew doing in there?"

Arro smiled fondly and patted his hand. "Wee bump is doing good. We both are."

"When do we find out if it's a boy or girl?"

"We don't."

Arran frowned. "You want to be surprised?"

"We do."

"Robyn and Lachlan are going to find out. And soon, I believe."

"Well, I don't know what to say, Arran. Just because it's highly possible your sister and brother had sex with their partners at the same time and got pregnant at the same time doesn't mean we're going to do everything at the same time when it comes to our babies."

"This is a weird fucking family," he murmured.

"The weirdest. We're also the most awesome." She patted his cheek teasingly. "Just don't get Ery pregnant at the same time as Thane gets Regan pregnant, or we'll start attracting those folks who travel the world looking for strange and paranormal stories to write about it. Now I'm off. Bye, love-birds!" She shot us a grin before hurrying across the street to where she'd parked.

I barely managed to say goodbye—I was reeling from the mention of Arran getting me pregnant.

The thought wasn't nearly as scary as it should be, which was, ironically, terrifying.

"You finished for the day?" Arran asked, drawing me out of those thoughts.

"Uh, no. I need to get back to work, actually."

His gaze moved to where Arro was pulling out of her space, noting my car next to hers. It was a miracle we'd found parking today. Arro waved as she passed us.

"I'll walk you over," Arran said, taking my hand.

I chuckled. "It's literally right there."

He shrugged and pulled me across the street. When we got to my car, though, he positioned my back up against the driver's door, his hands on my hips as he pressed the length of his body to mine. This kiss was slower, sweeter than the hungry kiss he probably shouldn't have given me in front of his sister.

After a while, he broke away with soft brushes of his mouth against mine, but he didn't move. "I need to tell you something."

At the seriousness in his tone, I tensed. "What is it? Has something happened?"

Arran gave my hips a reassuring squeeze, but replied, "Aye. It's probably nothing, but I don't want to have secrets between us."

"All right ..."

"A few years back, I started getting these strange emails. They'd come every few months, always from different email addresses, all along similar lines. Just a sentence or two telling me they hadn't forgotten me or what I did."

My pulse raced. "What?"

"I have no clue what they mean, if they mean anything."

"Why didn't you tell me before now?"

"I honestly thought they were just a prank. So I deleted them. But I got one a few weeks ago, and with everything that's been happening here over the past few years, I decided to have Lachlan's team look at it."

"And?"

"They couldn't trace the email. Something about dummy IP addresses. So Lachlan gave it to his hacker."

"Nylah?"

He frowned. "You know her?"

I nodded, glancing around to make sure no one was close enough to overhear. "She's the one who uses a system to find any mention of me or my sister online and then takes the pages down."

"Right." His grip on me tightened. "Well, Nylah traced the email IP address to an internet café in Bordeaux, France. I don't know anyone there, Ery. And I haven't had an email since."

I forced myself to be rational, to not panic out of instinctual fear. The truth was, the emails *could* just be a prank. Someone who sent creepy messages to random email addresses to get a rise out of people. Especially if

Arran didn't know anyone living in Bordeaux. "Who would want to prank you? Who would have something against you?"

He shrugged, his focus drifting over my head. "I honestly don't know. I can't think of any instance that I pissed someone off that badly."

Perhaps it was because I didn't want to be dragged out of our bubble so soon, but I smoothed my hand over Arran's chest and said, "It's probably just a prank. But keep me posted. I'm glad you told me."

He seemed to relax under my touch as he studied my face. Then he pressed a sweet kiss to my nose. "You're awfully calm about this considering..."

I shrugged. "I can't be paranoid about every little thing, Arran. It's no way to live, and I don't want to do that anymore. And neither can you. So let's just *live*. And if something else happens, we'll deal with it."

Arran's eyes gleamed with something that made my breath catch. "You're amazing, you know that?" His voice was hoarse with emotion.

And it was turning me on. I squirmed against him. "Don't look at me like that when I can't do anything about it."

The cocky bastard grinned and then kissed me. Hard. Hungry. Completely inappropriately. When he finally let me up for air, my body throbbed with need.

"Now look what you did," I said breathlessly, and then gave him a little shove. "You better go, or I am not going to make it to work on time."

"Apologies." He was still looking far too smug as he stepped back to let me get into my car.

"Just for that, you're doing all the work tonight." I slid behind the wheel, but before I could close the door, Arran grabbed it.

He leaned in and pressed a quick kiss to my lips before

murmuring, "I'll keep my head buried between your thighs all night if that's what you want."

My belly flipped low and deep at the imagery. "Sounds like a plan."

"But I'm guessing you'll want my cock inside you before very long."

My cheeks burned at his crudeness and even more so at how much my body loved it. Trying not to give his ego any more reason to inflate, I raised an eyebrow and pushed him out of the car. "Let's just see if your tongue keeps up first before we think about offloading some of the work to your cock."

Arran laughed loudly in delight, surprise glittering in his eyes.

I tried not to break my sassy scowl, but my lips betrayed me, twitching with amusement. Closing the door, I pulled on my seat belt while outside my window, Arran grinned down at me.

My return smirk made him grin harder before I backed out of the space.

I felt his eyes on my car until I disappeared out of his sightline.

30

ARRAN

I kept my promise and did most of the work that evening.

The scent of sex permeated Ery's bedroom as we laid tangled together in a heap of damp, hot skin. Her head rested on my shoulder, for once her mass of curls not tickling my face as she still wore the thick twin braids she'd deftly plaited this morning. Ery's fingers traced a gentle pattern across my pecs while I caressed her upper arm.

Our breathing had finally normalized after our energetic activities of five minutes ago.

Staring at the ceiling, I couldn't help but think of all she'd confessed to me in this room less than a week ago. The truth was, I hadn't been able to think of much else. I wished that wasn't her history. I couldn't imagine losing a sibling, let alone my bloody twin. The closest to that would be losing Brodan, and that would destroy me. It would kill me to lose any of my brothers or Arro.

I glanced down at the top of Ery's head, marveling, not for the first time, at her strength. She'd lost so much. First her mum, then her grandmother, and then her sister. All of her family.

Something occurred to me, and I hesitated to say it, but curiosity, the need to know everything about her, compelled me to. "I know you said there were no leads on your dad, but have you ever considered asking Lachlan to have someone look into it? He knows a private investigator."

Ery was quiet for a moment, and I wondered if it was the wrong thing to ask. However, when she released a sigh, her warm breath fluttered across my nipple. "I've thought about it, but it was never safe to do that. I didn't want to bring unwanted attention to myself that way."

"Right. Of course." Fucking Ezra Jefferson. I'd asked Lachlan if there was anything we could do to bring that bastard down, and Lachlan said Ery had specifically asked him not to, fearful it would alert him to Ery's whereabouts. I understood that. But I hated it.

"Ultimately, no. I don't want to know my father." She sat up to look at me, a small frown between her delicate brows. "I know that sounds weird. I didn't always think that way. I went through a phase of bugging Granny about him, asking her if she was sure she didn't know just one tiny detail about him, and she was always patient and gracious. Kia hated me asking about him because she'd decided he was not worth her energy, her curiosity, her longing. But me ..."

She exhaled, and I smoothed my hand down her arm in comfort. "After Kia died, I thought about finding him again but decided I couldn't ... and then sometime in the last eight years, I stopped wanting to know. He could've abandoned my mom, for all I knew. Maybe he never knew we existed, or ... there are so many possible reasons this man has never been a part of my life. And I don't need to know anymore.

"Maybe it's being surrounded by you all and how you've made a family without parents. I just ... the truth is, it hurt for a long time not knowing my father. I think my heart decided it was hurting enough over the people I'd lost and that I didn't need to waste that pain on someone I never knew."

I drew her down to press my lips to hers. Soft, comforting. "You amaze me, Eredine Willows."

I felt her smile against my mouth, and I swear to God, it made my heart swell to three times its size. When she again settled beside me, my gaze moved across the room to where she'd tied the ribbons of her ballet shoes on the handle of the closet.

They were no longer hidden.

A few days ago, I'd walked into her bedroom and spotted them there. Just like I'd worried about her birth father, I was concerned Ery was missing something she needed to be totally happy. "How long has it been since you danced?"

She stiffened against me. "Uh, why do you ask?"

"Just curious."

"It's been awhile. It's ... I tried a few years ago. I put on my pointe shoes and let myself into my studio on the estate after hours. But every time I was about to move, I felt afraid. And alone."

Everything rebelled inside me at the thought of Eredine ever feeling lonely or scared. An idea formed, and I blurted it before I could think, "Take me with you."

"What?" She lifted her head again, expression confused.

"Let's go. Now. To the studio. You can dance again, and I'll be there, so you're not afraid or alone."

Her beautiful eyes grew wet. "You'd do that?"

"Of course." *I'd do anything for you.*

Ery looked over at the shoes. "What if ... what if my body has forgotten how?"

"It probably has forgotten a little, gorgeous, but muscle memory is a powerful thing. It'll come back to you. And I'll be there."

She was silent so long, I was about to reassure her there was no pressure—and then she whispered, "Okay. Let's try."

That was when I knew she missed dancing. Such quick capitulation to the idea.

I hated that she'd given up something that had obviously been so vital to her, and I wondered if anyone other than Lachlan and Mac even knew Eredine was once a ballerina?

"C'mon." I kissed her nose and then slid out of bed to get ready to accompany her to the estate.

THE GUARDS at the gate knew me and Ery well enough that they didn't question it when she said she'd left something she needed at the studio. We drove through the dark woodlands and out onto the estate. The sprawling, manicured lawns were also a golf course. Solar lanterns provided a dim light, leading us toward the castle. Lights along the castle's exterior cast an eerie, warm glow up the sandstone brick walls.

When I visited the home I'd grown up in, it sometimes felt like our childhood had been part of another life entirely. We'd never thought it strange that we grew up in a damp old castle until we got a little older and people seemed fascinated by that fact.

Ery parked, drawing my focus back to her, and we got out to make the ten-minute walk to her studio. It could only be reached via a path that led toward Loch Ardnoch where the studio and staff residential cabins were situated.

More solar lanterns illuminated the way around the loch. Lights were on in the staff cabins beyond, and we tried to keep our footsteps as quiet as possible on the gravel surrounding Ery's studio. She let us in and switched on the lights.

It was basically a rectangular box with a few skylights.

The wall overlooking the loch was entirely glass, the perfect space for yoga and Pilates and mindfulness. Floor-to-ceiling mirrors that had been replaced after they were destroyed during Fergus and Lucy's harassment took up the wall opposite the entrance. A door in the corner led to Ery's private changing and shower room.

Stuffing my hands in my jeans pockets, I waited, my pulse racing as I watched her nervously take off her jacket and then sit to pull her ballet shoes out of her handbag. Ery wore calf-length black leggings and a T-shirt knotted at the waist.

"You all right?" I asked, my words loud in the empty studio.

Ery looked up at me as she unwound the ribbons. She gave me a nervous nod and then gestured to the back wall. "You can sit there, if you like."

Nodding, I sat with my back against the wall, my knees drawn up, my hawklike gaze on Ery. At the first sign she was too upset to do this, I would get her out of here.

I waited, fascinated by her every move, as she did warm-up exercises. Her flexibility didn't surprise me in the least after the things we'd gotten up to in the bedroom. Plus, flexibility was kind of in her job description as a yoga and Pilates instructor.

After a while, she seemed to take a deep breath before she pulled the first worn shoe on with its flat toe. I held *my* breath as she paused a second. Then she wound the ribbons around her slim ankle and calf with nimble precision, as though she'd done it a million times before.

And she had. In another life.

Once both shoes were on, she pulled her phone out of her bag and tapped the screen twice; a classical piece soared from the speaker. Then she got up, and everything about her posture seemed to change as she walked toward the room's middle, the shoes loud against the hardwood floor.

Her whole spine seemed to elongate as she took up position.

Ery drew in another deep breath and did a few gentle squats, except they were too graceful for mere squats. Her arms floated in a routine pattern. Every inch of her, down to her fingers, formed pure elegance. "These are pliés and much easier to do with a ballet barre," she informed me quietly.

"Right," I managed through the sudden lump in my throat.

Abruptly, she pushed out her right leg, up on pointe, and spun, her calf muscles flexing as she balanced on her dominant leg. Ery stumbled out of the spin, wincing. Frustration crossed her pretty face, and I forced myself to stay quiet.

Over and over, she repeated this until she was spinning on one foot, spin after spin around the studio. My pulse raced even harder as I witnessed her transform into a dancer before my eyes.

I didn't know how long I sat there, mesmerized, as Ery grew more and more confident. Then I knew the moment she slipped into a routine, some performance buried in her memories. Emotion glimmered in her eyes, joy and relief emanating from her very soul.

Fuck, she was the most beautiful thing I'd ever seen in my life.

That lump in my throat grew bigger. My skin felt too tight and too hot as tears slipped down Eredine's cheeks. She danced as if she were an extension of the music.

Finally, she slowed to a stop, chest heaving, sweat gleaming on her skin. Her T-shirt was stuck to her. She looked at me and whispered, "Thank you."

And I knew in that moment that I loved her.

I was in love with Eredine Willows.

Pushing to my feet, I bridged the distance between us and pulled her into my arms. She held on so tight, sobbing against me. I'd have been worried if I didn't understand her so completely. These were good tears. Cathartic.

Her feet were red and blistering when she took off the dance shoes, but she told me that was normal, that her feet would bleed and shred before they were strong enough again for dancing on pointe. I didn't like the thought of that, but it wasn't my place. If dancing made Ery happy, then it was worth the pain.

I held her hand as we walked in silence back to the car a little while later. It wasn't until we were out of the gates and heading through the village when I said, "You're a beautiful dancer. Thank you for letting me be with you for that."

She reached over and squeezed my knee. "Thank you." Then she gave a huff of dry laughter. "And my technique is all over the place. I don't know if I'll ever get that back."

I frowned. "You looked good to me."

"It can look pretty to someone who doesn't know ballet so well, but trust me, no dance company would ever take me on in this condition. I'm too old now, anyway."

"At thirty-two?" I scoffed.

"Yeah. Thirty-two is old in the dance world. I don't want to join a company. I just ... I wanted to see if it still felt like it used to."

"How did it used to feel?"

She considered this and then replied, "I imagine how it feels to be an actor or even a storyteller. Pure escapism into another person, into another story. It sparks my imagination like a beautiful piece of music does, or my favorite book. I've missed that feeling."

"So then dance for yourself. You don't need to dance for anyone else."

Ery was quiet a moment. "Do you think Lachlan would let me install a barre? I'd pay for it."

I reached over to take her hand and squeezed it. "Of

course. But you know he won't let you pay for it, and I know *you* won't let *him* pay for it. It'll be fun to see who wins, though my money is on you."

She laughed, and the sound only emphasized the magnitude of my feelings. When we got home, Ery practically jumped me. She kissed me and pulled at my clothes as we stumbled into her bedroom.

I didn't want frantic, though.

I wanted to memorize every inch of her.

I wanted to make love to her.

So I did.

We held each other's eyes, tension and intensity heightening our desire as I moved slowly, gently, inside her. It took time to build the pressure, so agonizingly good that I knew the payoff would be fucking fantastic.

And it was.

Ery came around me so hard, I felt every voluptuous throb of her inner muscles around my cock. My orgasm hit with such force, I bellowed her name as I came.

Holding myself over her, my face pressed to her throat, trying not to crush her with the full weight of my body, I felt those three words bubbling up inside me.

Christ, I wanted to tell her so badly.

But this was all still new between us. Although we'd known each other for a year, Ery had only just shared her past with me a week ago.

I was afraid if I told her I loved her now, it would chase her off.

So instead, I kissed her. I kissed her as if my lips comprised those three words, and when I finally pulled back to look into her eyes, I saw tears of amazement in them.

It was as if she'd felt every syllable of my silent declaration.

31

EREDINE

"I think this leaving the bride before the wedding day is nonsense." Thane's words carried down the upstairs hallway.

I was in the guest room Arro and I would be sharing for the night. The wedding dresses were safely hidden in here, along with Robyn's and my bridesmaid gowns.

"It's tradition, so you don't see the bride in her wedding dress before the big event," Regan explained unnecessarily. She giggled, and I raised an eyebrow. "Thane, you can handle a night without me. In fact, I bet you're looking forward to it."

"Never, *Mo leannan*." There was silence, and then a female moan.

My cheeks colored. Had they forgotten I was up here too?

"Okay, okay," Regan said breathlessly. "We have to stop. You need to leave."

"Stupid bloody tradition." I heard Thane murmur. Then louder, he said, "You're already my wife in my mind and in my heart. You know that, right?"

"I do. And just to freak you out, you've been my husband

in my head since my first day officially as your nanny when you found me in the kitchen making the kids' lunches."

"That soon, hmm?" I heard the rumble of amusement in his voice and was starting to feel very guilty for eavesdropping.

"That soon. And now it's really happening, I can barely believe it."

"Do you know how happy you make me, *Mo leannan*?"

"As happy as you make me."

I grimaced at the obvious sounds of a passionate make-out, looking for an escape where there was none. Thankfully, however, Regan broke free and forced Thane downstairs.

Now that I knew I wasn't about to be forced to listen to them having sex, I could smile at what I'd accidentally overheard. Anyone who met Thane Adair would never believe he was sappy and romantic with his fiancée. No wonder Regan was head over heels.

I'd watched him during family events and occasions looking at her as if she was the most perfect thing he'd ever seen, but to hear him be so free with his affection was heartwarming.

And tomorrow Regan would finally be his wife on paper, too, and I couldn't be happier for them.

For the double wedding, it was decided that all the girls would stay at Thane and Regan's the night before, and all the boys at Lachlan and Robyn's. Robyn and Regan were sharing a room, and Eilidh would probably join them, while I was sharing with Arro. It would be like a giant jittery slumber party. It had always been nice to be included like this by the Adair family, but now that I was with Arran, it felt *more* somehow. And it brought me the kind of peace I hadn't dared hope for in such a long time.

As I crossed the room to go downstairs, now that it was

safe to emerge, I caught sight of two people out the bedroom window. Arro and Mac were on the back lawn.

An ache, the good kind, flared to life inside me. Mac had Arro's face clasped in his hands. They pressed their foreheads together while Arro clung to his waist. I didn't know if words were being exchanged or if they were just holding each other. Even from up here, I could feel the love between them. It was so special. Then Mac lowered to his haunches to speak to Arro's belly. Whatever he said made Arro throw her head back in laughter. She didn't see the look on Mac's face when he stared up at her. But I did. My God, did that man love her. It was epic.

He stood and drew her into a kiss that turned so passionate, I moved away from the window to give them privacy.

My smart, kind, strong, loyal friend had waited a long time for Mac, and I was so beyond thankful he had worked so hard on himself to offer her the life she'd wanted with him.

Yeah, I thought, a small smile on my lips as I walked downstairs toward the raucous sounds of the whole family together, *I feel content*.

Everyone I loved was happy, and that was more than anyone could hope for.

THE LAST TIME I was inside the reception hall of the Gloaming, it had been dark, despite its high ceiling. That had a lot to do with the wood paneling on the walls, now completely gone. Arran's team had replaced the paneling with light stone brickwork and revealed a vault in the high ceiling by opening it up so the beam supports were visible.

Garlands of fairy lights, attached to three large hoop lighting fixtures across the ceiling, draped like a canopy and were connected to the walls on either side. The tables were dressed simply in white linen, the wicker chairs unadorned. Copper lanterns with white candles inside served as centerpieces, surrounded by elegant wreaths of white peonies.

A ceilidh band had played during the wedding dinner, but now as people mingled and danced on the newly replaced dance floor, music blared from the deejay station.

I stared around at the mostly familiar faces. Regan and Thane chatted with Regan and Robyn's mom and Regan's dad (Robyn's stepdad) Seth. Eilidh and Lewis were out on the dance floor with Robyn and Lachlan. Arro and Mac swayed out of sync to the too-fast music, oblivious to anyone but each other.

Both Regan and Arro had chosen elegant, simple wedding gowns. Regan's was white crepe with delicate straps, a V neckline, and a silhouette that skimmed her slender curves and then flared at the knees. The only detail was its scooped cowl back and row of buttons down her derriere and train. It was almost like a simplified version of Robyn's wedding dress. If Regan looked like a Hollywood starlet, Arro looked like a fairy-tale princess. Their dresses couldn't have been more different.

Arro's dress had cap sleeves that, like the bodice, were made from an off-white material cut into leaves and flowers. They were delicately sewn onto the sheer bodice fabric and cascaded down over her baby bump into a sheer tulle skirt. It had a silk underskirt, so she wasn't naked under the tulle, but that, with her delicate silver floral crown the stylist had woven into her platinum waves, created an overall ethereal look that suited Arro to a T.

Mac had teared up when she walked down the aisle toward him, while Thane had looked impatient for Regan to reach him, as if he was desperate to have her be his wife as quickly as possible.

Neither groom had been able to take their eyes off their brides, and it was a miracle I noticed because I was distracted by the fact that Arran couldn't take his eyes off me.

Like Robyn, I wore a pale lavender bridesmaid gown that suited both brides' aesthetic.

My gaze sought out Arran now.

He'd left for the barroom to get more drinks. With the ceremony concluded, the speeches done, and dinner finished, everyone was relaxed and looking to get happy. A guest I didn't recognize, a young woman and her female companion, had caught Arran, and from where I was sitting, it looked like he was flirting with them.

I knew he meant nothing by it, and I tried not to be bothered, considering I was certain I was the only woman he cared about. Arran had made that perfectly clear.

The flirting was just second nature to him. He couldn't help it.

My eyes narrowed as he laughed at something the pretty brunette said.

"This seat taken?"

I looked up at the familiar voice, and a mix of affection, discomfort, and concern filled me at the sight of Brodan Adair. He'd flown in last night. And although he'd look gorgeous in any situation, the dark circles under his eyes and the general haggard strain on his features worried me. If the glances his siblings had been throwing him throughout the day meant anything, I'd say they were concerned too.

The man looked exhausted.

And sad.

"Please, sit." I pushed out the chair next to me with my foot, and he slumped into it.

Once upon a time, Brodan could tongue-tie me. He was technically the most classically handsome of the Adair siblings, with a Captain America thing going on, massively broad shoulders, tapered waist, and long legs. He used to be clean-cut, but the last time I saw him, he had scruff, and today he was sporting an unkempt beard that Arro said was for his current film. His usually vibrantly pale-blue eyes were bloodshot.

"Are you all right?" I asked as he unbuttoned his kilt jacket and shot me an assessing glance.

He shrugged, his gaze dipping down my body, and back up to my face. "You look well. Happy."

"I am," I said truthfully.

"Arran?"

I nodded, even though talking about his brother made me uncomfortable considering the years-long flirtation that had gone on between Brodan and me.

But Brodan smiled wearily. "I am glad. For you both. My brother's a good man."

Relief moved through me. I knew they had a rough history with Monroe, and I was soothed to hear it wasn't affecting Brodan's opinion of Arran.

I looked past his shoulder to where Arran was still talking with those women. Brodan followed my stare and then looked back at me.

I shrugged. "I wish he'd flirt less, but that's an Adair trait, I think."

"He's not flirting. Believe me." Brodan sighed. "He's just social."

"It looks like flirting to me, but it's okay. I trust him."

"You should. I've never seen my brother look at a woman the way he looks at you." He glanced over his shoulder at Arran, and we discovered he was looking our way. Brodan sighed and turned back to me. "I've watched him all day with you. You have nothing to worry about when it comes to other women."

"I know that." I leaned over and touched his arm. "Brodan, are we okay?"

"Of course, we're okay. Ery, I just want you to be happy."

At the abject misery I saw buried behind that Adair twinkle, I pushed. "Are *you* okay?"

For a moment, something flickered across his gaze, and he hesitated. But before he could respond, Arran slid up to the table with our drinks and set them in front of Brodan.

He clamped a hand on Brodan's shoulder. "Sorry, Bro, didn't get you anything. Want me to go back and order something for you?"

Brodan shook his head and stood. "Nah, I think I'll go spend some time with my niece and nephew."

He was gone before another word could be exchanged.

Arran narrowed his eyes on him and then took his seat. "Everything all right?"

"Between us, yes. But with him …" I watched Brodan pick Eilidh up and spin her, squeals of delight cutting through the music. "I'm worried about him."

"Me too." Arran moved closer to me, stretching his arm around the back of my chair. "He looks fucking exhausted."

"He's working too hard."

Studying my face now, Arran asked, "He say anything else?"

"Not really. He was just keeping me company while you flirted." I wrinkled my nose at him.

He smirked. "I wasn't flirting. It's called conversation with a member of the opposite sex."

"It looked like flirting from here. She kept touching your arm."

"*I* wasn't flirting." He kissed my nose. "I promise."

"I don't mind if you were. You can't help yourself. But I trust you."

Instead of this pleasing him, Arran scowled. "I can't help myself? I wasn't flirting, Ery."

Surprised at his vehemence, I held up my hands defensively. "Okay, I'm sorry."

Suddenly, he gripped the nape of my neck and pulled me none too gently toward him. His lips crashed down on mine. It was a hard, sexual, claiming kiss, and extremely inappropriate in public. But I couldn't seem to yank myself out of it.

It was only when we heard a voice yell, "Get a room!" over the music that we parted. Flushing as wedding guests laughed, I caught Arro turning on the dance floor to smack Will playfully across the biceps. Will was Regan's friend, fiancé to Jock, one of the estate security guards. Jock had a son from a previous relationship and was a single father when Will, an artist, arrived in Ardnoch and swept Jock into a romance he'd never expected. When Regan was nanny to Eilidh and Lewis, she'd met Will at the school gates, and they'd formed a fast friendship.

I didn't know him that well, but that didn't seem to stop him from catcalling us.

"Sorry," Arran murmured, his gaze searching mine. "Just … I know I was a player before, but that was long before you. There's been no one but you in months, and I never want you to think that this isn't serious for me or that I think it's okay to flirt with other women."

Lord, now I felt bad. "Arran, it's okay. I'm sorry. I misinterpreted it and … I'm sorry."

He brushed his mouth over mine. "You're all I see."

My breath caught, my pulse racing. "You're all *I* see."

A cry broke the moment, and we turned to see what the ruckus was.

Shock jolted through me as Arran cursed and lunged from his chair.

Brodan laid sprawled on his back in the middle of the dance floor while Eilidh sobbed and Arro bent over him, searching his neck for a pulse.

32

ARRAN

Brodan stared belligerently at Lachlan, quite a feat considering how knackered he was. I had Arro, still in her wedding dress, tucked into my side as Lachlan glowered down at our brother. Thane stood behind Lachlan, arms crossed over his chest, wearing an equally pissed-off expression.

Mac was outside the private hospital room in the nearby waiting area with Regan, Robyn, Ery, and the kids.

"It was nothing," Brodan insisted.

Lachlan looked like he was ready to pop a vein, and I didn't blame him. "You're on a fucking drip because you just collapsed from exhaustion at your siblings' weddings."

"And I'll feel better soon." Brodan looked between Thane and Arro. "I'm sorry I ruined your reception."

"You didn't—"

Thane cut Arro off. "You didn't ruin the reception, but you are ruining our peace of mind. What the hell is going on with you, Brodan?"

"I'll tell you what's going on with him." Lachlan looked at us and then back to Brodan. "I've had a word with your

267

manager and your agent, and your manager is running you ragged. He's a soul-sucking vampire, and your agent is a weak arsehole for not speaking up."

Brodan sighed heavily. "I'm a big boy. I can handle the work."

"He says from a hospital bed. Well, it's done. I fired your manager an hour ago."

Whoa.

"You did what?" Bro asked, his voice lethally quiet.

Our big brother didn't even flinch. "You heard me. I'm your temporary new manager, and my first order of business is to clear your schedule for the next few months so you can recuperate."

"You high-handed bastard," Brodan snapped.

"Aye, I'll take on that role. I'll be the bastard. But at least my wee brother will be looked after."

Brodan moved to get off the bed, and Arro rushed forward to press a hand to his chest. "Please," she begged.

His eyes widened at her tear-filled plea, and he softened. "I'm fine, Arro."

She shook her head. "You're not fine."

"This isn't just about today," Thane added. "You've been avoiding this family for over a year. Acting cagey. Distant. It isn't like you. Christ, it's like you and Arran switched personalities."

"Hey," I grumbled.

Brodan shot me a pleading look, but I was with my brothers and sister on this one. I was worried as hell about Bro. He must have seen that on my face because he slumped back against the stiff pillow. "I have to finish the film I'm in the middle of."

Lachlan considered this. "Fine. You finish the film, and then you come home to recuperate afterward."

"Lachlan—"

"Brodan, you've made more money in the last few years than anyone needs. And to be frank, some of these films you've signed on to in the coming months have awful scripts. You've not been paying attention to what that fucking manager has been agreeing to, have you?"

"And how do you know? You can't possibly have read the scripts in the two hours since I passed out."

Our big brother at once looked a little guilty. "I might have talked to your agent a few weeks ago and persuaded him to let me see them."

"Then you might as well fire him too." Brodan glared. "You do realize I'm a grown fucking man."

"Who has changed before his family's eyes in the last few years, and we don't know why. What I *do* know is that you've been on some kamikaze mission to work yourself into an early grave, and it stops now. I don't care how old you are. I am the head of this family. You could be seven, thirty-seven, or seventy-seven, and I would still be here to pull your head out of your arse when necessary."

"Oh, Christ, whatever." Brodan closed his eyes and sagged into the bed.

I didn't want to piss off Lachlan even more, but I felt bad for Bro. "Maybe we can finish this discussion once he's not in the hospital?"

Everyone reluctantly filed out of the room, leaving me and Brodan alone. I sat on the chair next to his bed and drew it closer.

He opened his eyes. "You know I'm just playing along. There's no way I'm letting that son of a bitch take over my life. Once I'm out of here, it's back to filming."

"Don't call him a son of a bitch."

Brodan winced. "Sorry."

"I'm not going to argue with you." Mostly because I knew there was no way Lachlan wouldn't follow through on trying

269

to manage Brodan's life and yank him out of the crazy schedule. I trusted Lachlan to take care of our brother. "But can I ask why you're so set on doing this when you're clearly miserable? I've never seen you this unhappy."

He looked up at the ceiling. "I'm fine."

My frustration grew. "You know everything about me. I trusted you with that. Why can't you trust me?"

"It's not that simple."

"So, there is something going on that I should be concerned about?"

"Nothing's going on. I'm fine."

Angry, I pushed out of my chair. "When you want to talk, I'll be here. But I will not sit and take it while you lie to me."

"*That,*" he snapped. "That is why I can't be here."

"Why?"

"Because you'll all pester the fuck out of me to talk when there's nothing to talk about."

Lies.

But his words halted me in my tracks. "Okay. What if I could guarantee none of us would do that ... would you come home?"

"Lachlan can't help himself."

"Lachlan, believe it or not, is pretty preoccupied by his pregnant wife at the moment and will be even more so when the baby arrives. Same for Mac and Arro. The kids keep Thane busy. And you're missing it all, Bro. For shit that I can tell doesn't even make you that happy anymore. I think you miss us as much as we miss you."

Emotion glimmered in his eyes, and he swallowed hard. "Of course, I miss you all."

"Then come home. I will talk to the others, and I will make sure they know pestering or interrogating you is not on the menu."

He sighed heavily again. "It's not that simple. Lachlan is

making it out like it's simple, but I can't just walk away from films I've signed on for."

"Aye, you can. It happens all the time."

Brodan scrubbed a hand over his face and admitted quietly, "I am so bloody tired."

"Then come home."

After what felt like the longest minute ever, he gave me a wee nod. "I'll think about it. I promise."

I nodded at Brodan's bodyguard, Walker, who stood outside my brother's private room with another bodyguard I didn't recognize. After a quick huddle with my siblings in the waiting room where I explained what I'd promised, they reluctantly agreed that they wouldn't push Brodan away by pressing too hard to know what was going on with him.

"Maybe being home will make him naturally want to confide in you," Ery offered quietly.

"Exactly what I was thinking," Regan agreed.

"Fine." Lachlan nodded. "I'll back off. Unless he doesn't come home after this job, and then I will physically haul him back. Or my security team will."

Robyn rolled her eyes. "You can't force him to do something he doesn't want to do."

"Aye, I bloody can."

"When are they discharging him?" Mac asked. He held Eilidh in his arms, and she'd fallen asleep. Lewis dozed on a dull vinyl chair beside us.

"A few hours. You guys go." Lachlan waved them off and reached for a sleepy Eilidh. "Go enjoy your wedding night. Robyn and I have the kids."

"And I'll stay here," I said. "I'll make sure Brodan gets home."

"I'll stay with you." Ery caressed my arm.

"You sure?"

"Of course."

I wrapped my arm around her and pulled her close. She wore my kilt jacket over her flimsy bridesmaid gown.

We walked our family out of the hospital. I felt like shit for the newly wedded couples for how their big day had ended, but I imagined Brodan felt worse. Thankfully, both couples had booked honeymoons later in the year, so they wouldn't have to fly out tonight worrying about Bro.

I stood off to the side as Ery hugged Arro for a long time, and my phone vibrated in the sporran attached over my kilt. Pulling it out, my pulse skittered upon seeing the email notification. I tapped it, and the email opened.

Told you I hadn't forgotten about you. And now I see you've found yourself a girl. Eredine. Such a pretty name. I'd like to get to know her better.

Fuck.

Fuck. *Fuck.*

Hands shaking with rage, I stalked across the car park to where Lachlan had just eased Eilidh into the back seat of an Ardnoch Range Rover. Drivers from the estate had arrived at the Gloaming to take us to the hospital, since we were all too drunk to drive.

I grabbed my brother's arm after he closed the car door.

He frowned. "What is it?"

I showed him the email.

His expression darkened. "This is all we need."

"I know."

"Forward it to me. I'll have Nylah look into it." He glanced over at Ery, who was talking quietly with Regan now. "Maybe don't tell her until I know more. No point worrying her until we have some solid information."

"You think?"

"Ultimately, it's up to you. But it's been a long day, and she might not sleep if you show her that."

I didn't want to keep things from Ery or treat her like she

was fragile. Yet part of me wondered if Lachlan was right. Maybe it was better to hold off telling her until we knew where the email came from. Damn it. "I won't be able to let her out of my sight now."

"Try not to act strange, or she'll know something is up." He clamped a hand on my shoulder. "Call me if you need me."

"I will." But I hoped to God I didn't need to.

33

EREDINE

The few days since the wedding and Brodan's collapse had been a whirlwind of Adair family activity. While I got back to work at the estate, Arran was rushed off his feet at work with tourists piling into the Gloaming during the day and work moving toward completion in the guest rooms. We'd barely gotten an hour or two together at night. Brodan flew back to Vancouver for the movie he was shooting, but Arran told me that Lachlan offered Walker, Brodan's longtime bodyguard, who was staying at the estate with Brodan's private security team, a bonus for keeping Lachlan informed of Brodan's well-being. Walker had refused the money, shocking in itself, but he'd promised Lachlan he'd look out for their brother.

Arran told me about the conversation in the hospital room and how Lachlan *had* fired Brodan's manager and temporarily taken over managing Brodan's career. I knew Brodan well enough to know that he would have put up more of a fight if he hadn't been amenable to Lachlan managing him. Which told me, beneath his stoic utterances of "I'm fine" and his distant behavior, he still needed and wanted his family around.

Lachlan pulled Brodan out of unsuitable projects and cleared his schedule after the movie in Canada. He was supposed to do a press tour for a big movie coming up, but Lachlan was planning to cancel that too. He already had Brodan's flight booked to return to Scotland in six weeks, once shooting finished.

I personally thought it was too high-handed of him, considering Brodan was a grown man, but Arran seemed on board with the plan to force his brother to take a break in Ardnoch. Which told me he was really worried about Brodan.

As for the rest of the Adairs, well, I hadn't seen and barely heard from Arro and Mac, who had shacked up in their bungalow for a little mini honeymoon. Regan and Thane were as busy as ever with the kids, and Regan was helping Robyn design the nursery.

Everything was somewhat back to normal, which was probably why I'd forgotten about the strange emails Arran had been receiving. And why, when I returned home from work the following Tuesday evening, that the vase of vibrant flowers sitting at my front door didn't register as anything ominous.

I grinned as I walked up the porch, thinking Arran one of the most romantic men I'd ever met. Squatting, I breathed in the scent of the gorgeous, long-stemmed red roses and plucked the card from their midst.

Cold nausea prickled over me as I read the typed words on the card.

You didn't think I'd forget about you, did you? I never forget what's mine. See you soon.

Arran's emails immediately came to mind. I dropped the card like it might be covered in poison and ran back to my car. Locking myself inside it, I fumbled for my cell, adrenaline shaking my hands as I pressed speed dial.

"Pick up, pick up, pick up," I gasped as the line rang out.

Then click. "Gorgeous, can I call you back—"

"Someone left flowers on my porch with a creepy card in it."

"Where are you?" Arran barked.

"In my car, in my driveway. My doors are locked."

"Get out of there now. Drive toward the village. We'll meet in the middle."

THIRTY MINUTES LATER, we were back at my lodge. Arran had checked every inch of the place, and now we were scrolling through CCTV footage.

We watched as a car pulled up to my house around midday and a woman got out. She took the vase of flowers out from the back and walked to the porch. Her face was clear as she knocked on my door.

"That's Beth." She owned Bethany's Flower Pot, the florist situated on a lane off Castle Street.

"We'll need to call her and see if she can give us any information," Arran said, his features strained with worry as he turned to me. "I need to tell you something."

I nodded, not liking his tone.

"I got an email. On Saturday night while Brodan was in the hospital."

I tensed. "A creepy email?"

"Aye. But this time it mentioned you by name." He pulled out his cell, tapped the screen a few times, and then held up the email. I read it, the earlier nausea returning.

Looking up from the email to Arran's face, indignation flooded me. "Why didn't you tell me?"

"I was going to. I just … I wanted to wait until Nylah found something. She's going to trace it for us, but she's in the middle of something for another client. But when Lachlan gets here, I'll ask him to pressure her to deliver. Now that"—he scowled at the bouquet on my dining table—"things have escalated."

Arran had called Lachlan and Mac, who were on their way right now. But I didn't care about that at the moment. I cared Arran had kept this from me. "You should have told me."

"I was going to. I was never keeping it from you."

"You should have told me when you got it."

"I didn't want to pile it on. We'd had a crap night with Brodan, and I thought if I showed you the email, you'd freak out, and I didn't want that for you."

And while I understood where he was coming from, I needed him to understand something. "Now that we're in a relationship, I know things are different between us and that you want to protect me from anything hurtful, just as I want to protect you. But you have never treated me like I'm not strong enough to handle the truth, and I really don't want you to start now. Do you know the reason I let you bulldoze your way into my life within weeks compared to the years it took Arro and the girls?"

"Bulldoze?" He frowned.

I smirked. "Yes, bulldoze. I let you in faster than anyone. Partly because of this amazing connection between us, but mostly, at the time, because you treated me like I wasn't a delicate little flower everyone had to tiptoe around. You made me feel seen in a way I hadn't for a long time. You didn't keep anything from me. You were always honest. I need that from you, Arran."

"You have that from me." He held me by the arms and

dipped his head to look deeply into my eyes. "I will never keep anything from you again."

Hearing the sincerity in his voice, I nodded, and he sagged with relief, pulling me into his arms where he held me while we quietly pondered what this new threat could mean.

NOT LONG LATER, after a call to Beth, who told us the flower order was made online but that she couldn't give out details unless the police were involved, Lachlan and Mac arrived.

They were grim-faced as they walked into my lodge, and I was engulfed in one hug after the other, my promises that I was doing okay seeming to fall on deaf ears. Yes, I was freaked. Of course, I was. But I was determined to remain calm while we figured this out.

After they studied the card and then shared a look, Lachlan turned to us. "Nylah contacted me this morning. She discovered a video of you and Eredine on a social media platform. Nylah's software program only detects keywords, and so she does a more complex check herself once a month. The video was posted by that annoying fucking journalist who was hanging around Ardnoch this summer. It's a montage of you and Ery kissing, walking together, and talking on Castle Street. She named you both in the actual video. Nylah has deleted it, but she said it was up for two weeks before she found it, and it had over half a million views. I was going to come and tell you tonight, but then this ..." He gestured to the flowers.

And there went my calm.

Full-on panic threatened to take me out. Buzzing sounded in my ears as I stumbled away from them, trying to catch my breath.

"Ery?" Arran touched me, but I jerked away, feeling claustrophobic.

The flowers and the card took on a whole new meaning now.

He'd sent flowers and gifts and creepy cards to Kia before—

"It's him." I turned to glare at Lachlan. "It's Ezra, isn't it?"

Lachlan held up his hands, palms outward, as he walked toward me, as if approaching a frightened animal. "The first thing I did was check his whereabouts, and he's in Washington. I didn't want to mention this, but I've been trying to dig up as much dirt on this guy as possible over the years. It hasn't been easy, but he's hurt a lot of women, Ery. The evidence is mounting, and I hope that soon we'll have enough witness accounts to go after him."

"You said you wouldn't dig!" I cried, not reassured at all. "You'll bring him here!"

"He doesn't know it's me. I've hired private detectives who are very discreet and good at what they do. This isn't something I went into lightly. And it's taken me a long time to get close to where we are right now."

"Why didn't you tell her this? Or me? I asked you directly, and you lied," Arran said in a quiet manner that sent a chill down my spine. He looked at Lachlan like he wanted to rip off his head.

"I lied because I was worried you'd tell Ery, and I didn't want her to panic or get her hopes up."

"She's not made of glass, Lachlan. She can handle knowing the truth. You shouldn't have kept this from her."

Mac joined the fray. "This isn't likely to be Ezra. Arran has been receiving these odd emails for years, and this is the only time Ery has been mentioned in them. It's rational to assume whoever is sending the emails saw the video online and is using Ery to scare Arran. That's where our focus should be."

His words penetrated, and I forced myself to process what Mac was saying. He was probably right. Everything added up to this being the person harassing Arran. Yet I was still so pissed at Lachlan.

"Fine." I clenched my fists. "We'll focus on that. But, Lachlan ..."

He gave me a tender, worried look.

Yet I had to say this.

"I am more than grateful for what you've done for me—"

"Ery—"

"No, let me finish." I held his gaze. "Nothing you ever do will take away that gratitude. But you have to stop treating me like I'm a delicate flower that will break in half at the slightest breeze. I'm a grown woman. Your brothers and sister are grown-ups too. And while I think we will all always need you, you are not solely responsible for fixing our problems. I'm not fragile, and they're no longer kids who need a parent. It doesn't have to be all on you. Let us be a team now. Keep us in the loop. Make decisions *with* us, not for us. Okay?"

Lachlan stared at me, stunned.

After a moment of awkward silence as he looked to Arran and over his shoulder at Mac, Lachlan turned back to me and nodded slowly. "All right."

It was easier to merely concentrate on the morning breeze caressing my sweat-slickened skin. To watch the golden sand compact under my feet, feeling the rhythmic, gentle rush of the water to shore, inhale the salt air, and watch the sun break through the clouds in rays of soft light.

Dark green hills loomed in the distance where the earth jutted into the sea, reminding me I was running away from Ardnoch.

That thought cut through my intense focus on the run and my surroundings.

Ery.

I glanced to my side and noted she was nowhere to be seen. Panicked, and I stumbled, glancing over my shoulder. Relief replaced the panic as I saw her about a hundred yards behind.

Uneasiness shifted through me. I wanted to keep running, but I forced myself to stand still, to wait for her to catch up. Then I noted the time on my watch and realized we needed to head back, anyway. Jogging to meet her, I couldn't look at her face for too long. Behind her, a dog ran into the water.

Their owner was a dark dot farther down the beach toward the caravan park. This place would be busy by midday.

"You just took off," Ery said as we met.

"Sorry," I mumbled. "We need to get back." Before she could ask any questions, I ran. Guilt stopped me from outpacing her, and we kept stride as we headed back down the beach toward the car park.

I could feel her looking at me, but I didn't want to think about it. I didn't want to think about the fact that I was staying with her at her lodge because she'd received a new gift every day since I got the email mentioning her. All the gifts came with cards that insinuated the person would see her soon. Ery was handling it better than I might have imagined, considering her traumatic past. But she was quiet and despondent, her fear hidden behind the forced smiles.

All of it because of me.

I'd brought this shit back into her life. I'd blithely ignored that I had famous brothers and that people took photographs of me. It wasn't the first time. I'd had peace from it in Thailand, but after Lachlan became a big action star, Arro and I ended up in magazines and online articles too. It didn't happen often, but it happened.

And I'd come home and acted like that stuff didn't touch me, even knowing there was an arsehole journalist kicking around the village. So focused on being a fucking caveman and making sure everyone knew Eredine was mine, I'd kissed and held her in public without thinking of the consequences. Without thinking about her need to stay out of the limelight, her need for privacy.

Just like when I ran into the water in Thailand four years ago because all I was thinking about was myself and what I wanted in that moment. And Colin died from my selfishness.

Now I'd put Ery in danger too.

I'd break if anything happened to her. And if anything

happened to her because of me, that was the kind of break I'd never come back from.

We still had no answers to who was behind this. The latest email tracked to the same internet café in Bordeaux, so Nylah was trying to access their CCTV. She would send me footage from the exact moment the email was sent so I could check to see if I recognized anyone. Until then, we were in the dark.

Before I knew it, we were running up dunes and back into the beach car park. I kicked my toes against one of the SUV's tires to loosen the sand from my running shoes and was aware of Eredine on the passenger side doing the same.

We got into the car, and as I switched on the engine, she touched my forearm.

I stared at her elegant hand instead of her beautiful face.

"Arran ... what's going on?" she asked quietly, worry a tremor in her voice.

Swallowing against the lump in my throat, I couldn't muster up a fake smile and a "nothing" for her.

All I wanted to do was to protect her from whoever was harassing me.

And that meant getting her out of the line of fire.

EREDINE

MY NERVES WERE SHOT as I dressed for work. Arran had been distant all week, but this morning was worse. He'd run ahead of me on the beach, as if he'd forgotten I was there. And then he'd refused to talk in the car on the way back. I was beginning to feel like a ghost, and I was losing my patience.

Anger and frustration bubbled up, mostly because anger was easier than fear. Frankly, I was terrified I was losing Arran. I didn't know why, but I knew when someone was pulling away from me.

"You ready?" He strode into the bedroom.

He'd taken to not quite looking at me, and that was pissing me off too.

I scowled, snatched up my cell, and shoved past him. I heard him follow as I marched into the living room and grabbed my favorite pair of work sneakers off the shoe rack by the door.

"Ery?"

Afraid I was seconds from exploding, I ignored him. Instead, I pulled on my shoes and then grabbed my purse from the dining table.

"Ery?" Arran came into my line of sight.

I glowered up at him as he frowned down at me. "Oh, so now you want to talk? Now you want to make eye contact?"

Arran blanched and looked away.

Fear made my pulse race. "What is going on? You've barely said a word to me all week, locked up inside your own head."

"You've been quiet too."

"But not in the shutting-you-out kind of way. I'm not the one who tenses every time you touch me." It was true. The last few days, he'd pulled away from my touch, and I hated how much that hurt.

Scrubbing a hand down his face, he sighed, like this entire conversation was trying his patience. "Can we talk about this after work?"

"No, I want to talk about it right now. What the hell is going on with you?"

Finally, he looked me in the eye.

But his expression made me feel cold.

A lot roiled in his gaze, but the guilt scared me. I'd had boyfriends wear that look right before they broke things off.

I felt sick.

"I think ..." The muscle in his jaw ticked as he hesitated. But then, "I think we should put some distance between us. Just while all this is going on. That way, whoever this is who's harassing me will think you mean nothing to me anymore. You'll be safe."

He couldn't be serious. "You want to break up with me ... to save me?"

"Exactly."

"And what happens when we find this person and it's all over? Do we just get back together and pretend like it never happened?"

Arran stared grimly at me but didn't respond.

Oh.

A horrible pain cut through me, flaring into a burn below my breastbone. I wanted to rub the spot, to ease the sensation. But I didn't want to give him the satisfaction of seeing how much this hurt.

The whole stalker thing was just an excuse to break up.

He wasn't man enough to tell me that this was permanent.

I wanted to ask why. Why really?

Had he grown bored already?

Was he really just a player, after all, not cut out to be someone's boyfriend?

"I want you to move in with Robyn and Lachlan or Mac and Arro. Just until we figure out this situation. I don't want you alone here."

I was alone here. He'd made certain of that. And I stupidly allowed myself to depend on him. I'd let myself get used to his presence.

"I've already stayed with Robyn and Lachlan because of this stuff in the past, and I won't be a burden to them again."

"You're not a burden," Arran insisted, aggravated.

Fuck him and his aggravation. "I'm tired of running. Of hiding. I'm staying here. If you want to use this as a pathetic excuse to get out of this relationship, you do that. But I'm going to continue to live my life."

His nostrils flared. "Pathetic excuse? That's not what this is. I'm trying to *protect* you. Even if that means protecting you from me."

What did that mean? I narrowed my eyes. "I don't even know what's going on in your head right now. Do you want to clue me in?"

He shrugged. "I just told you."

"Okay. Well, that's bullshit, and I thought we were past this. If you want to leave, Arran, leave. But *never* come back."

I thought something like anxiety flashed across his face. "Ery—"

"You heard me." I grabbed my purse and keys and strode across the room, my heart hammering. "Stay. Or get your stuff together and get out of my life. For good." I slammed the door behind me and hurried down the porch to my car.

I peeled out like I was in a car chase, and it was only once I was on the road that I let the tears fall.

They fell so hard, I had to pull over.

35

ARRAN

"*If you want to leave, Arran, leave. But never come back.*"

Eredine's words pounded in my head over and over as I sat in Lachlan's kitchen, nursing the beer my eldest brother had set before me.

I kept trying to tell myself that this was for the best and that once all this was over, I could convince Ery to give me another chance.

If I was worthy of another chance.

If I could learn to be less selfish and think before I took what I wanted.

My gut churned, and the beer didn't help, but still, I swallowed another sip.

Arro and Mac had promised they'd go to Ery's and convince her to stay with them for now. Arro said she would text to let me know once they had her home with them, safe and sound, but I hadn't heard anything yet.

"I'm going next door to spend time with Regan." Robyn brought my head up from my phone. I sat on a bar stool at their kitchen counter. Robyn gave me a worried look before leaning up to kiss the corner of Lachlan's mouth.

His hand automatically grazed her belly as he bent his head for her, and I envied him as he shared a tender look with his wife.

When she was gone, Lachlan sat on the stool beside mine. He studied me, brows creased with concern. "Why are you here and not with Ery?"

"She's safe," I promised him. "Mac and Arro are with her."

"That doesn't answer my question."

"Let's wait on Thane." I'd asked my brothers to meet me tonight because after that horrific showdown with Ery, I was desperate to solve this god-awful mystery. I wanted to know who was after me and why.

There was only one thing in my past I could think of that might have provoked this, and by not confessing it to my brothers, I was hindering our investigation.

I just hoped they didn't think too badly of me once I told them the truth. I had to hope that I'd proven myself enough in the last year, that they'd know I was trying not to be such a fuckup.

And failing.

I was fucking things up to an epic degree with Eredine.

I missed her already.

The sound of Lachlan's front door opening broke me from my miserable musings. "Just me!" Thane called a few seconds before he appeared.

He took one look at us, at our beers, sighed heavily, and yanked open the fridge. We waited as he took out a beer, popped the cap, and leaned against the counter opposite us. "What now?" he asked after a quick swig.

Lachlan gestured to me. "Ask Mystery Man here."

Thane turned to me.

I exhaled nervously.

Before I could overthink it, I told them about what happened to Colin in Thailand.

By the time my words trailed off, my head was bowed in shame. It didn't matter that Brodan and Eredine had shown me compassion, that they'd tried to tell me it wasn't my fault. I couldn't let go of the blame. And part of me was waiting for my elder brothers' condemnation to validate my own messed-up feelings.

Instead, I felt Lachlan's hand curl around my nape. He gave me a squeeze and bent to press his forehead to mine.

He didn't say a word.

And I swear that act of quiet comfort and compassion broke me.

I turned into him, like I was that three-year-old who'd clung to him after our mother died or the twenty-seven-year-old who'd felt like a boy again when our father died.

I gripped my brother so tight as I tried to hold back tears. "I'm sorry," I choked out.

Lachlan's voice was gruff as he said, "You've nothing to be sorry for."

I wanted those words to be magical. To erase my guilt like I'd always imagined they might. They didn't. But they eased my fear that I'd lose all that I'd gained with my family in the past year. Releasing my big brother, I sank back onto my stool and shot a look at Thane.

His eyes were bright. "I wish you'd told us you were carrying this around. But at least Brodan was there for you."

"Aye. It's actually a relief to hear that." Lachlan sighed. "I can't make you think you're not to blame for this, Arr. You'll need to work through that. But for now, we can look into the people involved. I'll need Colin's family name."

I nodded. "And he had a pretty serious girlfriend. She outright blamed me for his death."

Lachlan raised an eyebrow. "We'll definitely need her name."

"Does Ery know?" Thane asked.

"Aye, I told her before we got together. The night of the ceilidh when Lachlan and I got drunk ... that was the anniversary of Colin's death."

"Fuck," Thane huffed. "I wish we'd known."

"We know now." Lachlan studied me. "Have you told Ery you're worried there's a connection between Colin's death and the harassment?"

My stomach lurched. "No. I ... uh ... I fucked up again. Just like with Colin." I explained about my need to be public with my affection for Eredine after weeks of having to keep our relationship hidden. "It was so fucking caveman of me. I wasn't thinking about anything else but what I wanted. And I should have known better. I put us out there."

Thane scowled. "Wait a minute ... Does Eredine not have a part to play in this? Is she not a grown woman who knew exactly what she was doing kissing you in public?"

"It's not the same."

"I'm pretty sure she'd feel like it was," Lachlan said, raising an eyebrow. "Or were you not present when she gave me that speech?"

Renewed guilt flickered through me. "I ... I broke things off with her today."

The mood in the room changed swiftly, and I could feel my brothers' combined anger.

I hurried to explain, "If I put distance between us, then maybe whoever this is will back off Ery if they think she's not important enough in my life to use against me."

My brothers shared a knowing look that annoyed the shit out of me. "And what did Eredine say to that?" Lachlan asked.

"If you want to leave, Arran, leave. But never come back."

I flinched. "She told me not to bother coming back. Ever. But that's just the heat of the moment. I can convince her after this is all over to take me back."

They were silent for so long, my already weak confidence

crumbled.

"Right?"

Lachlan took a sip of beer before saying, "We understand more than anyone the guilt and need to protect the woman you care about. Thane and I have been there. But from our experience, all you'll do is push her away. She specifically said she doesn't want to be treated like glass. I think that infers she also doesn't want to be treated as a problem that needs solving. You don't want her to get hurt, and I understand that. But"—he laid a hand on my shoulder and squeezed as he offered harsh words in a gentle tone—"you probably just hurt her more than anyone could. She probably feels more alone now than ever."

EREDINE

WHEN I WOKE, I had a moment of panic. The pillow didn't smell like my perfume or Arran's cologne, and the room was darker than it should be. As my eyes adjusted, I remembered where I was.

Arro and Mac's guest room in the bungalow, currently filled with boxes. Their new house was almost ready, and they'd started packing for the move.

That meant Arran's house was almost ready too. We hadn't talked about anything as serious as me moving in, but the fact he'd wanted my opinion on fixtures and finishings had given me hope he was contemplating the idea.

A wave of profound sadness flooded me.

And with it, indignation.

Shoving off the duvet, I sat up and swung my legs out of

bed. According to the alarm clock on the bedside table, it was just past five in the morning. Plenty of time to go for my morning jog.

I'd been beyond wounded when I'd returned home to the lodge to find Arran gone and Mac waiting for me. He asked me to pack a bag and pulled the "Arro is pregnant, and I don't want her stressing about you being here alone" card. So I grabbed what I needed and spent the night here with them.

Not once did Arran call or text.

So I guessed he'd made a decision regarding my ultimatum.

I rubbed the pain in my breastbone, fighting back tears. Reaching for my phone, I switched the screen on, and I froze at the sight of Arran's name on a notification banner.

Despite the fact that I sort of wanted to ignore him, I didn't. I swiped open the text message. It was long.

I'm sorry. I shouldn't have walked out. I just didn't want to be the reason you got hurt. I have a meeting this morning, but can we meet for lunch? Let me apologize in person?

The tears I'd been blinking back spilled over as relief flooded me. I'd never really been one to hold a grudge, unless the act committed against me was completely unforgivable. Kia had been the grudge holder between us, which was why I'd been shocked it had taken her so long to recognize Ezra Jefferson's toxicity.

But once she'd made up her mind about something, she stuck to it.

And she'd made up her mind about Ezra. She was never taking him back. He'd killed her for that.

Arran Adair was Ezra Jefferson's opposite in every way. While I was afraid he'd used the harassment as an excuse to get out of our relationship, that was just my own insecurities talking. It didn't mean I wasn't still hurt—I wanted an apology. But I didn't want to lose him either.

I hit the reply box.

Okay. Let's meet at my place, though. I don't want to talk about this in public.

He didn't respond right away, but he could be sleeping or showering. If he was already awake, maybe he was planning a run on the beach. Maybe I would bump into him there, and we could discuss everything so I wouldn't have to wish my morning away.

As quietly as possible, I dressed and left the bungalow. When I pulled up to the car park on Ardnoch Beach fifteen minutes later, it was empty.

Arran's SUV was nowhere in sight.

I tried not to lose hope because he could still show up while I was running.

Long summer days meant the sun was already well on the rise as I jogged onto the lonely sand. There wasn't a person in sight as I ran along the shoreline. Today's morning dawned brighter than yesterday's, and I took that as a good omen.

I used to run with earbuds in before I started running with Arran. But our jogs together had gotten me used to enjoying the sounds of the coast, a perfect symphony not even the best song in the world could beat.

A few miles down, just as I neared a break in the sand with nothing but rocks and water, I turned and started back toward the car park.

The sight of a figure in the distance made my pulse race faster with hope, but as I drew closer, I could tell by the person's shape it wasn't Arran. In fact, it wasn't a guy at all. Another woman jogged down the beach toward me.

Robyn was the only other person I knew who ran along the beach, but Lachlan had asked her not to run without him while she was pregnant, and it was a concession she'd made for him. They'd taken to running together along on the estate's shoreline after the doctor said it was safe for her to keep up the exercise since she'd always been a runner.

So it wasn't Robyn up ahead. Disappointed it wasn't Arran, I kept my eyes trained on the path in front of me where some of my footprints were still visible from my race along the shore. My calves and thigh muscles burned, as did my lungs. It was always worth it, though, for how it felt once I finished. There was nothing like that adrenaline. Dancing was the same.

That reminded me—Lachlan had agreed to install a ballet barre in my studio (we were still fighting over who would pay for it), and it was arriving next week, which was exciting. I hadn't danced since that night with Arran, but once the barre was installed, I planned to practice there in the evenings.

The stranger on the beach drew near enough I could make out her blond hair and navy workout clothes. I didn't recognize her face, so I assumed she was a tourist. As we neared, just about to pass, I gave her a friendly smile, but she wasn't looking at me.

It was a shock, then, that as we passed, I saw movement in my peripheral and reflexively turned toward it just in time to see the woman swing at me.

Stumbling out of the run, I raised my arms on instinct to block the punch and cried out at the stinging pain that sliced across my forearm. That was when I saw the knife, now bloodied.

She slashed me, I thought, stunned.

No time to freak out, however, because she lunged again with the knife. Like the muscle memory that had come back while I danced only a few weeks ago, the memory of Robyn's self-defense lessons took hold, and I dodged her attack and spun around her to slam my foot into the back of her knee.

She cried out, falling to the sand and losing her grip on the blade.

I didn't hesitate.

I pinned her chest down to the sand and grabbed the weapon to throw it behind me, out of reach.

"Get off me!" the woman yelled.

Time for questions would come. For now, I struggled to keep her secured while I fought for the phone in my yoga pants pocket. Every time I loosened my hold to do it, though, she almost fought free.

I ignored her insults, railed at me like a banshee, and my eyes darted around us as I tried to think.

Then, like heaven-sent angels, a couple walking hand in hand approached in the distance.

I yelled, glad there wasn't too much wind to carry my words away from them.

After what felt like forever, the couple seemed to realize I was screaming for help. They picked up their pace, running toward us.

Relief made me tearful as I tried to explain what had happened over the ranting denials of the insane woman beneath me. When they gaped at my arm, that was when I realized how much I was bleeding. Until that point, I hadn't even felt the pain. But as soon as I saw the long wound, a blaze of fire shot up my arm.

Deducing I was not lying, the couple called the police, and the man helped me hold my attacker down until assistance arrived.

Unfortunately, just as we saw the police Jeep driving along the beach toward us, the blood loss and shock became a little too much. At least I assumed so because one minute I was sitting on the crazy woman who'd slashed me, and the next I was waking up in an ambulance.

36

ARRAN

I was running after Ery through woodlands. Something was chasing her I needed to protect her from, but every time I'd call to her, she'd keep running. Every time I thought I was gaining on her, she'd slip from my grasp.

Now there was a banging sound in the forest, and my terror increased tenfold as she moved farther and farther away.

The banging grew louder.

"Arran! Wake up!"

My eyes flew open.

The annex. I was in my bed in the annex.

Relief made me sag against my sweat-dampened pillow. It was just a stupid bloody nightmare.

"Arran!" *Bang. Bang. Bang.*

What the fuck? I jumped out of bed at Lachlan's hammering. A quick glance down at my boxer briefs reminded me I wasn't completely naked, so I yanked open the door and squinted against the daylight pouring in.

Lachlan scowled at me.

He was dressed for the day in one of his expensive three-piece suits.

"What time is it?" I muttered, scrubbing at my tired eyes.

"Six o'clock in the morning. I thought you were an early bird?" My brother strode past me inside.

"Usually I am, but I took ages to fall asleep last night." I'd texted Ery at around midnight asking her to meet me, but she hadn't texted back. On that thought, I moved past Lachlan and lunged across my bed for my phone like a desperate man.

Hope gave me a burst of adrenaline when I saw I had a text from Ery asking me to meet at her place this afternoon. My shoulders relaxed as I typed out a reply. Maybe I could fix this between us after all.

"I didn't come here to watch you moon over your phone."

I looked up at my brother. He appeared so imperious this morning. "What's up?"

His imperiousness turned to seriousness. "I have news. One name you gave me, Maranda Peters, the girlfriend of your friend Colin ..."

"Aye?" I dropped my phone, giving Lachlan my full attention.

"She's working at the University of Bordeaux. Something to do with marine biology."

"Bordeaux?" Where the emails had originated from.

"The internet café is on the campus there."

"Fuck." Goose bumps prickled over my skin at the thought of Maranda holding Colin's death against me for so long. I'd never liked the girl, but I'd felt awful for taking Colin from her. "Maranda? All this time?"

"It's looking that way."

"What do I do now?"

Before Lachlan could answer, my phone rang.

It was Eredine.

"I have to take this."

"Of course."

"Hey, gorgeous, I need—," I answered, ready to blurt out everything we'd discovered.

"Uh, is this Arran?" an unfamiliar woman interrupted. She had a Scottish accent.

Alert, I stood from the bed, giving Lachlan a look as I replied, "This is Arran. Why do you have my girlfriend's phone?"

Lachlan's head jerked at my words, and he took a step closer, so I switched on the speaker.

"My name is Ashley. I promised your girlfriend I'd call you to let you know she's in the hospital at Golspie. She was attacked by a woman with a knife on the beach this morning. My husband and I stopped to help."

I barely heard anything after the words *attacked by a woman with a knife.*

"Arran?" Lachlan bent his head into my face. "Arran?" Scowling, he peeled the phone out of my hand and barked at the woman for details.

THANKFULLY, the hospital in Golspie was only twenty minutes from Caelmore. I couldn't have been in the passenger seat of Lachlan's Range Rover any longer than that. As it was, we'd already sniped at each other four or five times over my wanting him to break the speed limit and him refusing to do it.

"I'm worried about Ery, too, but I don't see how killing us will improve matters!" he'd eventually yelled.

I shut up then but was a jittery mess, and as soon as he swung into a visitor's parking spot, I jumped out of the car.

"Arran, wait up!" he called, but I was already jogging

across the car park and through the main entrance of the small community hospital. That she'd been brought here instead of airlifted to Inverness meant her injuries weren't severe, and Lachlan said the stranger on the phone had explained as much.

But rational thinking wasn't taking hold of the reins right now.

I just needed to see Ery.

I hurried over to the reception desk. "My girlfriend?" I asked without preamble. "She was brought in with a knife wound. Eredine Willows."

The receptionist gave me an abrupt nod and checked her computer. "Yes, she was brought in half an hour ago. The doctor is with her. If you'd take a seat, we'll let you know when you can see her."

"I need to see her now."

She pursed her lips. "She's being treated by the doctor, so I'm afraid that's not possible."

"I need to know she's okay."

"Sir, she was admitted with a minor knife wound. We'll update you beyond that as soon as possible."

Fuck that.

I turned to find Lachlan marching across the reception. "They won't let me see her, but she said her wound was minor."

He jerked his head and walked out of reception toward a set of double doors to the rear left. Hurrying to follow, I fell into step beside my brother as we entered the wide corridor.

"Where are we going?"

"Minor injury unit."

I slapped him on the back in thanks before we pushed through another set of double doors into the department. We each took a side and peered into the wards as we passed.

Before we even reached the third set of wards, I heard a familiar American accent.

"She's there." I hit Lachlan on the arm, and we both hurried toward the ward and burst into it in unison.

Eredine was upright on a bed, looking at the ceiling, chatting as a doctor stitched up her forearm.

"Fuck me." I practically melted into a puddle in relief as I scanned her body and saw she was otherwise unscathed.

Her gaze flew to me as the doctor turned to scowl at our rude entrance. "Arran?"

"Gorgeous."

Her lower lip trembled, and tears brightened her eyes.

My heart broke at the sight of her fear.

I hurried over to her other side.

"Be careful," the doctor warned as I leaned in to hold her. "I'm trying to work here."

"You're okay," I whispered over and over, more to myself than to her, as I peppered her cheek and temple with kisses. "I've got you."

And I did.

I would never put distance between us again.

"I'M REALLY OKAY." Eredine reached out to squeeze my hand. "You can stop fussing."

A snort behind me made me look from my girlfriend on the couch pushing off blankets I'd tucked around her to Lachlan, who leaned against Ery's dining table with a giant smirk on his face. "What's your problem?"

My brother shook his head. "Nothing. Just never thought I'd see this day."

"What day?"

"The day my wee brother fell into the same trap Robyn set for me."

"Christ, man, don't let her hear you call it that." Mac shot him a warning look.

"Oh, it's a trap I willingly fell into."

"Rewriting history now?" Eredine asked.

I chuckled because she'd told me all about how Lachlan didn't want to admit he'd fallen in love with Robyn Penhaligon.

"How did this get turned around on me?" Lachlan huffed.

"Because you were being a smart-arse." Mac gave him a wry look and turned to Ery. "How are you feeling?"

"Seriously, I'm okay. I don't need blankets." She grinned. "It's summer."

I gave her a sheepish smile.

Since we'd returned from the hospital, I *had* been mother-henning her.

"Pain okay?" Mac asked. "A slash like that can hurt."

He would know. I frowned at Ery's arm. It was a long wound, but thankfully, it wasn't too deep. The doctor had stitched her up and bandaged it to protect from infection.

"I might need some painkillers in a bit, but I'm okay at the moment." Ery gave me a reassuring nod and then turned to Mac and Lachlan. "You have news about who that woman was this morning?"

Fury shot through my veins at what Lachlan had relayed while I waited for Ery's discharge paperwork. I sat next to Ery and kept her hand in mine as Lachlan talked.

"Before Arran got the call you were in the hospital, I'd just come over to tell him we'd discovered Maranda Peters, the girlfriend of Colin, the man who died in Thailand that night with Arran—"

Eredine squeezed my hand, and I gripped on to her silent comfort.

301

"—Is living in Bordeaux and working at the university there. The emails were coming from the internet café on campus."

"It was her on the beach," Eredine deduced.

I squeezed her hand tighter, guilt threatening to consume me. Eredine's brows drew together in concern at what she saw in my eyes.

My brother continued, "I've spoken with the police, and yes, Maranda is the woman who attacked you on the beach. They ran her prints and discovered that two former boyfriends back in Ireland had filed reports of harassment against her. From what our guys have been able to deliver in the last few hours, it seems Maranda has been living in Bordeaux since Colin's death. She was arrested for assaulting a boyfriend, but the charges were later dropped. Considering her previous history, and that she confessed to attacking Ery as revenge for Colin's death, the police are holding her without bail. They said they'll be in touch to interview you both soon, so expect a knock on the door."

"I knew I never liked her," I growled. "Colin was too good for her. You know he was going to propose ... you have to wonder how that might have turned out if he'd lived." I tried to pull my hand from Ery's to stand up, but she held fast.

Her gorgeous eyes pinned me to the couch. "You are not running away again."

I was the reason she'd been attacked, for fuck's sake. Every time I visualized what that must have been like for her, I flinched.

"Hey." Ery soothed a hand up my arm. "I'm okay. And we have Robyn to thank for that."

"Robyn?" Mac and Lachlan asked.

Ery grinned proudly. "I remembered her self-defense lessons. They just rushed back, and honestly, it took seconds after Maranda swung to take her down." She looked back at me. "It wasn't some harrowing fight. I promise. It was over before it started."

"I still brought this into your life."

"And you want me to blame you?"

I glowered and looked away.

"Hey." She tugged on my arm again. "Do you want Thane to blame Regan for Austin assaulting me and hurting the kids?"

"Of course not."

"Or Arro to blame Mac because someone tried to shoot her?"

I looked over at Mac who still, quite rightly, appeared pissed off at the mention of his past coming back from Glasgow to take revenge on him with Arro getting caught in the crossfire. "You know I don't."

"So, why on earth would you think I'd blame you for this? Arran, this family has attracted some crazy people—"

Lachlan snorted unhappily, and I smirked at the understatement.

"We could have our own show. And I'm including myself in it because I have an ugly past too. Baggage. Everyone comes into a relationship with it. I will never blame you for what happened today. It was Maranda's fault, and I pretty much hate her for bringing this all back up for you when I've been trying so hard to make you see that what happened with Colin was just a terrible accident."

"I love you," I blurted out unexpectedly.

Her fingers tensed around my arm as her eyes widened at the pronouncement.

Fuck.

I huffed. "And I blew that too. I didn't exactly plan to say that for the first time with my brother and brother-in-law standing at our backs."

Despite the throat clearing behind us, I didn't dare look

away from Eredine.

Her eyes welled, and a smile prodded at her full mouth. "Does that mean no more running away from me for my own good?"

I moved closer. "I promise. I'm sorry for doing that to you in the first place."

Ery grinned that beautiful, knee-weakening smile. "I love you too."

"Thank fuck for that," Lachlan muttered.

"Aye, that could have been awkward," Mac said.

While Eredine giggled, I looked over at my brothers. "Do you two mind?"

"Leaving." Mac grabbed Lachlan, who was watching me like a proud bloody father. "We'll let you know when we hear more about Maranda."

The door had barely closed behind them when I pulled Eredine toward me to kiss her until we were both panting. "I love you," I repeated against her lips.

"I love you too. So much."

I groaned into another kiss as her words filled an empty place inside me I hadn't even known existed until then. Feeling her fingers slip under my T-shirt, I reluctantly curled my hand around her wrist to stop her. Breaking the kiss, I leaned my forehead against hers to compose myself. The combination of adrenaline and Ery reciprocating my sentiments had made me harder than I'd ever been. "Fuck. We can't. You need to rest."

"But—"

"Please." I stroked her cheek. "Tomorrow. We can wait until then."

"I hate waiting for you." She pouted uncharacteristically, and fuck if it wasn't adorable. "I feel like I've been waiting my whole life for you."

Grinning with pure joy, I nodded. "I feel the same way."

37

EREDINE

I woke an hour before the alarm was set to go off and blinked sleepily, the vision before me clearing.

Arran lay beside me on his stomach, one arm stuffed under the pillow, the other over the top of it. Not for the first time, I noticed his long lashes, but you almost couldn't see them because they were so fair. His features were soft in sleep, his mouth looking fuller, more tempting. My gaze stroked his angular jawline and down to the hard muscle of his biceps. His arm from the elbow was hidden by the pillow beneath his head.

Need pulsed between my legs. Not just lust or desire, but pure need.

Noting that I felt no pain in my arm this morning, I smiled. Despite Arran's promise that we'd have sex the day after we'd finally confessed our love to each other, we hadn't. It was day four after the attack, and because I woke every morning needing a painkiller, he'd evaded my attempts to seduce him for fear of hurting me.

But I was free of pain this morning.

I'd given another witness statement to the police, and

Arran had given his. They had charged Maranda Peters with attempted murder upon her own confession, and she was undergoing a psychological evaluation. Whatever happened, I was quietly confident she wouldn't be bothering us again.

With her incarceration, the creepy gifts had stopped, and it really felt like the dark clouds over our heads had drifted away. Relief made me buoyant.

And my hot, sexy, kind, protective boyfriend made me feel several levels of turned on.

Biting my lip to stop my wicked smile, I sat up to remove my nightie, trying not to overdo it with my arm because it still stung when I stretched it too much. Once my nightie was off, I moved closer and caressed Arran's side. He was lying on his front, which made it difficult to slip my hand down his boxer briefs, but I was determined.

Arran groaned in his sleep, and my skin heated as he instinctively turned his hips toward me, giving me better access.

Fondling him, I felt him grow hot and hard in my grasp and brushed a kiss across his sleepy mouth. When I pulled back, his eyes were at half-mast with sleep and arousal.

"What are you doing?" he asked, his voice hoarse and grumbly.

My hand squeezed him as my belly flipped in reaction.

"What does it feel like?" I murmured and kissed him again. "No pain this morning."

And just like that, Arran was fully awake.

I laughed as he lunged and suddenly found myself flat on my back.

He moved over me, straddling me, his hands braced at either side of my head. His heat engulfed me as he stared into my eyes and smoothed his hand up my naked thigh.

My inner muscles tightened. "I love you, Arran."

His expression darkened. "I'll never tire of hearing it. I love you so fucking much, woman."

I grinned at his guttural words, happiness flooding me. And then more than happiness took over as Arran slid his thumb between my legs, watching me with all the love and desire in the world. My breath caught as he circled my clit, tingles moving through me as I lifted my hips.

He stopped teasing and slid three thick fingers into me and grunted, his eyes flaring when he felt how wet I was. My inner muscles clamped around him in desperate need. "Ery, fuck." His hips undulated a little, mimicking his fingers. "You are spectacular." He thrust his fingers faster in and out, and my toes curled into the bedding.

"Arran—oh!" He caught my clit with his thumb again, sparks of pleasure shooting through me. "Don't stop."

But he did, his eyes filled with a fierce desire that made me breathless with anticipation. I felt overwhelmed by the size of his body, and I loved it.

Arran bent his head to mine, and that masculine, spicy scent rushed over me, sending a new set of tingles straight to my nipples.

My mouth begged for his kiss, and his lips touched mine. His tongue pushed between my lips, and we danced in a dirty, deep, wet kiss. My hips pulsed toward him at the feel of his hard cock rubbing against my belly.

And then he was gone, taking his mouth from me. His fingers trailed teasingly down the soft skin of my inner arm, under my arms, and down the sides of my breasts as he stopped to stare at them. I loved how Arran adored every inch of me.

A tugging ripple low in my belly caused a rush of wet at the heat of his mouth wrapped around my left nipple. Arran licked and sucked.

Hard.

He hadn't shaved in a few days, and the scruff scratched my skin in the most delicious way as my body writhed, bucking off the bed. Forgetting my wound, I wrapped my arms around his shoulders, stroking his hot, smooth skin. My fingers curled tightly into his hair as he tormented my nipples until they were swollen, almost painful, buds. He brought me to the edge of orgasm again and then stopped, kissing them sweetly before returning to suck on them.

"Arran," I groaned, tugging on his hair.

He ignored me and focused on kissing his way down my body, moving down my stomach, his tongue licking my belly button before moving south. My stomach clenched, and my legs parted in invitation. I heard his groan of satisfaction seconds before his tongue touched my clit.

Need slammed through me, and my hips pushed into his mouth. He gripped them, pressing my pelvis back to the mattress, and then the torture truly began.

As his scruff scratched and tickled my thighs, he suckled my clit, pulling on it hard, just what he'd done with my breasts. He tortured me. He studied my body, my reactions, and just when I was about to come, he'd lift his head and tell me he loved me.

And I couldn't even be mad about it.

"Arran," I begged.

His grip on my hips became almost bruising.

And then his tongue was back, this time licking inside me. I shuddered, but it still wasn't enough. Hearing my whimpers, he returned to my clit and thrust two fingers inside me.

"Arran!" I jerked against him. "Yes, yes! Don't stop!"

But abruptly, he was gone. I cried out in indignation, wondering where he thought he was disappearing to. My body relaxed when I saw he was pulling a condom out of his bedside table. I'd never seen Arran so hard and throbbing.

Still, he took his time with it, stroking his cock as he put on the condom, his hot eyes dragging over every inch of my body.

"Arran, please."

A muscle ticked in his jaw, and he nodded. But before he moved, he said, "Sometimes I can't believe you want to be here with me. You're something out of a dream."

Emotions overwhelmed me even as my body throbbed impatiently. "Arran."

And then he was over me again. His lips brushed mine, softly, sweetly, surprising me. He he pushed up onto one hand and curled his other around my thigh, opening me, and thrust inside.

Hard.

I gasped his name in utter pleasure. Our eyes held as my breath scattered and as he moved inside me, thick, hot, deep, so deep. Every time he pulled out, tingles exploded down my lower spine. I whimpered, and his grip on my thigh tightened.

He let go only to lift my legs so my hips and ass came up off the bed. His large hands held the backs of my thighs, keeping me at this angle as he got up on his knees. And then he powered hard into me.

It was our favorite position because Arran always hit my G-spot like this. Incredible pleasure seized my whole body. I was acutely sensitive to the heat flushing through me, the slickening of my skin, the feel of Arran's hard muscle beneath my hands, and of him pounding into me, hitting that perfect spot.

I wasn't cognizant of anything. I knew I was saying words, but they were incoherent. I heard his grunts; I heard my whimpers. I smelled his cologne and sweat mingling with mine. The bliss built and built inside.

And then I shattered, an exquisite release undulating

through me. "I love you!" I cried, my eyes fluttering as it rushed through my entire body. My inner muscles clamped around Arran, the sensation so sexy, I never wanted it to end. It felt like it *would* never end.

Expletives fell from Arran's lips as his hips slammed hard against mine. Stilled. And then they jerked as he throbbed inside me with his release. "I love you!" he cried out in return and then fell over my body, his face buried in my neck as he shuddered long and hard.

Our chests rose and fell against each other as we tried to catch our breaths. Love consumed me as I curled my fingers in his hair and whispered his name. Arran lifted his head, and we gazed at each other, recognizing the miracle of this, before our lips drew together. I kissed him, sweet and deep. He kissed me back, and I rolled until I was on top of him. His hands caressed my back, my hair, my ass as we kissed, and I writhed against him, needing more, wanting him hard again, ready.

I didn't have to wait long, and this time I explored him, feeling possessive, almost like I had ownership over his body. I rode him slow, the desperation of our need eased by the explosive wake-up sex. Dragging my nails down Arran's hard stomach, I moved up and down on him, and I felt my power as he gripped my hips and devoured the sight of me on top of him.

"Fuck, fuck." He squeezed me harder. "I fucking love you so much."

I would never get sick of hearing it.

In fact, whatever he saw in my face made Arran climax first, and as his hips bucked beneath mine, his features tight with pleasure, I came just from the sight of him losing himself in me.

310

38
EREDINE

I had three different people in my classes that day ask me what had put me in such a good mood. Since I couldn't tell them my boyfriend had given me multiple orgasms that morning and told me he loved me for the millionth time, I just smiled and said it was a good day.

It was an amazing day.

Maybe it sounded cheesy, but it almost felt like the first day of my life really beginning again. That meant Kia and Granny were on my mind too. I knew Granny would be more than happy that I'd found a place with the Adair family. She'd grown up in a big family, but tragically, three of her five siblings died fairly young, and her remaining brother and sister left the country for new lives in Australia and the UK. They traded letters back and forth over the years, but Granny never got on a plane to visit like she always said she would. Then she passed away, and it was too late.

I knew she'd missed having a big family around, and when she talked about Kia and me giving her great grand-kids, I knew she was wishing for that feeling again. It broke my heart that I hadn't been able to give that to her in time,

311

but Granny believed in Heaven, and so I liked to think of her looking down on me, so happy I'd found that big family she'd always wanted for us.

And Kia would've loved Arran. She loved anyone who treated me well. She might even have been a little envious because she and I were possessive of each other's affection. We were happy for the other to be in a romantic relationship (except for Ezra Jefferson, of course), but I think we secretly never wanted the other to meet someone we might fall intensely in love with for fear it might change our twin connection.

I'd fallen intensely in love with Arran Adair. But I knew now it would never have changed me and Kia. I would've given anything for Kia to be alive, to watch her find her own Arran.

But that was an impossible dream, and I had to make do with knowing she was in Heaven with Granny, relieved I'd found love and security. Joyful that I was on the road to finding peace.

Blinking back tears of sadness and joy, I tried to let go of the sadness and think of Arran. I thought of him coming home to me tonight and having my way with him again. Apparently, I was insatiable.

He told me yesterday his house was almost finished. When I got excited for him, he grew quiet, observing me as if he wanted to say something.

I had a feeling he wanted to ask me to move in with him but didn't want to push.

And I didn't broach the subject in the off chance I was wrong and I freaked him out because … I might love my little lodge, but I'd love even more to live with Arran in that beautiful house near his family.

Our family.

So lost in my thoughts, I wasn't really paying attention

when I pulled up to the lodge ten minutes later.

That was the reason I didn't see the gift on my porch until I was practically on top of it.

For a second, it didn't register.

I thought the gift might be from Arran, and it was only as I lowered to open the box that I thought how weird it was for him to do this, considering the scare I'd gotten from Maranda's harassment.

My blood turned ice-cold as I opened the box and saw the photo of Kia and Ezra taped to the inside. Items had been piled inside: a necklace with a gold *K*, lipstick.

Was that a . . .

Bile rose, and I gagged as I launched to my feet and backed away.

A lock of hair.

Kia's?

Footsteps sounded over the rushing blood in my ears, and my head jerked toward the sound. Fear suspended me as Ezra Jefferson appeared around the side of the house.

Although he'd lost some of his dark hair since I saw him last, I recognized his face. Once upon a time, I might have thought him handsome. But evil had made him ugly.

He wore a polo shirt and slacks. His posture was relaxed as he slid his hands into his pockets and grinned as if he'd never been happier to see anyone. "Kia," he called to me. "My love, it's been too long."

I bolted for the house as I heard his feet kick up to give chase. My fingers shook around my keys as I got them into the lock and fell into the small foyer. I slammed the door shut in his face and flipped the lock just as he crashed against the exterior. I screamed in fright.

The door began to give, so I turned frantically to the security panel on the wall, yanked down the cover, and hit the red panic button Lachlan had installed. A light next to it blinked to let me know the alarm had been sent.

Which meant an alarm was now sounding on Mac's and Lachlan's phones.

The door was seconds from crashing in against Ezra's rage-filled battering.

Blood rushing in my ears, body trembling, I tried to get hold of my fear. The sound of my cell blaring from my purse on the porch grounded me. It would be one of the men checking to see if I was okay, and they'd come here when I didn't answer. Plus, Lachlan could patch into my CCTV.

They'd definitely come for me.

I just had to hold Ezra off until they arrived.

Racing into the kitchen, I grabbed a butcher knife out of the block and then hid the block in the oven so Ezra wouldn't have easy access.

Upon a shattering noise, I stood and whipped around. The door had collapsed inward, and Ezra walked through, his forehead glistening as he brushed invisible lint off his polo shirt. He glowered at me as I backed up to put the island between us.

"I have to tell you, my feelings are hurt, Kia. I'd thought after all this time, you'd be happy to see me."

Kia.

"You made it so difficult to find you. How did you get out of the country with a false name? I know you didn't make it legal because I couldn't find your new name in the system. Nothing new under Kia Washington anywhere in the system."

Oh my God. He really was goddamn deranged. "I'm not Kia. You killed my sister. Remember that?"

Ezra blinked, stupefied. "Why would you say such a thing? You're right here. In front of me. And I've been looking for you for a very long time, Kia."

Stall him, I heard my sister's voice in my head. *Keep him talking. You know the asshole loves to talk.*

"How … how did you find me?"

"Why do you have that knife? Put it down."

"How did you find me?" I repeated, not, in fact, putting the knife down.

"A vapid girl on social media posted a video of you, and a friend sent it to me when he recognized you, Kia." His expression darkened. "She gave you a different name, and you were kissing another man. Do you want to explain yourself?"

After all these years, all the paparazzi that had descended on Ardnoch and my cover had been blown by a nosy social influencer.

Reining in my rage, I gritted my teeth and told him, "I'm not Kia, Ezra. You killed Kia."

"Stop saying that!" he bellowed.

I skittered back, hitting the wall. Arm shaking, I held the knife out as he prowled toward me. "Stay back!"

His gaze caught on my stitched-up arm. "Look, you've already injured yourself, so just put the knife down. I'm not here to hurt you, Kia." He gestured toward the porch. "Didn't you get my gift? Didn't you see how much I think about you? I've kept everything. I've never forgotten you."

Ezra had been volatile and violent all those years ago, but he'd lived in reality. Something had snapped in his mind. He was living in his delusions, truly believing, I realized, that I was Kia. That he'd never killed her.

That scared me even more than the thought of a violent Ezra.

I shifted from the wall, moving around the dining table to head toward the exit.

But he moved in the opposite direction to cut me off.

So I stopped at the head of the dining table as he halted at the opposite end, blocking my way out.

Impatience flexed in his jaw. "If you don't come to me, Kia, I'll make you sorry, my love." Before I could respond, he rushed up the side of the table toward me.

I huffed out a petrified cry and ran toward the kitchen to round the island, but my head was yanked back as he grasped my ponytail. Roaring with outrage, I whirled and slashed the knife at him.

Ezra jumped back to avoid it, and I hunched over in a defensive stance, knife out.

"What did you think would happen here?" I tried again to keep him talking.

But he was done talking.

He lunged and I slashed again, forcing him back. But then faster than I could compute, he grabbed hold of my wrist and slammed it against the island. An awful pain loosened my grip on the knife.

In seconds, he had me pinned to the kitchen floor. "Play nice," he murmured in my ear, and I could feel him hard against me. Nausea roiled in my stomach as memories flooded me. Terrible memories of discovering Kia's naked body. The bruises around her neck from where he'd strangled her. But first, he'd raped her.

He'd raped my sister and then strangled her.

Years of terror and fury blinded me, and I struggled and cried out as he slammed my wrists into the floor and bellowed at me to calm down.

Calm down, I heard Kia's voice again, and I shuddered to stillness at hearing it after so long. *Where is the knife?*

The knife.

"Good, good girl, Kia," Ezra groaned and buried his lips against my neck as he ground his erection into me.

I swallowed back bile, tears slipping down my cheeks as I

looked past him, craning to see the floor beyond us. My breath caught.

The knife was within reach.

"Mmm, you like that, Kia?" He misinterpreted the sound.

Distract him.

I forced out a moan as he undulated into me, and his breath hitched with excitement.

"I knew you missed me too." He lifted his head, eyes bright with madness and desire. To my relief, he released my wrist closest to the knife in order to squeeze my breast. Forcing my revulsion down, I arched into him and let my arm fall by my side. Ezra was so busy fumbling excitedly with the tight waistband of my yoga pants that he didn't feel me reaching for the knife.

Just as his fingers slipped into my underwear, I screamed like a raging banshee and used every ounce of my strength to shove the knife into his gut.

His face slackened with shock, and he rolled off me to wrap his hands around the blade's handle.

Scrambling from under him, I raced toward the door and stumbled onto the porch just as Lachlan and his armed security poured out of two SUVs parked in my driveway.

My knees gave way with utter relief, and I hit the porch hard.

39
ARRAN

Helmsdale. Fucking Helmsdale.

I'd traveled north to see a blacksmith in Helmsdale. Months ago, I'd commissioned him to make the staircase and outside balcony railings for the house. And I'd stopped by before the end of the day to make sure everything was ready to go for the delivery at week's end.

When Lachlan called to tell me Ery had hit the panic button in her lodge, I cursed my fucking plan.

I was too far away.

And she wasn't answering her phone.

My brother assured me he was on the way with his security team.

But that did nothing to stanch my terror.

I sped recklessly down the coast, cutting the usual forty-minute journey in half. My underarms and back were soaked with sweat as I skidded to a stop in Ery's driveway, clotted with police cars and flashing blue lights.

And an ambulance.

Feeling sick rise in me, I staggered out of my SUV and

rounded the cars toward the ambulance in time to see a man, cuffed to the stretcher, being lifted into the van.

I recognized that face.

Ezra fucking Jefferson.

Roaring with fury, I lunged toward the bastard only to feel strong arms band around me, hauling me back.

Through my rage, I heard Lachlan's order in my ear to calm down.

"She's all right, Arran. Calm, brother. Ery is fine."

Shuddering, I gave an abrupt nod, aware of the police officer who'd stepped forward, wary gaze alert. Shrugging away from Lachlan, I forced myself to settle as the ambulance doors closed behind the murderous fucker. "Where is she?"

"Inside."

I hurried up the porch, my wrath gathering steam again at the sight of the smashed-in door. Blood smeared the frame, and my vision almost went black.

Only her voice saved me. "Arran!"

She sat on the couch beside a policewoman. Even disheveled, Ery looked calm, stoic.

But holding my eyes, I saw her break.

She sobbed, and I lunged over the couch to get to her. I didn't know who shook more as I held her while she cried.

"Be careful of her wrist," the policewoman said as I met her gaze over Ery's shoulder. "She sprained it in the struggle."

The struggle.

My hold on her tightened. "What happened?"

I'D NEVER WANTED to harm another human being before. Not in any real or permanent way. Fuck, I still hadn't forgiven myself for Colin's accident.

However, Ezra Jefferson changed me in a fundamental way. After Eredine repeated what went down in her lodge that day, I wanted to find the insane motherfucker and gut him until the light bled from his eyes.

It shocked me a little. How bloodthirsty I felt.

How much rage boiled inside me.

Thankfully, love and pride in Eredine were stronger emotions, or the former might have eaten me alive.

The paramedics had insisted Ery get checked over, so I drove her to the hospital after the police were done interviewing her, Lachlan, and his men. Lachlan showed up just after Ery had stuck a knife in Jefferson, and the security team held Ezra at gunpoint until the police arrived.

The police took the CCTV footage from the porch, which could only prove that Jefferson broke down the door. Hopefully, it was enough. After a few hours at the hospital, where the docs X-rayed and splinted her sprained wrist, I took Ery back to the annex. She slept fitfully in my arms, renewing my desire to kill Ezra Jefferson.

Since Lachlan had called to ask us over to his place that morning, Ery and I walked from the annex. As soon as Robyn saw Eredine, she immediately engulfed her in a tight hug. "You're a warrior," she said, and I wholeheartedly agreed.

"Thanks to you." Ery gave her a wobbly smile. "And Kia."

Robyn frowned. "Kia?"

"My sister."

Robyn's face registered her surprise, telling us that Lachlan had kept Ery's story from even his wife.

Ery squeezed Robyn's shoulder. "I'll tell you about her soon."

Accepting that, she slid an arm around Ery's shoulders and led her over to the breakfast table where a pile of food awaited. My belly grumbled at the sight. I had eaten nothing since before I got the call about Ery.

"Let's eat and talk," Lachlan suggested, and we joined the women at the table.

"You have news, then?" I asked after I'd eaten half a pancake.

Lachlan sighed. "Mac got some information from his contact at the police. Ezra's family tried to buy him out of custody, but bail hasn't been set while Ezra recovers in the hospital from the attack. His family wants to press charges against Ery."

I sucked in a breath while Ery paled.

"But don't worry, there's no way. That doesn't mean his family will not try to make this difficult. Once he's recovered, I fully expect him to be extradited to the States. By then, however, he'll be facing several charges of sexual assault and harassment. One of his victims is the daughter of a US senator. She's spoken with her mother, with her family, and they want her to go public."

"Jesus Christ," I muttered, feeling sick to my stomach at the evil this guy had perpetrated.

"I'm sure the lawyers will want to reopen Kia's case, Ery," Lachlan said gently. "Are you prepared for that?"

"Oh my God." Understanding dawned on Robyn's face, and tears of sympathy glimmered in her eyes.

Ery reached over to squeeze her arm in comfort, and I swear to God, I thought at that moment, I couldn't fall any harder in love with her. Until she turned to Lachlan and made me do just that by lifting her chin defiantly. "I will do what it takes to finally get justice for Kia."

"It'll be a long road. Not an easy one."

"She has me." I curled my arm around Eredine's shoulders. "You have me," I promised.

"You have all of us," Robyn added.

Ery's lips trembled. "Then we'll get through it together."

EPILOGUE

EREDINE

Eighteen months later

This was not what I had in mind when I thought about enjoying the view from the master bedroom in our new home. Arran's house became ours days after my ordeal with Ezra Jefferson. He'd wasted no time asking me to move in.

And now we were fully settled into the beautiful space.

The master bedroom looked out over the North Sea with a wall of bifold doors that led onto the balcony.

I hadn't imagined enjoying that view with my naked body pressed against the glass while Arran moved languidly inside me from behind. His palms were pressed to the glass above my head, while my cheek felt the smooth coolness against my skin.

No one could see us, despite the less than private, slightly kinky slow lovemaking.

As I grew closer to climax, however, I pushed off the glass, arching my head against his shoulder, desperate for him to speed up.

Suddenly, I was on my hands and knees on the decorative faux fur runner in front of the doors, and Arran was no longer making love. He was thrusting into me with hard, deep drives.

He'd already pushed me close to the precipice, so it wasn't long before I cried out and came around him in tight throbs.

"Fuck, fuck, fuck." His grip on my hips tightened as he pistoned against my ass. And then I felt him jerk before he pulsed inside me.

We collapsed on the rug, panting for breath, naked, sweaty, tangled limbs reaching for one another.

Soon, I was cuddled into Arran's side, staring up at the ceiling as he made lazy circles on my shoulder. The wood burner in our bedroom crackled as the real fire filled our room with a cozy heat that warded off the winter chill.

Sliding my fingers through Arran's, I looked down to catch sight of my engagement ring winking in the light. He'd proposed this morning. It came days after we'd been running on the beach, and Arran had stopped and blurted out, "I want to spend the rest of my life with you. I want kids with you. When we're ready. Do you want that too?"

Since we'd really only had four months of blissful relationship time, considering Ezra's trial had taken a while to get going and then weeks to conclude, we hadn't talked about the future. I think we'd both wanted to put the past behind us first.

The accusations of sexual assault against Ezra were

terrible but my sister's story particularly horrified people. Ezra's father became a pariah as people deduced he'd used his power to cover up his son's crimes.

However, Ezra wasn't tried for Kia's murder. That he genuinely believed I was my sister had called his sanity into question. Five women, including the senator's daughter, came forward as witnesses in his trial. Jefferson was convicted of three counts of sexual assault, because there wasn't enough evidence in two other cases, as well as assault and attempted sexual assault against me. Any charges against me for stabbing him were dropped since it was self-defense.

In the end, it didn't matter. Ezra Jefferson hung himself days before the trial's end. An investigation into his death ruled it a suicide.

And I was finally free of him. Kia might not have seen justice while she was alive, but the world now knew what he'd done to her, and I hoped it was enough.

His death made me feel like I could breathe again.

Except this time, I was breathing the kind of fresh air I hadn't encountered in nine years.

It was for that reason that Arran and I had enjoyed spending the last four months together with no heavy conversations or worries about the future. Until he'd asked me on the beach if I wanted to spend the rest of my life with him and start a family together when we were ready.

Of course, I wanted to, which I told him with much enthusiasm that morning.

I smiled, remembering it.

"What are you thinking about?" he asked softly.

"Just how happy I am, and how sometimes I need to pinch myself."

"Aye?" He cuddled me closer. "Well, that's my aim in life, you know. To keep my wife happy."

I chuckled. "I'm not your wife yet."

"Almost." Then he groaned. "We need to get up soon, and I don't want to. Maybe we can skip family lunch for once?"

"Nope," I said immediately.

It was a life rule for me that we never skipped out on a family get-together unless there was an emergency. Not just because I was grateful beyond anything to be part of this family, but because everyone was so busy, yet they made an effort to be there. Arro and Mac and Robyn and Lachlan were rushed off their feet, taking care of their one-year-old girls (yes, they both had girls), and Thane was ever a support to his wife and children as Regan juggled full-time motherhood with finishing her business degree. She was close to opening a preschool here in Caelmore, and I couldn't be prouder of her. Or Arran. He'd turned the reopening of the Gloaming into an immediate success with tourists, and all it took to get the villagers back on his side was him hosting this year's anniversary ceilidh in the reception hall.

Even Brodan was happier than I'd ever seen him.

But that was a story for another day.

"We're going to lunch," I insisted.

"Okay," my fiancé grumbled and then crawled over me, peppering me with ticklish kisses that made me squeal with laughter. "But not until I have my wicked way with you, Eredine Willows Adair."

I laughed loudly. "I'm not an Adair yet, you ravenous beast."

He grinned down at me, his eyes glittering with affection. "Aye, you are. You've been an Adair for years. I'm just the one lucky enough to make it official."

Love and affection so big it made me feel explosive surged as I stared up at this man who had changed my life. I relaxed beneath him, opening myself to him as I replied huskily, "Then I guess I'm yours already."

He swallowed hard at that before he bent his head to

whisper across my lips, "Good. Because I've been yours for longer than you know."

COMING SOON

Only You (The Adair Family Series #5)

ONCE UPON A TIME, *Monroe Sinclair was Brodan Adair's best friend, but now he's a stranger and one of Hollywood's leading men...*

It took Monroe Sinclair eighteen years to return home to Ardnoch after a fateful night that devastated her friendship with Brodan Adair. She fled her unrequited love for him, as well as her difficult family life, and tried not to look behind her. Only a daughter's guilt could lure her back to the Highlands and the assumption that Brodan Adair rarely ever sets foot in their hometown. She can handle seeing the rest of the Adairs so long as she can avoid her ex-best friend and the only man she's ever loved.

Nothing is more important to Brodan than family, and only his demons have the power to keep him from them. For years, acting was something he was lucky enough to be good at, yet it wasn't his priority—Ardnoch and his siblings were. But when a ghost from his past returned out of the blue, Brodan tried to outrun its haunting, taking him further and further from home. When exhaustion finally forces him back to the family fold, the last thing he wants is to encounter another ghost. But that's exactly what Monroe Sinclair has been to him.

When a promise to his nephew obliges Brodan to work with Monroe, it forces them to face their past. The explosive connection that has always existed between them resurrects truths long buried. Yet, just when they might be on the brink of a second chance, the ghost from Brodan's past finally catches up to him and threatens not just their happiness, but their very lives.

Preorder for less!
Out February 21st 2023

Amazon
Apple Books
Kobo
Nook

CPSIA information can be obtained
at www.ICGtesting.com
Printed in the USA
LVHW032000211222
735680LV00004B/447

9 781915 243065